Recent Titles by Anna Jacobs

A FORBIDDEN EMBRACE
HIGH STREET
JESSIE
LIKE NO OTHER
OUR LIZZIE
SEASONS OF LOVE *
SPINNER'S LAKE

* available from Severn House

A FORBIDDEN EMB

A FORBIDDEN EMBRACE

Anna Jacobs

This first world edition published in Great Britain 2001 by
SEVERN HOUSE PUBLISHERS LTD of
9–15 High Street, Sutton, Surrey SM1 1DF.
This first world edition published in the USA 2001 by
SEVERN HOUSE PUBLISHERS INC of
595 Madison Avenue, New York, N.Y. 10022.

British Library Cataloguing in Publication Data

Jacobs, Anna
   A forbidden embrace
   1. London (England) – Social life and customs – 19th century – Fiction
   2. Love stories
   I. Title
   823. [F]

ISBN 0-7278-5646-4

Typeset by Palimpsest Book Production Ltd.,
Polmont, Stirlingshire, Scotland.
Printed and bound in Great Britain by
MPG Books Ltd., Bodmin, Cornwall.

One

March 1818

T he lawyer finished his cup of tea and turned to Cassie.
'Could I speak to you in private, if you please, Miss
Trent?'

'In private? But why? My mother's will surely has no
surprises for anyone here?'

Aunt Sophie was avoiding Cassie's eyes. 'Why don't you
take Mr Hurley into the dining-room, my dear? You won't
be disturbed there.'

'But—' Cassie stared at her aunt, then led the way out.
Perhaps this had something to do with bequests for her
aunt and uncle, or her two cousins? Yes, of course. That
would be it.

She sat down at the long polished table. 'Please take a
chair, Mr Hurley.'

He obeyed and placed a pile of papers on the table. 'Now
– ahem – I have something of a surprise for you. Pleasant,
I hope.' He fiddled with his papers. 'The question of your
guardianship.'

'But surely my aunt and uncle—'

'Not Mr and Mrs Trent. Your mother has nominated your
other aunt and uncle as guardians.'

'*What?*' Cassie jerked forward in the seat. 'But my
mother's family disowned her when she married my father!
There must be some mistake.'

'No. No mistake. Your mother very much wished for you
to have a London Season, just as she had done, and Lord and

1

Lady Berrinden have the entrée into polite society, which Mr and Mrs Trent do not.'

'They didn't even write to my mother when my father was killed. I want nothing to do with them.' Cassie could hear the anger in her voice. 'Besides, they won't agree to it.'

'Ahem. I think you will find that they do agree. You see, there are some legacies involved for their own daughters if they do so.'

'But that's bribery! I don't believe it! My mother wouldn't have done such a thing.'

He continued to stare at her steadily.

Cassie could feel tears threatening and stood up hastily. 'I still won't go to them. Bardsley is my home and they're complete strangers. Excuse me, please.' She made her way up to her bedroom, hating the thought of anyone seeing her in such an emotional state.

Her mother's maid was waiting for her there, standing by the window with arms folded. Seeing the expression on the older woman's face, Cassie stopped dead in her tracks. 'Did *you* know what was in the will, Mary Ann?'

The maid nodded. 'Aye. But your mother thought it'd be better if you heard it from Mr Hurley.'

Tears were now streaming down Cassie's face. 'Well, it doesn't make any difference who told me – I won't go to them!' She let Mary Ann draw her over to the bed and hold her until she had stopped weeping, for she had not given in to her grief before.

After a few minutes, the maid pulled away, saying briskly, 'It wouldn't hurt for you to give it a try. It's only for a year, love, less than that, for you'll be twenty-one in a few months.'

Cassie scrubbed furiously at her eyes. 'It's only the shock that's upsetting me! I *despise* people who turn into watering pots.' She stood up, peered into the mirror and winced at the sight that met her gaze – her eyes were reddened, her heavy brown hair looked duller than usual and strands had fallen down around her face, while her normally smooth complexion was blotchy.

Mary Ann picked up the pretty blue and white jug from the washstand and poured some water into the matching bowl. 'Here, love. You'll feel better if you wash your face.'

Cassie went to obey her, then looked down at her black gown and sighed. 'I miss Mother so much.'

'All the more reason to try a change of scenery.'

'But Mary Ann, whatever would I do with myself down there in the south?' It might have been the moon, so far away did the fashionable world her mother had grown up in seem from a bustling cotton town in Lancashire, with its smoky chimneys and rows of terraced dwellings.

'Why, you'd do what all the other young ladies do, Miss Cassie. Find yourself a husband.'

Cassie stiffened and turned round, her eyes flashing. 'I'm not going to hand over my fortune to a useless nobleman who'll scorn the way my father made his money – and will probably scorn me, too. If I ever marry, it'll be for love, like my parents.'

Mary Ann went over to the dressing table and began absent-mindedly picking the melted wax off the candlestick. 'Your mother was fair set on your having a Season, lass. She often talked about it to me during those last few weeks and wished she could see you all dressed up in your hoops and feathers for presentation to the Queen. She wanted you to have a wider choice of husbands than you'll get in a small town like Bardsley.' Her own eyes full of tears for the mistress she had served for over twenty years, she turned round and said firmly, 'It's all you can do for her now, love, carry out her last wishes.'

There was silence for several minutes, then Cassie confessed, 'One day, just before she died, I promised Mother to do as she had asked in her will. I thought she meant me to see about the bequests to servants and . . . and things like that.'

3

'No, she meant the London Season. And you can't go back on your word now, can you, lass?'

'I suppose not.' Cassie looked at her pleadingly. 'But you'll come with me to London, won't you, Mary Ann? Be *my* maid now?'

'Just let anyone try to stop me!'

That same day in London, two gentlemen dined together in the Giffard town house. Not until the covers had been cleared and the port was low in the decanter did Simeon Giffard sigh and share his news. 'Susannah Berrinden is to come out this Season.'

'Ah.'

Simeon stared down into the glass. 'She's grown quite pretty . . .' his voice tailed away.

'But—?' his friend prompted.

'Have you ever been in love?'

'No.'

'Neither have I. But . . .' Simeon shook his head. 'Always that *but*, Albert.' He hesitated, then asked in a low voice, 'There ought to be some warmth of feeling at least, don't you think, if one is to marry someone?' He had seen no warmth in his parents' marriage – on the contrary, their quarrels had made his childhood hideous – and he did not wish to make the same mistake as they had made.

Albert didn't pretend to misunderstand him. 'And you don't feel any warmth for her?'

Simeon shook his head. 'No. Oh, she's a nice enough girl, but she stirs nothing in me and her conversation is – well, insipid.' Which was a polite way of describing Susannah's vapid prattling. 'I sometimes fear there's something wrong with me, for no other woman has stirred me to the point of considering marriage, either.' He took another sip, then added, 'And I've been on the town long enough to meet quite a few of them.' To no one else would he have admitted this.

'Your mother been playing up again about your getting yourself an heir, old fellow?'

Simeon nodded, but did not comment. He did not need to. Albert knew what his mother was like.

'Well, at least if you got married, she'd have to move to the Dower House and you'd get a bit of peace.'

'Yes. That would be an advantage,' the only one Simeon could think of, 'though the place needs completely renovating. And she's right, really. I do owe it to the family to produce an heir, since I'm the last of the Giffards. But—' he broke off. It would be ungentlemanly to say that the thought of facing Susannah Berrinden over breakfast every day for the rest of his life filled him with dismay.

'You're blue-devilled, old fellow.'

'I am.' Simeon tossed the fine old port down his throat like water and poured himself another brimming glass.

'Maybe you could find someone you feel a bit – well, a bit warmer about?'

He had wanted to do that, but had not met anyone who attracted him, and time was passing. He looked at Albert. 'My mother has set her heart on Susannah.'

'Ah.'

Simeon grimaced. There was no need to explain matters further. For a weak and sickly woman, Flora Giffard knew how to get her own way, playing on her son's pity for her, after the years in which they had both suffered from his father's irrational and often unkind behaviour. There was also the question of her health, and the doctor's warning that she should not be upset, that the storms of emotion with which she sometimes reacted could be fatal for her.

In a sense, his mother was right. At thirty-three he ought to do something about providing an heir. He had put it off for the past few years, because he had been busy setting the estate in order after the years of neglect under his father. Now, you couldn't find a better-run estate in the whole of Hertfordshire.

And he had run out of excuses for avoiding marriage.

*   *   *

In a tall house in one of London's most prestigious squares, Henry Lord Berrinden and his family were at breakfast. He picked up a letter from the silver salver presented to him by the butler, stared at it with lacklustre eyes and slit it open. When he had finished reading it, he gasped and perused it for a second time. Then he crushed it, threw it on the floor and exclaimed, 'Damn the woman! She's even causing us trouble after she's dead!'

Then he realised what he had said and looked guiltily at his wife and eldest daughter.

In the heavy silence which followed, the butler picked up the offending missive, smoothed it out and replaced it on the silver salver, his face expressionless.

Amelia Berrinden breathed in deeply, annoyed to hear such language at her table. But for all her high principles and elevated breeding, she was as prey to curiosity as the next person, so she said quietly, 'Thank you, Meckworth. Susannah, you may go and visit your sisters in the schoolroom.'

As soon as the door had closed behind them, Amelia turned to her husband. 'To what, Henry, do we owe this shocking language?'

He cleared his throat. 'My dear, this is a letter from Mr Hurley, who is a lawyer from Bardsley in Lancashire.'

Lady Berrinden clutched the lace at her ample bosom. '*Bardsley!*'

After a moment, his lordship fumbled into speech again. 'It . . . er . . . it appears my sister has died and . . . and her lawyer has written to say he wishes to see me as soon as possible regarding her will and the,' he hesitated again, then finished in a rush, 'the guardianship of my niece.'

'But we do not even acknowledge the girl's existence!'

He observed her agitation with a certain perverse satisfaction. 'Gave me a bit of a start, too, I can tell you.'

'One cannot forget that you have a sister, Henry – nor can one forget the scandal she caused – but to speak of our becoming guardians to the daughter of such a misalliance . . . Why, the very idea of such an ill-bred person coming here is unthinkable!'

'Ahem – not exactly ill-bred. The Trents are landed gentry, after all.' He picked up the letter again, his lips moving as he read the words under his breath. 'What I can't understand is why this Hurley fellow should want to tip the girl's guardianship into our dish. Never heard a word from them over the years, apart from the announcement of the child's birth and Robert's death – and you decided not to reply to those.'

'I should think not!'

'So why can't *they* look after the girl now?'

'Why not, indeed?'

When Lady Berrinden held out her hand, he placed the letter in it, then re-arranged the crockery and drew patterns in some spilled sugar, while she read and re-read it.

After giving the matter some thought, she announced, 'You will have to go to the North and investigate this unsavoury business in person.'

'Eh – what? Go where?'

'Go to the North, Henry, to Bardsley.'

He wriggled uneasily. 'Is that really necessary?'

'What else can one do? This is not something we can entrust to anyone outside the family – think of the scandal! You must tell this Hurley person to settle the guardianship upon her paternal relatives. He'll probably have to draw up some papers to that effect. You can sign them before you return.'

'Er – well, if you say so, my love.'

Lady Berrinden stood up, her thoughts already turning to her day's engagements. 'And I cannot think of a more inconvenient time for you to be away, just as the Season is about to begin! Still, what can one expect from a woman who eloped with a person whom she met in a bookshop? Your parents were quite right to forbid her to marry him! She should not even have spoken to him in the first place.'

Becoming aware of the time, she whisked away to complete her toilette, don a new lace cap and summon her daughter. The two ladies then arranged themselves in the drawing-room to wait for the callers who never failed to attend upon a woman so well connected in the ton.

After due consideration, Lady Berrinden informed Susannah of the reason for her Papa's departure.

'*I have a cousin?*'

'A cousin whom we do not recognise,' Lady Berrinden said firmly. She made no mention of the guardianship. Henry would simply decline the responsibility, then they could all forget the idea had ever been broached.

'But Mama, shall we not have to go into mourning?'

'For a relative the family has disowned? I think not. I do not intend to mention this to anyone else and neither should you. I am telling you merely because you are almost grown-up now and entitled to know.'

'Yes, Mama.'

Her ladyship then put the whole annoying business from her mind until her husband should return, and devoted herself wholeheartedly to the pleasures of this Season to which she had been looking forward for many years. She had no doubt that, by the end of it, her lovely eldest daughter would be safely engaged to a gentleman of impeccable breeding and respectable fortune – and she rather fancied she knew which man it would be.

The Season was not yet in full swing, but by the time Lord Berrinden returned to the bosom of his family a sennight later, her ladyship and Susannah had attended a reception, a musical evening and two pre-Season dancing parties especially organised to give those in their first Season a chance to accustom themselves to the etiquette of the ballroom. The two ladies had also visited fashionable shops to make last-minute purchases of stockings, silk flowers, ribbons and other trifles essential to a lady of fashion, as well as having some final fittings for gowns designed to outshine those worn by other hopefuls and their mothers. In between, they had driven in the park and made morning calls on those persons whom her ladyship deemed worthy of such attentions.

Lady Berrinden saw the family carriage turn into the square as she sat by the window of the drawing-room, where she and Susannah were entertaining a gentleman caller. Simeon Giffard was the son of her ladyship's dearest friend, Flora, with whom she was in frequent contact by letter now that Flora was too frail to withstand the rigours of a London Season. Since their recent arrival in town, Simeon had, to her great satisfaction, called on them several times.

'So you think that—' Lady Berrinden drew in her breath sharply and stopped in mid-phrase as she saw her husband help a young woman in a crumpled travelling cloak out of the carriage and escort her up the steps to the front door.

'Is something wrong, Lady Berrinden?'

Simeon Giffard's cool voice recalled her attention and she managed to smile at him, while at the same time controlling a surge of anger. This unknown female could only be the niece from the North. Fury sizzled through her at that thought, though her expression of polite interest did not change. How *dared* Henry bring Harriet's daughter back to London?

She realised that her guest was still awaiting a response. 'I do beg your pardon, my dear Simeon. My husband's carriage has just drawn up and that distracted me for a moment. As you know, he's been away in the North all week on urgent family business.'

'Then you'll wish to speak to him privately, so I'll take my leave of you.'

But before he could do so, the door of the drawing-room was flung open and Lord Berrinden breezed in, followed by

9

a maypole of a girl in a dowdy cloak that even her ladyship's maid would have scorned to wear.

'Ah, there you are, my love,' his lordship announced unnecessarily. 'See what a pleasant surprise I've – . . . Oh, Simeon! Nice to see you again, my dear fellow.' Becoming aware of the thunderous expression on his wife's face, he came to an abrupt halt and stood like a fish stranded on a beach, mouth opening and shutting in a fruitless search for words that would fend off her wrath.

Cassie halted by the doorway, dismayed to find that the older lady, who must be her aunt, was glaring at her, that a fair young lady, Cousin Susannah no doubt, was looking very apprehensive, and that an unknown gentleman was staring at her with a disdainful expression. It was the latter who caught her attention and she could not resist staring as he rose to his feet.

He was very tall, well over six feet, with a presence you could not ignore. His lustrous brown hair was cut short and brushed into an elegant tangle, a style she later discovered to be called *coups de vent*. Fawn trousers were moulded over muscular legs and worn over gleaming half-boots. His sage green frock-coat was stretched across broad shoulders, with not a single wrinkle marring its fit, or that of the fawn waistcoat beneath it. A high and intricately tied neckcloth worn over even higher shirt points, gave his head a haughty elevation which perfectly matched the expression on his lean aristocratic face.

He was extremely handsome, or at least, Cassie amended mentally, he would have been handsome if he had not looked so bored and world-weary. Whoever he was, she decided, as the silence stretched across the room, she wished he'd stop staring at her. Turning, she saw her uncle put up a finger to ease his neckcloth as if it were choking him.

'Er – I'm back, my love,' he offered in greeting.

Lady Berrinden breathed in deeply.

It took him a few seconds to realise what she was waiting

10

for. 'Oh . . . ah . . . my love, this is my – I mean *our* – niece, Cassandra Trent, and Cassie, this is my wife and, er, of course she's your aunt – Aunt Amelia, that is.' His voice faltered to a stop.

For all her tiredness and embarrassment, Cassie had a sudden urge to chuckle. After several days in her uncle's company, she was aware that he lived directly under his wife's thumb and was terrified of upsetting her. Their time together had also shown her that he was not at all quick-witted. But he was a lord and, as a consequence, no one seemed to notice the slowness of his wits or the banality of his conversational offerings.

Cassie was given the merest tip of her ladyship's fingers by way of a greeting.

'And this is your Cousin Susannah,' added his lordship in a falsely hearty voice, beaming round at everyone. 'Suzie, come over and shake your Cousin Cassie's hand!'

Cassie watched her cousin move across the room, her carriage graceful and her voice as soft as a strand of silk. At least her smile seemed genuinely friendly as she shook hands and said, 'I'm so happy to meet you. I do hope you're not too tired after such a long journey!' before returning to her place on the sofa.

The strange gentleman cleared his throat.

Lord Berrinden jerked round. 'Oh . . . ah . . . Simeon, forgot you were there, old fellow. Pray let me introduce you to my niece. Cassandra Trent, Simeon Giffard.' In a hurried aside to Cassie, he volunteered the information, 'Families known each other forever. Giffard's got a seat in Hertfordshire close to ours. Excellent hunting. Dashed draughty house. In all the guide books, though.'

Cassie found her hand being shaken again and frowned up at Mr Giffard. He was so tall that he made her feel quite small, which was an unusual sensation for her. That must be what was making her feel breathless, she told herself, as she stood there with her cold fingers clasped in his warm hand.

'Delighted to meet you, Miss Trent,' he drawled, staring down at her with a frown wrinkling his forehead as if he were puzzled.

He started to turn away without venturing to offer a comment about her journey, as the merest courtesy would have demanded, and Cassie's temper began to rise. She had never met so many ill-mannered persons in her whole life! Any new-found relative, however distant, coming to the Trent household in Bardsley would have been made warmly welcome, not stared at like a bear in a sideshow. 'I'm equally delighted to make your acquaintance, Mr Giffard,' she tossed at him, her tone contradicting her words.

He froze for a moment, looking as if he did not know what to make of her. 'Indeed.'

'Yes, I've heard so much about *polite* society that I knew I should soon be made to feel welcome here.' Was that a softening of the expression in his eyes, she wondered, as if amusement were creeping in behind the boredom?

'I hope you will soon feel comfortable among us, Miss Trent. You must be tired after such a long journey?'

'A little tired, sir. Nothing that a good night's sleep will not mend.' She had the satisfaction, then, of being the one to turn away from him. She had not been invited to sit, but did not intend to stand like a supplicant, so took a seat on a fat overstuffed sofa and waited to see what her relatives would do next.

'I really must take my leave now,' murmured Simeon Giffard to his hostess.

The hint of animation had vanished from his face and Cassie wondered whether she had been imagining the amusement. She admired the address with which he shook his hostess's hand and made a swift exit from the room. Perhaps he could tell that a storm was brewing? The rigidity of her aunt's expression and body spoke volumes, contrasting as it did with the trepidation on her uncle's face and the way her cousin glanced from one parent to the other with wide, nervous eyes.

Lord Berrinden crossed to stand in front of the fire and remained there, shifting his weight from foot to foot and making a great show of warming his hands. 'Cold weather we're having, eh? And nearly April, too.' Under his wife's basilisk stare, his voice trailed away.

Cassie watched Lady Berrinden punish her husband by allowing the awkward silence to continue for a few moments before commanding, 'Kindly ring for the butler, Henry.'

She did not speak again until he arrived. 'Meckworth, pray tell the housekeeper to prepare a room for our niece, Miss Trent, who will be staying with us for a while. The room next to Miss Susannah's should be suitable.'

After the butler had left, her ladyship set one hand to her forehead. 'Susannah, kindly fetch me my vinaigrette. I feel a headache coming on. A *severe* headache.'

Lord Berrinden's expression became, if that were possible, even more apprehensive.

How ridiculous! Cassie thought. Why do they allow the woman to bully them like this? She leaned back on the sofa, wishing she were back in Bardsley.

Lady Berrinden's sharp voice cut across the room, 'A lady *never* lounges in her seat, Cassandra! Kindly remember that while you are under this roof.'

Cassie jerked upright, anger welling. This was worse than her blackest imaginings. If it were not for her promise to her mother, she would walk out this very minute and return to those who loved and wanted her.

As Susannah re-entered the room, carrying the little silver box of smelling salts, even Lady Berrinden's grim expression relaxed at the picture her daughter presented – silvery blonde hair, blue eyes, a delicate complexion and a slim figure, just a trifle lacking in height, perhaps. Above all, a sweetness of expression and a willingness to please that made her universally liked. Such a pity her sisters took after their father! Still, one should count one's blessings. Susannah was exactly the sort of daughter any mother would have chosen, just as Richard was exactly the sort of son and heir one would wish to have, though why he had insisted on going off to tour the Continent in that ramshackle manner just before the Season started, Lady Berrinden would never understand.

She sighed audibly as she studied her niece. Some might have described the girl as handsome with a well-proportioned figure, but Lady Berrinden considered her too tall. Why, the girl looked to be the about same height as Richard, and he stood five feet nine inches. Yes, and she had a pert look to her, too, decided her ladyship, meeting a steady gaze from across the room. Well, Miss Cassandra Trent had better mind her manners. This was London, not the wilds of the North.

Susannah smiled encouragingly across at her father, then gave her mother the vinaigrette, saying softly, 'I do hope your head gets better soon, Mama.'

She means that, thought Cassie in amazement. Is she too stupid to see that her mother is playing games?

The butler returned. 'Miss Trent's room is ready, your ladyship.'

'Thank you, Meckworth. Susannah, pray take your cousin upstairs so that she may change for dinner.'

'Yes, yes! You go with your cousin, Cassie,' added Lord Berrinden with a heartiness he clearly did not feel.

The jovial expression dropped from his face the moment the door closed behind the two girls.

'Pray explain yourself, Henry!'

He launched into a description of the journey North.

'Kindly reserve the no doubt interesting account of your journey until a more felicitous occasion.'

'Er – yes, my love. Well, I went first to see the lawyer. What's-his-name. Always forget what he's called. Thin little fellow, got a cast in one eye.'

'The letter was signed by a Mr Hurley.'

'Yes, that's it! Hurley! Anyway, what he had to say gave me a nasty shock, I can tell you!' He paused and took a deep breath.

Her ladyship rolled her eyes towards the ceiling. '*Do* get on with it, Henry!'

'Yes, dear. It seems the girl's grandfather, Robert Trent – well, her father too, come to that, they were both called Robert – anyway, the Trents are now rich. Talk about recouping the family fortunes! Used to be squires, then lost almost everything, so they took to trade and now they're as rich as Croesus. Couldn't believe my ears when that lawyer fellow told me! They own half the town now, you know. Well, perhaps not half, but a deuced lot of it. Not that you'd want to own a town like that. Dirty sort of place.'

Lady Berrinden permitted herself a loud sigh.

His lordship hurried on with his tale. 'Where was I? Oh yes. Cotton, you know. That's where the Trents get their money from now, but they were into canals as well, I believe, before that. And property. They used to own some country acres near Manchester. When the city grew bigger, they sold 'em at a juicy profit, that lawyer fellow said. Dashed ugly countryside round there. Surprised anyone wanted to buy. I don't like those moors at all. No trees, wind always howling and you'd break your horse's legs the minute you tried to gallop. And there's no game to speak of, well, there's no cover, you see . . .' He realised from his wife's expression that he had strayed from the point yet again and made a heroic effort to gather his thoughts together.

'So – it seems Harriet's husband died unexpectedly a few years ago – well, he was murdered, actually, by those damned – er, those rascally Luddites. Caught 'em trying to smash his new machinery and they turned on him. Shocking affair. Shot through the heart. Militia called out, but never caught the villains. Don't know what the world's coming to!

15

Didn't make old bones, did he, Robert Trent? Only forty-six when he died, younger than me.'

'And his money . . . ?' she prompted.

'I was coming to that. He left everything to his wife and daughter – as was only proper, can't fault the fellow there. Then the grandfather died shortly afterwards, leaving most of his fortune to the other son, Joshua – well, he *was* the elder, after all – but there were some rather generous bequests to all three grandchildren, as well. So Cassie came in for more of the old pewter – er, I mean, more money.'

Her ladyship's expression was bitter, but she said nothing. There was no justice in this world if someone who disobeyed her parents and eloped with a common northern millowner could be so richly rewarded.

'And then last month, after a long illness, poor Harriet died, leaving a rather surprising will and this letter for us.' Lord Berrinden hesitated, fumbled in his pocket and produced a crumpled piece of paper, which he handed to his wife with the air of one passing across a live coal.

As she read it, Amelia Berrinden's face turned a dull red. 'How *dared* your sister write us such a *vulgar* letter!' She tossed the offensive scrap of paper towards her husband, did not wait for him to pick it up, but jerked to her feet and began to pace up and down the room, firing remarks at him each time she passed.

'No one with the *slightest* sense of decency would have made such provisions in a will!'

Her rose-coloured skirts swished viciously. 'That some-one born a Berrinden could pen such words!'

'No, er, yes, my love. But it would be a nice little addition to our girls' dowries, would it not? Two thousand pounds each.'

No answer, just another flounce of Lady Berrinden's skirts and a curl of her lips.

His lordship tried again. 'It's a most generous amount,

isn't it? I mean, well, have we not always wished that we were a little better placed with regard to the girls' dowries?'

'It is blackmail! I am amazed that I did not faint clean away at the mere sight of that letter!'

'Yes, yes! Dreadful, my love. Dreadful. Though I don't know if I'd call it blackmail exactly. It's more a form of bribery, wouldn't you say?'

'I am no expert in such matters! And the one seems to me quite as reprehensible as the other.'

'Yes, er, no, my love. But it *is* a generous amount of money, very generous, and it's less than a year till Cassie turns twenty-one and then . . .' His voice trailed away as he saw his wife draw a deep breath.

'Your sister knew very well that we should not be able to refuse. Only the most unnatural of parents could turn away such a bequest for their children!'

Her husband waited for her to pronounce judgement.

'Well,' she said acidly, 'we have one consolation, at least, Henry.'

'My love?'

'We shall know that we are not only helping to provide for our daughters, but that we are behaving with true Christian charity in taking that *northern nobody* into our home.' The high moral tone slipped a trifle and she added waspishly, 'But goodness alone knows how she has been brought up and what her table manners are like!'

She sank into a chair, delicately applying a fine lace handkerchief to her eyes.

He stood beside her and patted her shoulder clumsily. 'I do believe, my love, that you'll find Cassie a polite and ladylike girl. Her behaviour on the journey down here was all that anyone could ask, I promise you. Why, she was as quiet and well-bred as our little Suzie. And her table manners are perfect, too, though she don't eat much, hardly a thing, in fact! Can't imagine how she grew so tall if that's all she eats.'

Her ladyship's tone was ominous. 'Her manners had better be impeccable, if I am to introduce her to our friends!'

'But I can see that it's all going to be very difficult for you, introducin' a girl with a trade background into polite society, not to mention the effort of gettin' her a suitable wardrobe and all the fallals you ladies seem to need. Perhaps it's too much to ask? Your welfare is, as ever, my first consideration, my sweet.'

She glared at him, bosom swelling with outrage. 'Difficult! *Difficult!* I can assure you, Henry Berrinden, that if I choose to introduce your niece to our friends, and *if* she proves to be well mannered, then there will be few difficulties. There is nothing like a fortune for smoothing one's path in the world! And after all, her father came from what was once a respectable county family, even if they have turned to trade. If there were not some good blood there, I could do nothing for her, were I the Queen herself.'

'My love, you are marvellous!' He took her hand and kissed it gallantly. 'I knew I could rely upon you. And about the, er, the legacies . . . ?'

She drew herself up. 'We accept them, of course. Let alone we have our girls' futures to think of, only the most uncaring of parents could turn down such bequests. No one could accuse *me* of not caring for my children's welfare, I hope!'

He kissed her hand again. 'You are the most devoted of mothers, my dear! Indeed, a model parent in every way! Cassie will be in good hands.'

Two

As she climbed the stairs with her cousin, Cassie was suddenly conscious that she ached in every limb after two days of jolting in her uncle's well-sprung chaise. She had not been offered any refreshments and was quite parched with thirst, but she was not going to ask for anything, because she was embarrassed at being foisted on the Berrindens.

She became aware that they had stopped outside a door and Susannah was waiting for a reply. 'Oh, I beg your pardon. I was lost in my thoughts and didn't quite catch what you said.'

'I said, I expect you're rather tired after all that travelling, Cassandra. I know I should be.'

'Do call me Cassie! Everyone else in the family does.'

'Cassie, then.' Susannah pushed open the door. 'This is your room. We'll ring for one of the chambermaids to unpack your things.'

'I've brought my own maid. If she can just be sent for . . .'

But Mary Ann was waiting for them, grim-faced and angular as ever, over fifty years old and clad simply in brown wool.

'This is my Cousin Susannah, Mary Ann.'

'Good day to you, Miss.'

Susannah found herself being carefully scrutinised by a servant, who stared openly at her more like an equal. She saw that Cassie had gone to stand next to her maid and had barely glanced at the bedroom, and suddenly found herself wondering what it was like to be thrown so suddenly among strangers. She knew she would be terrified if it happened to her.

Cassie asked, 'Mary Ann, how are you? Are they looking after you as they should?'

The woman nodded and patted her mistress's hand gently, a fond, familiar gesture that caused a pang of envy to shoot through Susannah, because she could not remember the last time anyone had touched her like that. Her new lady's maid was ferociously efficient and made Susannah feel nervous, and her mama didn't like the children to disturb her toilette. As for her father, often he didn't even notice his children as he passed them on the stairs.

The maid said bracingly, 'Now, do stop fretting about me, Miss Cassie, and get yourself changed. We're here now and it's what your mother wanted, so you must make the best of it.'

Susannah blinked in surprise. Had her cousin not wanted to come to London, then? She felt a surge of fellow feeling, for she had not wanted to be here, either, terrified of her first Season after all the lectures Mama had given her.

'I've laid out your black silk, Miss Cassie. I'll go and fetch some hot water. Your hairbrushes are over there.' Mary Ann nodded to Susannah, placed the petticoats she had been unpacking in an open drawer near the bay window, and bustled out of the room.

'I – perhaps you'd like me to leave you for a little while?' Susannah asked, not sure whether to leave or stay.

'If you're not too busy, I'd welcome some information about – well, about everything – times of meals, how you spend your days, anything you think I ought to know.'

Susannah's tender heart was touched by the sadness in her cousin's eyes. Enjoying the rare sensation of feeling superior, she perched on the edge of the bed and began to give an account of their daily routine and of Lady Berrinden's code of behaviour for young ladies.

As she spoke, she watched Cassie tidy her hair, then stand by the window and stare out. It was getting dark now and you couldn't see the square with its fenced central garden, only the reflection of the room in the glass, but Susannah saw her cousin close her eyes for a moment, as if weary.

Abruptly, Cassie swung round. 'My goodness, I don't see how you find the energy for it all!'

'Well, it is a little tiring, I must admit, but I'm getting accustomed to it now, for we started entertaining earlier this Season and – and Mama does sometimes let me rest in the afternoon, if I'm very tired or if we are to attend an important party in the evening.'

Susannah could not help sighing as she said that. She knew the whole purpose of this Season was for her to attract an eligible husband, but the prospect of that terrified her, too. She had spent most of her life with her sisters in the schoolroom, and wondered how one would converse with a strange gentleman day after day, as well as – the other things. She shivered at the thought of those intimacies. Raised in the country, she knew how animals mated and simply could not imagine the same act between humans. Female animals sometimes screamed. What if it hurt so much that she screamed or cried? How dreadfully embarrassing that would be!

She wished she were clever, like her sister Charmian. Mama said gentlemen did not like clever females, and if she confined herself to discussing the weather, fashions and London or the country, she would not err. But Susannah was sure any gentleman who was clever himself would soon become bored with her.

Mary Ann returned with the hot water and a cup of tea she had coaxed from the cook by the simple expedient of comparing the poor welcome she and her mistress had received in London to the welcome that would have been extended to a visitor by even the lowliest of housemaids in Lancashire.

Susannah excused herself, promising to return in a quarter of an hour to escort her cousin down to dinner. 'It doesn't give you a lot of time, I'm afraid, but Mama does like people to be punctual.'

As she walked away, she decided that whatever Mama said, she was glad Cassie had come to stay with them. There was something steady and comforting about her northern cousin, who had a very warm smile. Perhaps – perhaps she might even become a good friend. Susannah would like to have someone to confide in and discuss her worries with.

When Simeon Giffard arrived home, the butler drew his attention to a letter from his mother which a groom had brought up from Stovely Chase only an hour earlier, and also a letter from Dr Murray, sent at the same time.

'The groom has been told to wait for a reply, sir.'

Sighing, Simeon took the missives and wandered into the library. It was a while before he could bear to open his mother's letter and read the contents. Indeed, he felt he knew already what it would contain, and he was not wrong. It was, as always, spotted with tear stains and was heavily underlined in places, for she wrote as she spoke.

My dearest and *only* son

Today Jane had to call in Dr Murray because my palpitations were so bad. And the doctor was so worried that he has written to you as well. He was his usual gruff self, which always grates on my poor tattered nerves. However, you will be glad to know that he has assured me no harm will be done, as long as I continue to live quietly and *am not upset by anything*.

Oh, my darling boy, I long to hear the news you have *promised* me! Indeed, I lie awake at night with tears bedewing my pillow, so desperate is my longing for grandchildren. I have met no one as pretty and amiable as dear Susannah, in every way a *most suitable* bride for a Giffard. I cannot understand why you delay in this matter *so close to my heart.* I look forward to the day when we can all live together in harmony here at Stovely Chase – *as you have promised me.*

Do not let me down, my dearest son. Remember: a Giffard always keeps his promises.

Your loving mother, Flora, who prays that the Lord will spare her long enough to see her son *happily established.*

He cursed and flung the letter down on the desk. Why had he let her wring that damned promise from him?

But he knew why. She had fainted one day and turned alarmingly blue around the lips, something no one could fake. One could not ignore something like that. His mother had had so little consideration from his father that Simeon felt it his duty to make her declining years happier. To that end he had found her a companion, a sensible lady who was a distant relative fallen on hard times. Jane Canley ran here and there at his mother's behest, showed no resentment and appeared grateful to have a roof over her head.

The letter from the good doctor was brief and to the point.

My dear Mr Giffard

Your mother is fretting herself into a decline. I have never seen her so bad. If you can spare the time to visit and reassure her about whatever is upsetting her, it will benefit her health greatly.

Hamish Murray

23

Simeon threw that letter on his desk with the other. If Dr Murray, who was always so busy, was taking the trouble to write as well, she must be bad.

'She's definitely failing,' the gruff doctor had admitted during their recent chat, 'though she is perhaps not as ill as she claims, or as near to the end of her life. Still, it's best to keep her calm and happy if you can. Miss Canley does her best, but it's you who makes the most difference.'

Which, as far as Simeon could see, settled matters. He must do his duty, and soon. There was no escaping.

He felt impelled to visit his mother the following day, to judge her health for himself and also to set her mind at rest. He had assured his dying father that he would look after her, though his father had not asked it of him, and indeed, had let out a gasp of ironic laughter and said, 'She'll drive you mad.'

Simeon returned to London after a trying visit, feeling the trap closing tightly around him. He went up to his room and changed his clothes for the evening, saying little to his manservant and not even checking his final appearance in the mirror.

Unfortunately, he decided, as he sat in his town coach and waited in a long line of similar carriages to enter the house, having given his mother his word, he had no choice but to offer for Susannah.

From the moment Cassie entered the dining-room that first evening, she found herself to be under strict scrutiny and observation.

'Stop!' commanded Lady Berrinden. 'Turn round! Slowly, if you please.'

She did as she was instructed, too surprised to protest.

'Provincial dressmakers,' pronounced her ladyship, 'are always behind the fashions. You cannot be seen in public, Cassandra, until you are suitably gowned. If you will observe what Susannah is wearing, you will see what I mean.'

Cassie obediently turned to study her cousin, who was

wearing an evening gown of white silk muslin, with a fine satin stripe woven into the material. The gown had several tiny satin flounces round the hem and similar flounces round the neckline. It seemed almost to float around the matching satin slippers as her cousin moved. Susannah's hair was long, which must be a new fashion, for the ladies' fashion journals Cousin Sarah had borrowed from a neighbour in Bardsley had said that short hair was in style – though they had been rather out of date. Her cousin's silvery blonde hair was worn in a high knot, with a curled fringe already falling out of its tight curls and with ringlets hanging down the back. The knot of hair was tied with silver ribbons, bows of which also decorated the flounces of the gown.

'You look lovely, Susannah,' she said softly, smiling to see her cousin blush. The blush was becoming, a delicate shade of peach colouring Susannah's cheeks and showing off the large blue eyes that made even Cassie think of a fairy tale princess.

Sublimely unaware of her own rudeness, Lady Berrinden continued throughout the meal to analyse her niece's appearance and make plans for its improvement. Her daughter and Lord Berrinden each bravely made an attempt to divert her attention, but were cut short and requested to keep their minds on the matter under discussion.

Fortunately, Cassie's sense of humour came to her aid, and by concentrating on the ridiculousness of the scene, she was not only able to bear it in silence, but to enjoy it, too. If only her cousins, Will or Sarah, had been here to share that enjoyment. The three of them had grown up together and had always managed to find something humorous in difficult situations. Poor Susannah looked so dreadfully embarrassed by it all, Cassie intended to reassure her later.

At the end of the meal, Cassie was betrayed into a gurgle of laughter when told that her table manners were pretty enough. 'My mother did not forget how to hold a knife and fork when she married my father,' she said mildly.

Lady Berrinden saw nothing humorous in that statement. 'Well, one can be glad about that, at least. She certainly forgot her duty to her parents when she ran away with him.'

The desire to laugh vanished and Cassie almost made an equally sharp retort, but she had resolved in advance to endure without complaint the time she had to spend in London. However, she did not intend to put up with many more disparaging remarks about her mother.

Susannah managed to snatch a moment alone with her cousin before the Berrindens left for the theatre. 'I'm sorry if Mama – if she seemed overbearing. She – she means well. She is aware of the necessity for young ladies to appear to the best advantage, so that they can make suitable matches. It's only concern for you that makes her speak so plainly, I'm sure.'

Cassie had recovered her equilibrium by this time. 'What! Is our only aim in life to find ourselves husbands?' she teased.

Susannah blinked in shock. 'Well, of course! That's the whole purpose of the Season.'

'It's not *my* purpose!'

Susannah looked stunned. 'But – what else is there to do? Ladies must marry. They cannot live on their own, after all.'

'There must be more to life than getting married. And if I want to live on my own after I'm twenty-one, then I shall! Who is to stop me?'

Susannah could do nothing but gape at this heresy.

Cassie decided that she had shocked the poor girl enough and changed the subject. 'Bless you for worrying about me, Susannah, but I'm not upset by your mother, I promise you! I'm beginning to get Aunt Amelia's measure, and shall soon be able to deal with her quite comfortably.'

She heard Susannah gasp at this and wondered what there was about her aunt to inspire her own daughter and husband with a nervous anxiety verging at times upon outright terror.

As Cassie slowly climbed the stairs to her room, she began to review the evening in her own mind and came to the conclusion that one had to admire Lady Berrinden's taste in clothes, at least. Her aunt was wearing a magnificent turban with peacock feathers in it, and a high-waisted ball gown in dull purple silk, which only a woman with her presence could have carried off. In fact, her aunt's and Susannah's clothes were so flattering they brought home to Cassie the inadequacies of her own wardrobe.

It was a good thing she didn't feel the cold, though. Both gowns had décolleté necklines and short puffed sleeves in spite of the chill of the evening, and Susannah had been vainly trying to hide her shivers at the dining table. She had left wearing a white satin wrap lined with palest pink velvet to keep out the cold. The dresses barely reached the ladies' ankles, revealing shapely limbs clad in white silk stockings and satin evening shoes with rosettes. The shorter skirts must be much more convenient for dancing, Cassie thought, then was overcome by an enormous yawn, and abandoned any idea but that of sleep.

When Cassie went down to breakfast the next day, Lady Berrinden stared at her thoughtfully. She had been giving the situation some serious consideration. 'Black does not suit you, Cassandra. If you are to fulfil your mother's dying wish and have a London Season before you grow too old to find yourself a husband, it will be necessary to prevaricate a little about the date of her death.'

Cassie was obliged to stare down at her plate for a moment before she could recover her composure.

'And,' continued her ladyship, inspecting a platter of ham and nodding to the footman to transfer a large juicy piece on to her plate, 'you will *surely* not wish to ruin your cousin's first Season and prevent her from joining in the dancing and other activities by compelling us all to go into mourning with you? After all, Susannah has never even met your mother.'

Cassie took a deep breath. 'I'm sure you know best about what behaviour is acceptable in polite society, Aunt Amelia, so I shall do whatever you wish. In any case, no one in London would care about my mother, and I do not desire to parade my own grief before strangers.'

'Very sensible. Then you will put off your mourning immediately.'

'I suppose so.' Her mother had disliked the wearing of black anyway, believing it was what you felt in the heart that mattered not what you wore on your body. Cassie cut into her piece of ham with sharp, savage strokes which alleviated her feelings, though the food seemed to have little taste and in the end she left half of it on her plate.

The rest of the meal passed in near silence, broken only by one or two short monologues from Lady Berrinden, two hearty but unanswerable remarks from his lordship, who thought his niece looked a bit downish and needed cheering up, and a few 'Yes, Mama's from Susannah.

The morning's outing was the beginning of a few days of frenzied activity. At the terribly unfashionable hour of half-past nine, Lady Berrinden escorted the two young ladies on a round of visits to shops and dressmakers.

Their first visit was to a modiste whom Lady Berrinden patronised for special gowns. That her provoking niece could well afford Mademoiselle's extortionate prices for her whole wardrobe when they'd had to have some of Susannah's simpler day dresses made by the seamstress in the village was yet another source of annoyance, but her ladyship did not let that deter her from doing her duty and turning her niece out in style.

The modiste, who went by the improbable name of Mademoiselle Clunette, turned out to be a sharp-eyed woman, possibly of French extraction, but more likely not. When told that Miss Trent, who was wearing an old-fashioned blue round gown, needed supplying with a complete new wardrobe, she at first demurred.

'Expense, my dear Mademoiselle, is no object,' declared Lady Berrinden.

The modiste suddenly remembered a good seamstress, who might just be free to work on some garments. If Milady needed the dresses urgently, the woman could come as necessary to Bransham Gardens and perhaps Mademoiselle Clunette might just find the time to design a series of ravishing gowns – as a very special favour to an old and valued client.

Lady Berrinden nodded. She had expected no less, and as it was Cassie's money which would be paying for this, she did not even bother to inquire what this extraordinary favour would cost.

The two older ladies then forgot their social differences in the enthralling task of deciding exactly how many morning gowns, walking gowns, carriage gowns, ball gowns, cloaks, spencers, pelisses and other trifles of apparel would be needed.

When they began deciding which of the current fashions would best suit mademoiselle, however, Cassie took a hand. Smiling sweetly and ignoring her aunt's affronted expression, she stepped forward and joined the discussion, ignoring the tug Susannah gave to her dress and her cousin's warning shake of the head. While deferring to her aunt regarding current fashions, Cassie managed, in a way that baffled Susannah, to steer the choice towards her own preferences without bringing her aunt's wrath down upon her head.

'I prefer to see young ladies clad in pale colours only,' declared Lady Berrinden at one stage, bristling.

'But I'm not so very young, I'm nearly twenty-one, and pale colours definitely do not suit me.'

After several deep breaths, Lady Berrinden conceded, but only because she was forced to agree. She relaxed still further when she realised her niece was showing far more sense than her daughter did in her preferences. Susannah, if left to herself, would have chosen fussy garments more suited to an opera dancer than to a well-bred young lady.

From the modiste's, the three ladies went on to several other shops and warehouses which enjoyed Lady Berrinden's patronage, including Grafton House at Number 164 New Bond Street, which was appallingly crowded, but which stocked everything the fashionable heart could desire.

Here, Cassie found she could not remain indifferent, but thoroughly enjoyed choosing the shawls, hats, gloves, silk stockings, shoes, fans, reticules and other accessories which her aunt declared indispensable to a lady of fashion.

With a short break for luncheon in Bransham Gardens, which also allowed the servants to unload the mounds of parcels cluttering the carriage, they continued shopping right through until five o'clock, leaving Susannah behind during the afternoon to recoup her strength for another evening. Lady Berrinden, however, was indefatigable and it was not until they returned home that Cassie realised how tired she herself was.

Her ladyship, scorning such weakness, put her feet up for a mere half-hour, changed her dress, consumed a generous dinner and then left with Susannah for a ball. There, she casually announced the arrival of her niece to enough people to ensure that the news would spread and invitations would be proffered to coming events.

Once the gowns started arriving, Lady Berrinden delivered another of her decrees over breakfast. 'We are to entertain some friends to dinner on Friday night. I shall invite Cousin Clarence to make up the numbers and you, Cassandra, may attend.'

'How delightful, Aunt Amelia!'

'I dare say everything will be new and bewildering to you, but if you keep quiet and observe how persons of breeding comport themselves, you will no doubt manage not to disgrace us all.'

Cassie, who was growing tired of such remarks and was in danger of forgetting her good resolutions, had to subdue a spurt of anger before she could speak calmly. 'I've been out in society for two years now, Aunt Amelia, and am quite accustomed to dining in company, dancing at local assemblies and attending other social gatherings. Lancashire is not without genteel society, you know.'

Lady Berrinden looked down her nose. 'Provincial parties cannot be compared to those in London, any more than persons in trade can be compared to members of the ton.' A look of distaste crossed her face. 'I sincerely hope you will not bore the company you meet here in town with tales of such bourgeois gatherings.'

Cassie closed her eyes briefly and prayed for strength.

At seven o'clock on the Friday evening, the girls were inspected by her ladyship and pronounced fit to be exhibited to company. Susannah, indeed, was an ethereal vision in the palest pink muslin, with a broad satin sash in a slightly deeper shade of the same pink, and just one bias-cut frill around the hem. Real rosebuds graced her breast and hair.

Not for Cassie the pale muslins which so flattered Susannah. She wore a gown in summer gold silk, which suited her dark colouring to perfection.

'Yes,' said her ladyship when they came down to the drawing-room, 'that gold was an excellent choice, much better than the rose pink you would have chosen if left to yourself. We don't want you looking like a blowsy milkmaid at the midsummer fair.'

Cassie, who had only expressed a preference for the rose in order to obtain the yellow, feigned a cough to hide her smile. She felt very queenly, with her long dark hair dressed high in a chignon, from which a few ringlets had been carefully teased at the back, and with a garland of yellow silk flowers around the chignon to match her gown. The full skirts made a satisfying swishing sound as she walked.

'The pearls look very – um, tasteful.' In fact, they were so fine that Lady Berrinden had not been able to speak for several seconds when she first saw them, so bitter was the knowledge that she could not provide similar jewellery for her own daughters. 'I flatter myself that I have turned you out to the best advantage, Cassandra. It's a pity your figure is so well developed, though, and you will no doubt be quite plump by the time you reach thirty – but at least you have enough height to carry it for the time being. Thank heavens waists are slightly lower this year. The high waists of two years ago would not have flattered *you*. Now, kindly do not put yourself forward this evening. You are there to watch and to learn.'

I will not be rude to her, Cassie repeated to herself for the thousandth time. *I – will – not!* But it was hard, and likely to get more difficult before the evening was over, she was sure.

All but one of the guests arrived on time. The married couples were placed around the fireplace in attendance upon their host and hostess. The younger ladies, who consisted of Cassie, Susannah and the two Misses Dinnington, were formed into a group sitting at the other end of the room and left mainly to their own devices. Young Mr Heversley and Cousin Clarence remained standing and gravitated to and fro between the two sets of people.

Simeon Giffard had apparently been visiting his mother in the country again, but had accepted the invitation to dine before he left for Hertfordshire. When he had not arrived by a quarter past eight, Cassie noticed a little frown creasing her aunt's brow. Surveying this scene of superior social behaviour, she was suddenly betrayed by her sense of humour and broke into a chuckle, which caused her to choke upon her drink of fruit cup.

At this inauspicious moment, Mr Giffard made his appearance. Through tear-blurred eyes, Cassie became aware of his entry, and was relieved that his arrival had diverted Aunt

Amelia's glare from the niece who was showing herself up so badly.

When he had greeted his hostess, he came across to join the young ladies, but seemed a little distracted. 'So you're to make your come-out with Susannah, are you, Miss Trent?'

'Yes.'

'I'm sure you'll enjoy the Season. Young ladies are always fond of parties and balls, are they not?'

'Yes.'

'And are you enjoying yourself in London?'

'Yes.' Could he manage no better conversation than this? Or perhaps he didn't care to make the effort? Well, if he wasn't going to make an effort, neither was she.

She was glad when he threw her a puzzled glance and abandoned her for the over-effusive Dinnington sisters, who fluttered their eyelashes and displayed their gratitude for his attention in a way which quite disgusted her.

She watched him scornfully but had to admit to herself that he looked even more handsome in dark evening clothes with his chestnut hair gleaming in the light of the many candles. Why had he been invited tonight? she wondered. More important, why had he come? Lady Berrinden was his mother's friend, not his.

Then, as he turned his attention to Susannah, Cassie caught sight of her aunt's smug expression and realised exactly why. He was clearly a favoured suitor.

She studied her cousin again and saw that when she conversed with him, Susannah did not for one moment lose the air of slight nervousness which she wore most of the time in public. Susannah had not looked particularly glad to see him, either. Did she not realise what her mother was hoping for?

The food was excellent, without being lavish, the service discreet, and the guests restrained in behaviour. Cassie spent an eternity during the first course being lectured by Mr Heversley on the subject of lepidoptera. Butterflies and moths seemed to be his sole interest in life and he ignored her attempts to introduce other subjects of conversation.

After that course was over, she turned with a sigh towards her other neighbour, expecting nothing better from a man so sure of his own superiority as Simeon Giffard.

'Susannah tells me you're to stay with them for the next few months,' he began, in a voice so patently disinterested that Cassie's frustration overflowed.

'Yes, indeed! It's *so* kind of Aunt Amelia and Uncle Henry to have me,' she gushed, and had the pleasure of seeing him wince. 'I'm *so* excited to be here in London! I've been just *longing* for the Season to begin.'

When she saw that he was beginning to grow suspicious, she sent him a triumphant smile and lapsed into silence, addressing herself to her food with a suddenly revived appetite. A speculative sideways glance showed him to be engaged in a scrutiny of her face, which brought a little warmth to her cheeks and made her breath catch in her throat. He had surprisingly beautiful eyes, for a man, grey with long lashes – and why she was thinking about his eyes, she could not understand!

Simeon had realised by now that he had been treating Miss Trent as he treated most young ladies, and this clearly would not do. His interest was aroused. Miss Trent had a very expressive face, not beautiful like her cousin but yet with its own attraction, not the least of which was the intelligence sparkling in her hazel eyes.

'Are you by any chance mocking me, Miss Trent?' he asked, awaiting her response with interest – and not disappointed by it.

'Just offering you the sort of conversation you expected, Mr Giffard.'

It was then he decided that he'd like to make her better acquaintance. 'Touché. Perhaps we could start again?' Her liveliness would make a welcome change from young ladies who were either so nervous about doing something wrong that they hardly dared open their mouths, or so intent on making a lively impression that they became over-effusive.

Cassie studied him cautiously. His face had now lost its wooden expression and he was smiling. Goodness, he was *very* handsome in this mood! How could Susannah not be attracted to him? 'Whatever you wish, sir.' She waited for him to speak first, for she did not intend to hang upon his words, like those silly Dinnington girls.

'How do you like to spend your time when you have freedom to choose'?' A glance flickered towards her aunt and spoke for itself.

'I love to walk on the moors,' she said at once. 'Or ride. I live in a smoky little town and I love getting out into the countryside.'

'I, too. But the countryside near my home is very cosy, with woods and fields and pleasant vistas. It doesn't have the sweeping spaces of the moors.'

'You've visited the North?'

'Yes. Several times. I have relatives in Lancashire.'

She felt tears rise in her eyes. She missed her home so much, and her *real* family. With a deprecating smile, she said, 'We'd better change the subject. I'm still a little homesick.'

So he talked of his own home, which he loved, and saw her relax again.

And she found herself enjoying what he had to say about Stovely, regretting it when she had to turn back to Mr Heversley as the next course was served.

When the meal was over and everyone was reunited in the drawing-room, the two Dinnington sisters entertained the company with a duet upon the piano, with only a very few false notes, after which Mr Heversley sang 'The Rose She Wore' in a rather wobbly tenor voice, with a soulful expression in his eyes as he looked at Louisa Dinnington.

Cassie was not called upon to perform, as she had already confessed to a lack of musical skill, but to end the evening's entertainment, Susannah sang for them, to her mother's accompaniment. Her voice was quite outstanding, as beautiful as any Cassie had ever heard, and the applause afterwards was spontaneous and sincere. Susannah was prevailed upon to give two encores, which she did with blushing modesty, then, when she resolutely declined to sing again, the tea tray was brought in.

Within half an hour the party had broken up.

'Quite long enough,' Lady Berrinden stated as the front door closed behind the last guest. 'A very satisfactory little affair. But I'd be obliged if you, Cassandra, would take more care in future when drinking. You must learn to sip delicately, as a lady should. If you are thirsty, then quench your thirst before a function begins, but do not gulp your glass like a horse at the water trough.'

Cassie responded only with a nod, but she lay awake for a long time that night, wondering how she would endure the boredom of more evenings like that – and for how long she could continue to bite her tongue. If it had not been for Mr Giffard, she would have found no enjoyment whatsoever tonight, but she had very much enjoyed his quiet descriptions of Stovely – once she'd shown him she did not relish meaningless pleasantries. The man was a puzzle. He seemed so very stiff most of the time, then just once or twice he had relaxed and she had seen what she believed was the real Simeon Giffard – a much more likeable person.

But the rest of the guests had been dull, and if this were a sample of London high life, then the nine months until her majority would be even more tedious than she had feared. Safe behind her bed curtains, Cassie allowed herself the rare luxury of a few tears of regret for the happy family life she had led until her father's sudden murder three years previously.

After a few moments, however, she scrubbed her eyes fiercely on a corner of the sheet and reminded herself that this was no way to go on. She would do as her mother had wished and endure a London Season, but, she scowled into the darkness as she made the promise to herself, she did *not* intend to let her aunt push her into marriage with a stuffed shirt of a man like Mr Heversley, or worse still, one as arrogant as Mr Simeon Giffard could sometimes be.

And once she was twenty-one, she would live as she chose, though first she would have to think what to do . . . One didn't really die of boredom, after all. But she didn't think she could live in Bardsley again, with its sad memories. She would have to keep her eyes open and . . . She fell asleep on that thought, to dream of exhilarating encounters with Simeon Giffard, in which she came off winner every time, encounters in which he showed her his more attractive self.

Three

The next morning, punctually at eleven o'clock, Simeon Giffard arrived to take the young ladies riding. They set off from Bransham Gardens, with grooms following behind.

You would think we were expecting footpads to attack us, thought Cassie scornfully, but she could not maintain her ill humour and felt her spirits lifting in spite of the staid progress of the cavalcade, which went at a pace to suit Susannah's slug of a horse. The grey mare Cassie was riding seemed unused to city traffic, for a couple of times it took exception to passing carriages or people stepping carelessly off the pavement. She saw Mr Giffard look sharply her way once or twice and smiled at his patent uneasiness. The animal was a trifle frisky, but nothing she couldn't control. After a moment or two, he nodded as if in approval, and stopped watching her.

Although it wasn't a very warm day, she raised her face to the sun, enjoying the brightness of the morning. It was so good to be out of the house; good to be away from her aunt's strident voice and unceasing vigilance; good, even, that Simeon Giffard was giving most of his attention to Susannah.

In the park, they left the grooms near the entrance and the horses were allowed to move into a sedate trot.

They stopped almost immediately, however, to chat to the Dinnington sisters, who were then invited to join them.

Cassie had managed to fall behind her companions when

suddenly, a large dog darted out from behind a clump of trees and began to bark furiously at her horse. As the dog raced round and round her, barking, her horse began to dance about nervously. Someone was shouting, but Cassie could only concentrate on staying on the animal's back. The dog redoubled its efforts and with a jerk, the horse swung round and took off across the park.

The dog ran alongside for a moment, still barking, then a voice called and it ran back among the trees. Cassie knew she shouldn't be galloping here, but for a moment or two she gave the horse its head, enjoying the exhilaration.

Becoming aware of hooves pounding along behind her, she cast a glance over her shoulder and saw Simeon Giffard bearing down upon her. With a sigh, she began to slow her mount down, so that when he drew alongside, she had it under control and was trotting again.

He was very watchful, but made no move to intervene. 'Are you all right, Miss Trent?'

'Oh, yes. It was nothing. The dog frightened my horse, that's all.' Smiling, she turned and began to walk the mare slowly across to her cousin then realised in dismay that people were staring at them. 'Oh, dear! Have I quite disgraced myself by galloping in the park?'

'They'll have seen the dog upset your mare. No disgrace to that. You mustn't ride this animal in town again, however. It's clearly not used to crowds.'

Everything closed in on her again. 'No. I suppose not.'

'If your uncle has no suitable mount, I can send for a horse from Stovely.'

'No need to do that. I'll send for my own mare from home. We left in such a hurry I never thought to do that.'

Susannah was waiting for them, pale and obviously distressed by the incident. Cassie watched Simeon's impatience at her cousin's fussing, then intervened with a bracing, 'No harm done, Susannah. I'm fine.'

'But—'

Cassie could not keep the sharpness from her voice. 'I'm *perfectly* all right. Now, may we continue our ride, please? People are staring.'

Susannah flushed and rode on.

Cassie found herself riding behind with Simeon while her cousin conversed with her two dearest friends.

He was silent at first, then said abruptly, 'Where exactly in Lancashire do you come from, Miss Trent? Susannah didn't seem sure.'

They had both received firm instructions from Lady Berrinden not to bore people by discussing Cassie's antecedents. 'Near Manchester.'

'Where exactly near Manchester?'

'Oh, it's a very small town. You wouldn't recognise its name.'

'Are you prevaricating?'

She flushed and said through gritted teeth, 'No, Mr Giffard, but you must allow me to be surprised at your insistence on knowing. You're hardly likely to have heard of my small town.' She had the satisfaction of seeing him draw himself up a little at this blunt retort, so she followed up her advantage by adding, 'I come from a place called Bardsley.'

'Then I'm happy to tell you how wrong you are in your assumptions, Miss Trent. I do know Bardsley, or know of it, at any rate. A second cousin of mine has just inherited a small property there.'

'Moorthorpe Grange, that'll be. Old Mr Newborough died recently.'

'You know it?'

'Yes, of course. Bardsley's a small place.'

'Your father's family still live there, do they not?'

'Yes.'

At the thought of the Trents, she longed so desperately to see Sarah and Will that tears welled into her eyes. Breaking off the conversation, she cantered forward to join the others before she betrayed her feelings.

Simeon saw her flick the tears away with one fingertip and guessed that she must be feeling homesick. He felt suddenly ashamed of the way he had pressed her to talk about her family and her home. She was the most provoking young woman he had ever met, but he had not intended to hurt her.

He watched her chatting to Louisa Dinnington. She was smiling politely and yet her eyes were still over-bright. Could she be missing her family so much? From what Susannah had innocently let fall in conversation, Miss Trent could count herself lucky to be sponsored into the ton by Lady Berrinden, who was an old termagant, but whose birth and breeding were impeccable.

But even that thought annoyed him, because it was patronising. No wonder she had taken offence. What was there about this young woman that always made him feel uncertain of how to behave? Whatever it was, he wasn't sure he liked it. She was so unlike any other young woman of his acquaintance.

When the ride was over and the young ladies had duly thanked Mr Giffard for the outing, they went upstairs to change their riding habits.

'It was kind of Simeon to squire us to the park, wasn't it?' asked Susannah.

'I suppose so.'

Susannah stopped dead. 'Why, Cassie, you don't sound happy about our ride.'

'Well, Simeon Giffard can be very arrogant, don't you think? And I would prefer him to keep his condescension for those who are willing to accept it!'

With that, the homesickness welled up again, so Cassie muttered something about changing her clothes, hurried into her bedroom and closed the door behind her. She leaned against it for a moment, wondering why she had let herself get so upset by Simeon Giffard – only, no one else had really asked her about her home, not even Susannah. And she missed her family greatly.

She pushed herself away from the door and rang for Mary Ann. What did Simeon Giffard matter to her? What did anyone in London matter? She would probably never come here again once this Season was over.

After a few evening engagements and a couple of lessons from a dancing master, Lady Berrinden decided her niece would not disgrace herself or her family at a ball, and informed her of that fact. 'You had better wear the cream satin for your first appearance.'

Cassie immediately decided to wear a very striking red dress, about which her aunt had been rather dubious.

'Cheer up, lass,' said her maid that evening, while putting the finishing touches to her coiffure. 'You'll probably enjoy yourself.'

'I doubt it. Oh, Mary Ann, I think I'll go mad if I have to stay here till my birthday.'

'Get on with you!'

'Are *you* enjoying it here?'

The maid shrugged. 'Not so's you'd notice. These southerners have been making fun of the way I talk.' She grinned. 'I think I've managed to hold my own, though, and very fortunately, the housekeeper's mother came from Yorkshire, so I've found myself an ally. Funny, I've never thought much of Yorkshire folk before.'

She glanced sideways and added gently, 'What's the matter, love?'

Cassie shook her head. 'Nothing in particular. It's just – no one talks about anything *real,* Mary Ann. All they do is gossip about the Royal Dukes rushing into marriage and – and who has gambled away a fortune. Don't they know that poor people are starving? That the war they're so proud of winning has left men maimed with no means to earn a crust?'

'I dare say they don't. There's not many as care for their people like the Trents do. Now, hold your head still a minute!' Mary Ann fitted a confection of red silk roses and ribbons into the side of the high cluster of curls. 'There, that's got the dratted thing in place. Are you sure your aunt said you could wear this dress tonight?'

Cassie dimpled. 'I didn't ask her. And it's too late to change it now.'

Mary Ann shook her head, but she too was smiling broadly. 'Well, love, I'm glad to see you getting a bit of your old spirit back. Just don't let it get away from you.'

Planting a kiss on her maid's cheek, Cassie gathered her things together and made her way downstairs, feeling cheered up by their conversation. Of course she wouldn't let herself do anything impetuous here in London! She was not a complete fool.

When she saw her niece, Amelia Berrinden's sense of propriety fought a brief battle with her sense of style – and lost. The red crepe dress was ravishing on a tall brunette. With it, Cassie was wearing a diamond pendant and bracelet, which had belonged to her mother and which, Lady Berrinden saw at a glance, must have cost a small fortune. Even she had nothing to compare with them, for her husband's family jewels were old-fashioned and none of the stones was out of the ordinary. Had there been money to spare, she would have insisted on better ones; as there was not, she treated them as if they were priceless heirlooms and refused even to have them re-set in a more modern style.

'Oh, you do look magnificent, Cassie!' exclaimed Susannah. 'I wish I could wear a dress like that!'

'Red would make you look faded,' snapped her mother. 'And that's a rather vulgar shade, in my opinion. I don't know what I was thinking of to let you choose it, Cassandra. But there's no time to change it now. Well, are we to stand gossiping in the hallway forever, like the grocer and his wife?'

Pleasure at looking her best gave Cassie more confidence

and she gazed round the ballroom with interest, lifting her chin proudly when she knew herself to be under scrutiny. She was tired of trying to follow Susannah's example and intended to behave as she would have done at home, with the quiet confidence of a young woman used to meeting people, not like a shy girl just making her come-out.

Her manners won the unqualified approval of her hostess, and of several other society matrons who had sons looking to marry money.

'No smell of the shop about her,' one whispered to another, and prodded her son to ask for a dance.

'Well, her mother was a Berrinden, after all,' the second lady replied, and decided to give her nephew a nudge in Miss Trent's direction the next time she saw him. No one was quite sure of the exact extent of the Trent fortune, but Amelia Berrinden had assured them it was considerable.

Susannah watched her cousin's transformation wide-eyed, wishing she dare wear such a gorgeous garment and also that she knew how to make old Lord Arlen laugh so heartily.

Cassie did feel a little nervous when being led out for the first time, because, after all, she had never before displayed her dancing skills in such exalted company and there were a lot of people sitting round the sides of the huge room watching. She needn't have worried, however, because she found herself easily able to follow her partner's lead and she soon realised that the youthful Harry was also nervous, and was more concerned with minding his own steps than with watching hers. She suppressed a smile at his efforts to count his movements and still maintain some sort of a conversation with his partner, and had soon quite lost her own nervousness in encouraging him to relax.

Her ladyship, watching her niece with grim concentration, ready to pounce at the first sign of unbecoming or forward behaviour, nodded to herself. The girl would do. And after all, you couldn't expect a woman who was five feet nine inches tall, the possessor of a large fortune and

over twenty years old to behave like a shrinking violet of
seventeen.

Even Lord Berrinden commented that, 'By Jove, Cassie
looks well tonight, m'dear. She's a credit to you, indeed she
is.'

Lady Berrinden nodded acceptance of the compliment
and began to hope the next few months might not be too
hard to live through and her niece might even, with a
little judicious management, make a respectable match –
which was, after all, the purpose of the visit. She began to
consider more seriously who might be an acceptable suitor,
for her pride made her determined to earn those bequests for
her daughters.

The lovely Miss Berrinden was, of course, immediately
besieged by admirers wishing to engage her for a dance. Her
shyness did her no disservice with those young gentlemen
who were themselves up for their first Season and who
were striving so desperately to appear knowledgeable and
confident. Although they looked at Susannah's more magnificent cousin with admiration, few of them dared ask such
an elegant lady to dance.

As the evening progressed, a frown creased Amelia
Berrinden's forehead. Where was Simeon Giffard? He had
promised to be here tonight. She must tell Susannah to save
him a dance.

'The gentlemen flock to you like bees to a honeypot,'
commented Cassie as the two cousins stood together between
dances.

'Oh no! It's nothing like that. Harry lives near us in the
country and Freddy is distantly related on Mama's side.
They're simply being kind to me.'

'*Kind!* It's not just kindness that makes young men flock
to someone as pretty as you.'

Susannah turned a shocked gaze upon her, 'Cassie, I
haven't been acting in a flirtatious manner, have I?'

Cassie swallowed a teasing comment and patted her

cousin's arm. 'No, of course not, love. No one could ever accuse *you* of flirting.' In fact, Susannah seemed singularly uninterested in the gentlemen who flocked round her. 'Oh, look! Mr Giffard's just arrived. Is he always late?'

'Usually.'

'And does he always look so bored?'

'Yes. I dare say it's because he's been on the town for ages and knows everyone. My brother Richard is exactly the same. Simeon isn't – he isn't coming over here, is he?'

'No. He's talking to someone.'

Susannah sighed in relief. 'He says such cutting things at times that I'm rather afraid of him. I wish I were clever like you.'

Later, Cassie saw Simeon Giffard stroll over to join a somewhat plump gentleman. With this companion, his air of boredom vanished and he became quite animated, even laughing aloud. Intrigued, she watched unobtrusively. As she had noticed before, Mr Giffard looked different when he relaxed. He looked – yes, she had to admit it – truly handsome at the moment, which made his stiffness on other occasions puzzling.

Simeon caught sight of Lady Berrinden, who nodded at him imperiously. The animation left his face as he bowed to her from across the room, then brought his friend across to join them.

Once again he became coldly correct and the hauteur of his attitude set Cassie's teeth on edge. And yet, she was only too conscious of the tall strong body beside her, the delicate smell of his cologne, the candlelight shining on his burnished hair. She had never met anyone like him before, that must be why she found him so interesting to watch.

Lady Berrinden's attention was claimed by another acquaintance and Mr Giffard turned to Cassie. He opened his mouth as if to say something, then closed it again as he surveyed her more dashing appearance.

She did not appreciate this close scrutiny which made

her feel a little uncomfortable, so she stared right back at him.

Albert Darford watched in amusement as Miss Trent made no attempt to maintain a conversation, and his friend tried to cope with a hostile lady instead of the sycophants he usually encountered. At length, Albert took pity on him and filled in the awkward silence with a few easy remarks, to which Cassie at once responded.

The dance ended and Susannah rejoined her mother. Simeon turned with relief to her, for at least Susannah Berrinden was a restful companion. But her conversation seemed even more insipid than usual tonight, however pretty her face and attentive her expression.

After a few minutes' chat, Albert bespoke Cassie's hand for the next dance. 'Is something wrong, Miss Trent?' he asked as they met and parted, then met again during the lively steps of a Scottish reel.

She was so irritated by his friend, she forgot to mind her tongue. 'It's Mr Giffard. He looks so *bored*. That's not very flattering to Susannah.'

'Oh, you mustn't mind him. Bit shy, really, old Simeon, though you wouldn't think it to look at him.'

'He seems very arrogant at times.' Cassie realised too late that her tongue had run away with her and blushed in embarrassment. 'Oh, I'm sorry. I didn't mean to be rude about your friend.'

When they came together again, it was Albert who continued the conversation. 'It's his mother's fault Simeon's like that. The Giffards can trace their pedigree back to the dawn of history, you see, and so can the Laxleys, his mother's family. And she makes sure everyone knows it. Wait till you meet *her,* if you think old Simeon's arrogant! The thing is, he's been pursued by a great many females since his very first Season, which he doesn't enjoy. He's very eligible, you see. No brothers or sisters, inherited everything when his father died – house in town, estate in the country. Good looking, too, or at least, the ladies seem to think so.'

'Really?' Cassie pretended indifference.

Albert chuckled, but before he could speak again, they were interrupted as the ladies' partners for the next dance claimed them. As he watched Cassie walk away, his expression was thoughtful.

'Falling for the new heiress?' Simeon murmured in his friend's ear.

'Nice girl. Unaffected. Pretty, too.'

'If you admire pertness!'

'Don't you like Miss Trent?'

'Heavens, what does she matter to me?' Simeon changed the subject quickly.

At supper time he watched as Albert and Cassie chatted animatedly and suppressed his irritation when Susannah hardly contributed a word. After supper, she was immediately swept off to dance with another of her youthful admirers and Albert excused himself, being also engaged for that dance.

Cassie was left standing next to Mr Giffard until she could find her aunt. There was a moment's hesitation before he asked her to dance, and he sounded so unenthusiastic she felt anger surge up. 'No, thank you. You needn't feel obliged to dance with me!'

He looked taken aback by this remark, a reaction which filled her with satisfaction. She bobbed a mocking half-curtsey and rejoined her aunt without giving him a chance to reply.

When the wretched man followed her and asked for the honour of this dance, as if doing so for the first time, with her aunt nodding approval, Cassie felt obliged to say yes because she could imagine the scenes at Berrinden House if she dared to refuse Mr Giffard!

'You had no need to ask me again,' she hissed at him as he escorted her toward the floor.

'I couldn't resist it.' He smiled and held out his arms.

Only then did she realise this was a waltz. Surely – but a glance over her shoulder showed her aunt still nodding approval, so it must be all right to dance it. For a moment Cassie froze, looking up at him doubtfully, suddenly afraid to be held so close, but he pulled her towards him and swept her out on to the floor.

He was tall enough to make her feel small, and she was aware of the strength in the arms that were guiding her effortlessly in and out of the other dancers. She looked up to find him staring down, a hint of puzzlement in his expression. She couldn't think of a single thing to say to him, though she was not usually at a loss for words.

Dancing with him was different from dancing with other men. And dancing a waltz with him was – difficult.

His voice was a low growl just above her ear and his breath fanned her cheek as he spoke, 'Are you enjoying your first London ball, Miss Trent?'

She found her voice at last. 'Of course, Mr Giffard. Isn't everyone?'

They danced in silence for another half-circuit of the floor, then he said unexpectedly, 'You look well in that dress. Red suits you.'

Receiving a compliment from him was so disconcerting she could feel herself flushing. When he followed that remark by complimenting her on her dancing, and then said it was obvious her company in London was giving Susannah great pleasure, Cassie became suspicious. Was there a twinkle in those grey eyes? Could the great Mr Giffard be condescending to tease her?

She was suddenly filled with exhilaration. She looked at him limpidly and fluttered her eyelashes in an exaggerated way. 'Oh, Mr Giffard, it's *so* easy to dance well, when one has *such* a skilled partner. And your conversation is always *so* interesting, too!'

He was betrayed into laughing, which set her chuckling as well.

'All right. Cry truce, Miss Trent!' he said.

'Very well, Mr Giffard.' As he whirled her around in an intricate spiral, she leaned back against the strength of his arm and gave herself up to the pleasure of the dance. In truth, it was the first time she had waltzed with anyone except her cousin Will or the other young men she had known since childhood, and she was enjoying the sensation. That must be what was making her pulse race. It was still considered a very dashing dance, even in London, but now that the Prince Regent had allowed it at court, even the highest sticklers would hesitate to ban it at their balls.

'Ah, that was wonderful!' she exclaimed, as he led her off the floor. 'Thank you so much!'

'It was a pleasure, Miss Trent. You are an excellent dancer.'

She inclined her head. 'You too, sir.'

As they neared Lady Berrinden, she felt him stiffen again, and listening to him a few moments later, wondered at the brief metamorphosis she had experienced in his behaviour.

Albert, who had missed nothing, shook his head in mock reproof when Simeon rejoined him. 'Thought you were after the Berrinden girl. Leave the heiress for someone else, there's a good chap!'

The ball ended at two o'clock in the morning and it annoyed Cassie that she dreamed of Mr Giffard that night, of dancing with him in an enormous ballroom, where they were the only two people. She could feel her head spinning, delight shivering along her veins as they circled the floor. She wished the dance would last forever.

Goodness! she thought in the morning, recalling the dreams with embarrassment. These late nights are not good for one!

Susannah was so exhausted the following morning that Lady

Berrinden sent her back to her bedroom to lie down after breakfast. Watching, Cassie thought how unsuited her poor cousin was to the life of a lady of fashion, for the series of late nights had exhausted her, leaving dark circles in the delicate skin under her eyes.

Cassie herself felt bursting with energy and would have loved to take a brisk walk, but for the past day or two the weather had been grey and overcast, and anyway, Susannah merely dawdled along. Cassie had to spend the morning in yet another series of fittings for clothes, for Mrs Keeling, the seamstress employed by Mademoiselle Clunette, was still coming to the house at regular intervals and had produced a heroic number of garments in a very short space of time.

The poor woman was looking heavy-eyed today, but when Cassie asked if she were feeling quite well, she hastily denied any debility. A slight head cold, very slight. She begged miss's pardon for the annoyance that it might cause. It would soon pass and she promised it would have no effect upon the quality of her work.

At luncheon, during which the two of them were alone, Lady Berrinden took the opportunity to warn her niece not to let her behaviour become too pert. 'You mustn't let Mr Giffard's kindness to a young relative of mine go to your head, you know.'

'No, Aunt Amelia.' Cassie felt her eyes glaze over with boredom. There was no point in arguing with her aunt, who would never listen to anyone else's point of view once she had made up her mind.

'I didn't at all like the way you were laughing when you two were dancing. He spoke to me afterwards about your behaviour.' Actually, he'd said that he'd enjoyed Miss Trent's liveliness, but that had annoyed her ladyship, for he should only have been *enjoying* Susannah's company. 'You are to behave more modestly in future, if you please.'

Cassie said nothing, just concentrated on drawing breath quietly up her nostrils and picturing the odious Mr Giffard pierced by spears and arrows. How dared he complain when *he* had started everything by teasing her, and had seemed to enjoy her response, too?

When luncheon was over, she stormed upstairs to find Susannah awake again and waiting for her in the small sitting-room used by the young ladies in the few unoccupied moments allowed them by Lady Berrinden.

'Is something wrong?' Susannah asked as the door slammed and Cassie began pacing up and down the room.

'Not more than usual. Your Mama, my dear cousin, has been scolding me again.'

'Oh dear, what's wrong? I do hope she won't be in a bad mood for the rest of the day.'

'It's I who am in a bad mood, though I shouldn't be taking it out on you. But my aunt has just implied that I have been throwing myself at Mr Giffard.'

'*At Simeon!*'

'Precisely. If I were to throw myself at any gentleman, it would *not* be him, I can assure you!'

'Oh yes, I agree. Simeon is so very – well, so very severe.'

'Downright arrogant, in fact!'

'Yes. He's usually quite kind to me, but I'm a little afraid of – of offending him. He can be dreadfully sarcastic.'

'But I thought—' Cassie broke off abruptly. Was it possible that Susannah was unaware of her mother's aspirations? If so, she must be the only person in London who was.

'Simeon's mother is a very close friend of Mama's, you know. We are forever staying with them in the country at Stovely Chase. He's very proud of his home, but I think it's a dreadful, gloomy old place. They visit us at Fairleigh sometimes or, at least, they used to before Richard left and before Mrs Giffard became an invalid. Simeon and my brother were at school together, you see. They aren't as close as he and Mr Darford are, but they've known one another for a long time.'

Cassie let the matter drop. Not for her to prepare Susannah for her mother's ambitions, which, if Simeon Giffard's assiduous attendance at the same social functions was anything to judge by, were highly likely to be fulfilled.

They did not see Mr Giffard for the next two days, as he was visiting his mother again, for which Cassie was grateful. If he'd come near her after criticising her to her aunt, she'd have been strongly tempted to give him a piece of her mind and tell him frankly that her behaviour was none of his business. Indeed, she several times found herself indulging in mental exchanges with him, where she gave him a set-down and brought him to apologise. But these daydreams were not half as satisfying as an actual encounter would be, and she found herself listening for his name, so that she would be prepared when she met him.

In the meantime, Albert Darford called on them, and proved as pleasant as first impressions had suggested. He reminded Cassandra a little of her cousin, Will, and she felt at ease with him. The two of them chuckled over the absurdities of members of the ton, and he told her several tales of past Seasons and amusing mishaps.

This made her aunt look at her sharply at first, but Cassie ignored that. Did the ladies in London think of nothing but attracting men to wed? she wondered. How foolish!

She would have been horrified if she had realised her aunt was seriously considering his suitability as a marriage partner for her. Cassie had not for a moment regarded Albert as a suitor, but someone whose company she enjoyed. She didn't want any suitors, thank you very much. She was not sure what she did want from life, but there must be something beside an arranged marriage and a tedious round of social events.

In any case, she did not intend to marry anyone unless she fell as deeply in love as her parents had. On that she was quite resolved.

*   *   *

Lady Berrinden was in a gracious mood for the rest of the week, to her family's relief. Who would have thought it? she told her husband. Cassandra attracting Darford! But they need not be ashamed of that connection. And certainly the Darfords needed the money. The Trent fortune might as well go to a good cause.

Lord Berrinden wasn't so sure. To his mind, Albert was not the sort of fellow who ever got married. There were some like that, happy to remain pampered bachelors. You came to recognise them. Indeed, even envy them sometimes.

Besides, Cassie didn't look at Albert in a flirtatious way. But Lord Berrinden didn't say that to his wife, hoping she wouldn't realise it. Life was so much easier when Amelia was not upset. A dashed relief all round.

He made plans to spend the evening at his club, where he toasted his beautiful daughter and newly found niece a great many times. Nothing wrong with a fellow having a drink or two with his friends, nothing at all – whatever Amelia said.

Four

The days continued to pass in a round of engagements, some of which Cassie could not help but enjoy. The theatre had her enthralled and she made great use of the bookshops and a circulating library, reading voraciously works such as *Northanger Abbey* and *Persuasion*. Such a pity that Miss Austen, now revealed to be the author, had died so young!

Pride and Prejudice was one of Cassie's favourite novels and now that she was seeing the silly focus on match-making from close at hand, her delight in the author's mockery of it much increased.

Lady Berrinden inspected the first few books her niece brought home, then lost interest, so Cassie was able to indulge a certain low taste for gothic tales, and even to share this with her cousin without upsetting her aunt.

There were times, however, when Cassie longed to do something more worthwhile with her time, as she had in Bardsley, for there she and her mother had kept an eye on the welfare of the many Trent employees, visiting the sick, ensuring that promising children got an education, that people too old to work were not going hungry. It had been so very satisfying to feel oneself of real use.

Although trade had improved in the last twelve months, she knew from reading her Uncle Henry's newspapers – something he clearly did not often do – that many of the poor in the south were still in great want of the necessities of life, but when she mentioned that to her aunt and asked if there were anything she could do to help, Lady Berrinden was quite horrified and scolded her for a full ten minutes. So Cassie had to keep her restlessness bottled up and tell herself that a few months would soon pass.

One day, she could stand it no longer and summoned Mary Ann to her room early in the morning. 'I want to go out for a walk,' she fixed her maid with a determined look as she added, 'just the two of us, no footman trailing behind. And if we can manage it, no catechism from my aunt about where we're going.'

'She'll throw a fit, Miss Cassie, and it'll be me as gets into trouble.'

'I'll make sure she doesn't blame you.' She beat at the windowpane with a clenched fist. 'Mary Ann, if I don't get out, I'll go *mad*!'

'Best not to wear one of your grand cloaks, then. Your old travelling cloak is upstairs in your trunk. I'll fetch it. And wear something dark under it.' She frowned at her young mistress. 'And a bonnet with a veil, as if you're a widow. Then it'll not seem as unnatural for you to be out and about.'

Cassie's eyes lit up. 'And we'll go out the back way. Can you get us out of the house without anyone seeing?'

'Mebbe.'

As they were walking along the street, Cassie threw up her hands and skipped a few steps, joy radiating from her. 'Oh, Mary Ann, would you mind walking *fast* I'm so tired of dawdling.'

Which was how the two of them came to be in the park at the time when all the nursemaids were taking their young charges for walks.

Mary Ann glanced sideways at her mistress, whose cheeks were glowing with the brisk exercise and who was looking better than she had for weeks. Like keeping a frisky puppy chained up, it was, expecting Miss Cassie to sit around all day. No good could come of it.

The first two outings went well, with none of the servants noticing them creeping out – or perhaps they had looked the other way, not wanting to become involved.

On their third outing, however, the two women found a small child weeping softly to itself in the park, and of course Cassie had to stop and see if she could help. Which led to her throwing up her veil, and picking up the child, the better to comfort it.

Simeon Giffard had ridden past and admired the devotion of the young mother to her child before he realised who the lady was – upon which he reined in abruptly and swung his horse round.

'Miss Trent.' He raised his hat to her.

'Oh, drat!'

He blinked in shock.

Cassie glanced round and saw one or two people staring at them and hissed, 'Pray ride on, Mr Giffard, and don't tell my aunt you've seen me here today.'

'I – beg your pardon?'

The child began to cry again, upset by his sharp tone.

'Now see what you've done!' Cassie told him crossly.

He swung down and gave the child his whip to play with, a ploy which always answered with the children of his tenants.

Just then there was a shriek from behind them and a young woman came rushing towards them, snatching the child from Cassie's arms as if she had kidnapped her. 'What are you doing with Janie?' she demanded.

'I found her weeping for her mother and took her in charge until we could find you,' Cassie told her.

'Oh. Oh, dear, I beg your pardon, miss. I just turned round for a minute and she was gone.' She bent her head to kiss her young charge, saying fondly, 'Now see what you've done, you naughty girl!'

'No harm done. But see you keep a better eye on her in future.' Cassie turned away, with a curt, 'Good day to you, Mr Giffard.'

He grabbed her arm and pulled her back.

'Does Lady Berrinden know you're out, Miss Trent?'

'That, sir, is none of your business!'

'Then she doesn't know.'

Cassie wrenched her arm away, breathing unevenly. Once again, he had made her feel – uncomfortable, restless. 'I repeat – it's none of your business, sir.'

'I am making it my business.' He gestured to his groom, hovering a few paces away. 'Follow us with my horse, George. I'll escort Miss Trent and her maid home.'

Cassie swung round and set off at top speed, ignoring him.

He had to run to catch her up.

Mary Ann rolled her eyes at the groom as she set off more sedately behind them. George grinned and followed them, leading his master's horse – an indignity to which it took great exception, tugging and jerking in an attempt to get free.

'Your horse needs its rider,' Cassie said curtly, looking behind to see what the noise was about, 'and I have my maid to keep me company, so there is *no need* for you to force your company on me.'

'What are you doing out at this early hour? It isn't safe.'

She stopped and glared at him. 'If it's any of your business, I'm taking a walk.'

'But surely you can do that at the fashionable hour, with your cousin to keep you company?'

'That, sir, is a mere dawdle. I'm used to real walks and find myself in sore need of exercise.' She set off again.

He followed, amazed to see how fast she could walk, not to mention how pretty a glow this exercise lent to her cheeks.

Not until they neared Bransham Gardens did she stop again, to confront him, arms akimbo. 'I suppose you intend to report this to my aunt.'

He hesitated, knowing he ought to do just that.

'Well?' She was tapping one foot, anger radiating from her.

He threw wide his arms. 'Have it your own way, Miss Trent. But if I see you out without your maid, I shall certainly mention this to your aunt.'

She opened her mouth, ready to argue and it took her a minute to realise she had made her point. 'Oh. Well. Thank you.'

He raised his hat in a mocking gesture and signalled to his groom to bring his horse up. But although he mounted, he didn't move away until he had seen her turn the corner safely into her own street. He rode off very thoughtfully. She had looked magnificent. He had never met a lady who could walk so fast, and without getting out of breath, too. She was clearly not meant for town life.

Another picture came into his mind as he trotted slowly homewards: Cassie bending her head over the child, comforting it, not caring whether the snotty, tear-stained face smeared her cloak or not. 'You have to admit that she's – she's –' But he didn't finish his sentence, or answer the groom's query as to whether he wanted something, but rode slowly on, lost in thought.

He couldn't imagine Susannah, for all her tender heart, doing that – and as for his own mother, well, he had no memories of her ever cuddling him as a child, none whatsoever. And although he had had a very loving nurse until he was nine years old, when she had left to marry, that was not the same as having a loving mother. The child had looked up at Miss Trent so trustingly, clearly feeling quite secure in her arms. It made him think of what he had missed, something he hadn't done for years.

Two days later, Cassie was summoned unexpectedly to the drawing-room at eleven in the morning. She had been sitting with Susannah in the small parlour, where the two young ladies were supposed to be working on their embroidery – something Cassie loathed with a passion and which she mostly left lying untouched upon her lap.

In the doorway of the drawing-room, she stopped in her tracks as she saw her cousin Will sitting with Lady Berrinden, whose icy politeness was meant to show that she had no intention of encouraging any of her niece's northern relatives to worm their way into the ton.

'Will! Oh, Will!' Cassie rushed across the room to fling herself into his arms and startled everyone, herself included, by bursting into tears.

He held her close, patting her back and frowning at his hostess. 'Nay, Cassie, love, this isn't like you. Are you all right?'

She gulped and made a huge attempt to stop the tears, aware of the expression of distaste on her aunt's face and knowing there would be another scolding in store about her unladylike display of emotion later. 'I'm s-sorry, Will. It was just the surprise. I didn't know you were coming to London'

'It was a sudden decision. I had no time to write first.'

She went to sit down on a sofa and he joined her there, still frowning.

'How are you settling down here, Cassie?'

What could she say? Her aunt was sitting there listening to every word. 'Um – everyone has been most kind. We've been to a ball and riding in the park and—'

He gave a snort of laughter. 'Rather you than me. I wouldn't like to spend *my* life doing the pretty to strangers. Nor I wouldn't like all those late nights. Ten o'clock is quite late enough for anyone to go to bed. Especially a man with a business to run.'

Cassie saw her aunt's expression relax a little, and hid a smile. She knew Lady Berrinden was worried the rest of the Trent family might try to encroach upon their social life, but she was well aware that nothing could have been further from the minds of her paternal relatives. They would have been bored to tears by it all – as she was much of the time. 'What are you doing here, Will?'

'Our broader business interests need a little attention. As you well know, if we didn't have other strings to our bow, things would have gone hard with our operatives lately. You know what the textile trade's been like since the war ended.'

After listening for a few more minutes to their business talk, with an expression of frozen boredom and distaste on her face, Lady Berrinden intervened. 'Perhaps you would care to continue this discussion over luncheon, Mr Trent? I have an engagement which I cannot break, but I know Cassie and Susannah are free. I shall send my daughter down to join you.'

The moment her ladyship left the room, Will turned to his cousin with a determined look on his face. 'Now tell me straight, Cassie. *Are* you unhappy here? Because if you are, I'll take you back home with me when I go, and to hell with the lawyers.'

She laughed and hugged him again. 'Oh, Will, I'm fine, really I am, though this sort of life is not to my taste, I will admit.'

He nodded. 'Aye, well, it sounds a rubbishy way of going on to me.'

'It is,' she agreed soberly. 'But I suppose it'll give me time to get used to being without Mother. In Bardsley there were so many memories.' Her voice trembled a little and she had to take a deep breath before adding, 'And my cousin's a dear. You'll like her.'

That was a considerable underestimation of the effect Susannah had on Will. When she tripped into the room, well rested after a morning with no engagements, her silver-gilt hair lit up the sombre formality of the breakfast parlour and when she smiled shyly at the visitor with those lovely blue eyes, Will Trent could only stand and goggle, totally forgetting his manners.

Observing Susannah's instant and effortless captivation of yet another hapless male, Cassie couldn't help wishing that she herself made even a tenth of that impression on the gentlemen she met. Had it been anyone else but Will, she would have stood back and thoroughly enjoyed watching the encounter. However, it was Will, and apart from the fact that she was conscious of a little tug of annoyance that he should be just like all the rest, she was only too well aware that nothing could come of such an attraction.

He made a heroic effort to tear his gaze away from Susannah and, after helping her to sit down as if she were made of the most fragile glass, he resolutely gave his attention to his cousin, though his eyes kept straying back to Susannah from time to time.

Cassie wanted to know a dozen things. 'How is Sarah? And dear Aunt Lucy?'

'Well, as usual. Did you ever know them to ail?'

'Is Sarah missing me? I miss her quite dreadfully.'

'Well, she moped around at first. Then she got to know Newborough's sister – you know, the fellow who's inherited Moorthorpe Grange. The pair of them are getting as thick as thieves.'

'Oh.'

He patted her hand. 'Nay, Cassie, no one could replace you in her affections, and well you know it! Sarah's given me a letter for you. I've got it somewhere – yes, here it is! And I'm not to dare go back without a long reply from you!'

Cassie smiled a little mistily at him, holding the letter tightly clasped in her hand. Then, guiltily, she remembered her other cousin. 'I'm sorry, Susannah. We're being very inconsiderate, talking about people you've never met!'

'Oh, please don't stop for me! It's only natural that you'd want to hear about your family and friends. It's I who feel like an intruder – only Mama said . . .' Susannah's voice tailed away and she flushed.

'I can imagine exactly what Mama said.' Cassie turned to Will. 'Do you realise that Susannah is here to chaperone me because of you?' Her eyes were dancing as she spoke.

Will's horrified expression made Susannah give an involuntary gurgle of laughter, and that set Cassie off as well.

'It's all right you two laughing,' he said indignantly, forgetting his formal manners, 'but I never heard anything so stupid in all my life! A chaperone, indeed! As well chaperone me and my horse! Mind you set your aunt straight on that, Cassie – or perhaps I should do it myself. A chaperone! As if I'd want to marry *you*!'

And that masterly compliment set the two young ladies laughing again.

The atmosphere during the rest of the meal remained lighthearted. Cassie and Will, unable to resist the temptation to exchange news, seemed to find something humorous in nearly everything they talked about, even when the joke was against them.

Susannah, carried along on a tide of loving warmth, such as she had never experienced in her whole life, wished the meal would go on for ever.

But in the end, Will pulled out his watch, exclaimed that he would be late for an appointment in the City if he didn't set off at once, and took a reluctant leave of them. 'I'll call again tomorrow, if that's convenient, Cassie, Miss Berrinden.'

As the daughter of the house, Susannah took it upon herself to reply, 'We shall be very happy to see you at any time, Mr Trent. Perhaps you would take luncheon with us again tomorrow?'

'I'd love to – No, I can't! I'm engaged with some business colleagues, but I could pop in for an hour in the morning, if that's all right.'

Seeing Cassie's disappointment, Susannah had an inspiration. 'Perhaps you could come out with us for a drive the day after that, then, Mr Trent? That would give you a chance to talk to Cassie properly.' Without her mother glaring at them.

'I'd like that.' But his eyes were on Susannah, not his cousin, and there was a warmth in his gaze that worried Cassie.

'You did *what?*' demanded her ladyship, when informed of the invitation her daughter had extended.

'I – I invited Mr Trent to take a drive with us, Mama.'

Air hissed into her ladyship's mouth and she turned on her niece. 'Let me make it quite clear to you, Cassandra, that there is to be no foisting your paternal relatives on to our friends.'

Seeing a dangerous sparkle come into her cousin's eyes, Susannah nobly tried to divert her mother's attention, 'But it was I who invited Mr Trent, Mama!'

'At whose instigation, pray?' She shot another venomous glance at her niece, who was looking altogether too pretty lately and whose vivacity sometimes made her cousin look rather fragile and spiritless.

What her mother might have said or done had not visitors been announced just at that moment, Susannah hardly dared contemplate. She was glad to go and sit quietly in a corner, letting her pounding heart slow down again and wondering at her own rashness. But she couldn't regret the invitation, however much Mama scolded, for Mr Trent was such agreeable company. And he had quite taken the sad look out of her cousin's eyes.

'You are a goose, Susannah!' Cassie informed her later on, when they had been sent up to change their clothes for yet another slow drive round the park. 'You really shouldn't let your mother upset you so – especially when it concerns me and Will.'

'I know, but – well, he is your cousin, and he is so – so – well, gentlemanly. I – I mean . . .' Susannah lost herself in a morass of half-sentences, as she tried to correct any impression she might have given that she had expected Mr Trent to be anything other than gentlemanly.

'Dear goose,' said Cassie, putting an arm around her cousin's slender shoulders, 'I know precisely what you mean, and I can assure you that your mother's attitude causes me no more than a temporary irritation. Now, pray stop worrying and go and change, or we shall be further in her black books.'

Susannah looked at her wonderingly. 'You don't really care very much what she thinks, do you?' she asked a little hesitantly. 'And however great a kindness Mama feels she's doing you by introducing you to our friends, you don't care much about that either? I wish—' She broke off abruptly, not wanting to be disloyal to her mother. 'Anyway, I'm glad you came to stay with us,' she said and gave Cassie a sudden convulsive hug before hurrying off to her room.

The next day, when Will called to see them, Lady Berrinden remained in the room and her presence inevitably prevented them from recapturing the happy mood of the previous day. Conversation was stilted and laborious, and it was made very plain that her ladyship was not interested either in the doings of unknown and unimportant provincial persons, nor could she see anything in business matters to interest a group of ladies.

Susannah would have felt upset about this deliberate attempt to discourage Mr Trent from visiting them had she not received a friendly wink from Will when her mother was not looking, and had Cassie not squeezed her hand when Lady Berrinden made a more than usually disdainful remark. It made Susannah feel rather naughty, but she enjoyed the sense of conspiracy and, for the first time, her belief that Mama always knew best was a little shaken.

While Will was with them, Mr Giffard's card was brought in and Lady Berrinden felt obliged to have him shown in. He entered the room with his usual aloof air and, after greeting

the company and being introduced to Will, he presented
Lady Berrinden with a letter from his mother, engaging in
desultory conversation with the others while she excused
herself to read this.

Will did not like the newcomer's attitude and had no
intention of being spoken down to. 'Giffard,' he said,
wrinkling his forehead. 'Now, where have I heard that
name before?'

'Perhaps you know my relatives at Moorthorpe Grange?'

'Ah yes,' replied Will. 'That'll be it. Miss Dennaby is
always in and out of our house these days, but I'm a
busy man and I don't pay the attention I should to social
chit-chat.'

There was an audible intake of breath from Lady
Berrinden at this and a moment's silence, during which
Cassie pulled an expressive face at Susannah, who was
looking petrified.

Simeon looked at Will, then surprised them all by chuckling. 'Your point, Trent,' he conceded.

Will grinned back at him, in no way abashed. 'Aye, well,
I'll leave you on that note of triumph, then.'

'More – er – business?' asked Simeon.

'Can you doubt it?' Ignoring Lady Berrinden's icy glare,
Will turned to his cousin. 'There are some papers you need
to sign, Cassie, so I'll come a little early tomorrow and
we'll get that over with first. It'll only take a few minutes
– it's just routine stuff.' He then bowed to his hostess and
shook hands with Susannah, favouring her with another
wink, which made her feel warm and happy inside, before
he took his leave of them all.

Cassie sat quietly in a corner, puzzling over Mr Giffard's
behaviour. He was so disconcerting. One minute he was
being odiously patronising, and she could dislike him in
comfort, the next, he would smile at something, glance
in her direction, as if to share his amusement, and she
would find herself smiling with him – even when the other

people present did not see the humour. And he remained the easiest person to dance with that she had ever met, his steps matching hers far better than Albert Darford's or her cousin Will's ever did.

Her aunt's sharp voice interrupted her reverie. 'Cassie! Mr Giffard has just spoken to you.'

'Oh. I do beg your pardon. What did you say?'

'Simeon was speaking about our drive tomorrow,' Susannah explained hastily. 'Mama has just invited him and Mr Darford to accompany us.'

'Then you'll find yourself somewhat crowded, sir, since my cousin Will is also to be of the party.'

'Oh, it will be worth a little discomfort for the pleasure of furthering my acquaintance with Mr Trent.'

She looked at him suspiciously, suspecting a double meaning, but his expression displayed nothing but calm pleasure. When he was in a room, she could never quite relax, not sure whether he'd be stiff or friendly. And she was always far too aware of him, even when he was talking to other people – which annoyed her.

When he had taken his leave of them, Lady Berrinden gave full vent to her annoyance. 'Is it not enough that I must receive a person involved in trade in my own home, Cassandra? Must your relatives also be foisted on our friends?'

'It is rather Mr Giffard who has been foisted on our party,' retorted Cassie, determined not to let Will be maligned in his absence. 'But if you feel my cousin's presence tomorrow will be an imposition, that's easily settled. Will and I can take a drive on our own once we've completed our business.'

'Susannah cannot possibly go for a drive on her own with Mr Giffard and Mr Darford, as you very well appreciate.'

'Then perhaps *you* could accompany them, Aunt Amelia.'

'I have other engagements.' In fact, Lady Berrinden knew that if she did go with the party as chaperone, the pleasure of the two gentlemen would be sadly diminished and her daughter would hardly say a word. She had no desire to spoil things when they were going so well, for Simeon Giffard was paying marked attentions to Susannah, and it could only be a matter of time before he made a formal declaration. She knew his mother was pressing him to do this, because Flora had said so in her letter, but she wished her friend would let nature take its course, for gentlemen resented it if you pushed them too obviously in a certain direction. Besides, how could Simeon fail to be captivated by a girl as lovely as Susannah? She was one of the successes of the Season.

'I shall not say anything further at this time, Cassie, but I trust you will not involve your cousin with our friends again.' Then, before her provoking niece could say anything further, she swept from the room.

However, at dinner, Lady Berrinden launched a further shaft at her niece. 'If there are papers to be signed, I feel you should have the benefit of your uncle's guidance. After all, he is your guardian and a girl of your age cannot possibly be expected to understand such things. Business matters are totally beyond our female comprehension.'

As she was always present at her husband's meetings with his man of business, even Susannah felt this was going a bit far but, of course, no one dared contradict her publicly.

Lord Berrinden shot a glance of supplication at his wife, but finding her adamant, he said in a doubtful voice, 'Well, er, if you don't object, Cassie, I'll be happy to give you the benefit of my experience – if I think of anything, that is.' His voice tailed away.

'I shall be happy to have the inestimable benefit of your wise guidance, Uncle Henry.' Cassie's only regret was that she had no one to share this joke with. Even Simeon Giffard would have done, for he would have been quick to see the humour of the situation, as her cousin Susannah clearly did not.

In the event, having conducted his niece and Mr Trent into the library the next day, Lord Berrinden retired into a corner with the speed of a rabbit going to earth. 'Er – just start your discussion without me, while I attend to a small matter.'

He then disappeared behind a copy of *The Times* and did not emerge until it became obvious that all business was concluded. He could not avoid overhearing what they said, however, and later told his wife that Cassie was considerably richer than they had thought, and those dashed Trents had their fingers into a good many pies besides cotton.

His wife did not derive much satisfaction from this information and could hardly bear to address her niece civilly for the rest of the day.

The drive was more enjoyable than Cassie had expected. Mr Giffard was relaxed and friendly, with no sign of the hauteur he could display at times, Mr Darford was his usual pleasant self and Will was not one to be awed by any company.

Susannah was looking particularly radiant that day, sparkling with laughter at Will's gentle sallies and looking at him with such warmth in her eyes that Cassie began to have an uneasy suspicion that her beautiful cousin was as attracted to him as he was to her. This could lead to nothing but unhappiness for them both, so she could only hope she was mistaken, and felt relieved that Will would be leaving for the North next day.

It added to Cassie's unease in the days that followed when Susannah several times commented on how very much she had enjoyed Mr Trent's company – though she didn't mention him when her mother was present. Cassie could only hope this attraction would fade as time passed.

Albert Darford had also noted Susannah's gentle flowering as she conversed with Mr Trent and been mildly surprised, but as he had no interest in that direction himself, he merely observed the situation with his usual detached amusement. He had no doubt of his friend Simeon's ability to win over any female he chose, once he had decided to take the dreaded step into matrimony, but he was not sure Simeon had even noticed which way the wind was blowing, for during that drive he and Miss Trent had been holding a lively discussion about the plight of the poor and how best to ameliorate their distress – and had disagreed sharply on several points.

Albert himself was seriously considering paying court to Cassie Trent, this being the first time he had ever contemplated shackling himself for life. In her were combined a juicy fortune, an attractive appearance and a winning personality. Not that he was in desperate need of marrying an heiress! Certainly not. It was just that his mother and sisters had been going on at him a bit lately to settle down and produce an heir.

He sighed at that thought. He could see that he might have to do so one day, but he felt disinclined to give up his carefree bachelor existence yet. It would require considerable thought, even with a woman as charming as Cassandra Trent.

After a restless night, he came to the conclusion that for the moment, he would just take things gently. There could be no need for haste. She did not seem to be desperately on the catch for a husband, whatever her aunt's intentions. In fact, she showed not the slightest sign of feeling a tendre for anyone, himself included. Which was one of the most attractive things about her.

Five

One evening, when she had been out in polite society for over a month, Cassie overheard her aunt confide in her uncle, 'I've told Louisa Raineforth in the strictest confidence how wealthy that provoking chit is.'

Annoyed by this, Cassie could not help lingering near the doorway.

'But – doesn't that mean it will soon be all over the town, my love?'

'Exactly. That should *facilitate* matters. No one shall ever accuse me of not doing my duty by that girl!'

'Admirable, my love. Quite admirable,' he murmured. 'But – well, Cassie isn't makin' much effort to attract a husband, is she? What if she refuses 'em all?'

'Leave such things to me, Henry. I shall know how to bring her round if someone suitable offers.'

Cassie stormed up to her bedroom to confide her annoyance in Mary Ann but, after some heated expression of her feelings, allowed herself to be persuaded not to make an issue of it with her aunt. After all, no one could actually force her to accept an offer and she had met fortune hunters before, even in Bardsley, so could easily recognise the signs.

From then onwards, to her great dismay, Cassie found herself even more in demand at balls, with several gazetted fortune hunters besieging her with their attentions – though to give her aunt her due, they were given short shrift when they attempted to call on her at home – if you could call that mausoleum a home.

One day it occurred to Cassie that she might just as well use the resultant increase in her popularity to do a few things she really wanted. It soon became known that the wealthy Miss Trent had a penchant for antiquities, and that if you wished for her company, the best way to get it was to invite her to see some ancient monument or other. Gentlemen who had happily forgotten the very existence of the Romans when allowed to abandon their schoolboy Latin now perused guide books and arranged visits to see piles of mouldy stones or collections of battered statues.

Cassie did not attempt to correct the explanations they gave as they conducted her on such expeditions, though she did at times have a struggle not to laugh when told, for example, that a certain medieval church had been built in the fifth century before Christ by the Romans.

Simeon was paying a great deal of attention to Susannah, but could not persuade himself that she was responding as a young woman should to being courted. She was easily flustered in his company, offered only the most banal of conversation, and she clung to her cousin's side whenever she could. In duty bound, he asked Miss Trent to dance from time to time as well, and continued to find her the easiest woman to dance with whom he had ever met. She was graceful, lively and able to maintain a conversation on a wide range of topics without missing her steps.

He could not help observing how many suitors Miss Trent had and when he saw her on the dance floor in the arms of a man whom he did not respect, it disturbed him, to his own surprise. Well, he would not want his own sister – if he had one – to dance with some of those men, though Lady Berrinden kept the worst of the fortune hunters at bay, of course.

Cassandra Trent would make some fortunate man a good wife, he decided, adding hastily, just as Susannah would make him a good wife. Indeed the young woman he had chosen would make him a *better* wife, he was sure, for she was too gentle to cause quarrels and trouble in their home. However, he could not help noticing that even gentle Susannah had changed lately and was not nearly as docile as she had been, and he knew at whose door to lay that.

To his own surprise, however, he kept remembering how tenderly Cassie had bent over the lost child in the park and that memory troubled him. He realised that he wanted the woman he married to treat his children with similar warmth. He did not want them to have the unhappy childhood he had suffered, he was quite determined upon that. He felt that Susannah would not be unkind to anyone – but was that going to be enough?

'Oh hell, Albert,' he groaned one night, 'what's wrong with me? Richard's sister would make any man a good wife. She's pretty and pleasant natured. Why can I not bring myself to do the deed and ask for her hand?'

'Perhaps she's not the right wife for you, old fellow? Perhaps you need someone with a bit more spirit?'

Simeon shuddered. 'Spirit is the last thing I'm looking for in my wife, believe me. Imagine how a spirited girl would clash with my mother!'

Albert sighed. What could you say to that? He had tried to hint that it might be better to choose a wife to meet one's own needs, not to please one's mother, but he knew he'd be wasting his time. Simeon was determined to create a peaceful home life, after a childhood made hideous by his father's selfishness, rages and improvident behaviour, and was firmly convinced that this meant taking a wife of whom his mother would approve.

'I definitely shan't wed a female as provoking as Miss Trent. I sincerely pity the man who marries *her*, for she won't make a very comfortable wife at all. She's far too fond of expressing her own opinions and contradicting people.'

He and Cassie had had a sharp difference of opinion the last time he took Susannah and her cousin out for a drive, and Cassie's arguments had been unanswerable. 'What's more, her sense of humour might prove rather wearing in a wife.' He cocked an eye at his friend. 'So if you're thinking of offering for her . . .' He deliberately left the sentence unfinished.

'I might do. But I shan't rush into it. I've got enough brothers that I don't have to fling myself into Parson's mousetrap.' Albert rubbed his nose and frowned in thought. 'Never considered myself the marrying sort, to tell you the truth. But I have to admit that I enjoy Cassandra Trent's company.' He shrugged. 'We'll see. You'll be the first to know if I decide to offer for her.'

Simeon was puzzled that he couldn't bring himself to wish Albert good luck with the heiress. In fact, he decided after some thought, he didn't think she and Albert would suit at all. But of course you could not say that.

When his friend had gone, he sat on, staring at the ruby liquid in his glass. 'Oh, hell!' he said in the end. 'I'd better get it over with. I'll feel better once it's done.'

Surely he would?

Socially, Cassie had one more hurdle to cross. After much consideration, the lady patronesses of Almack's Assembly Rooms had decided to issue Miss Trent with vouchers. These would enable her to enter its hallowed portals and attend the Assembly Balls, held every Wednesday throughout the Season, which would, she knew, be a crucial stage in the ton's acceptance of her and – much more important to her – was something her mother had particularly wanted for her, even more than the presentation at Court. Though the latter had gone well enough – if you enjoyed such discomfort and pomp.'

The seamstress was instantly summoned back to make a new ballgown under Mademoiselle Clunette's direction, and an ivory silk was chosen for Cassie's first appearance.

'But ivory is such an insipid colour, aunt! Would it not be better to—'

'This is not a time to be trying for a dashing appearance. Oblige me for once, miss, by taking the advice of one who knows about such matters! And do not, whatever happens, dare to laugh while you are at Almack's! You are far too prone to levity, as I keep telling you. With your background, it is vital, *absolutely vital* that you show a proper respect for the conventions of our world.'

'Yes, Aunt Amelia.' What did it matter, after all?

'And why, pray, have you not done more to encourage Mr Salterby, who is the heir to an honourable line? Contradicting a man in public is no way to win his affection!'

Cassie bit her tongue and refrained from remarking that Mr Salterby was three inches shorter than she was and had a nervous titter that set her teeth on edge. She forced her fingers to uncurl before her aunt noticed the unladylike fists.

The tedious fittings recommenced, because Lady Berrinden deemed it sensible to order a few other gowns to be made up at the same time. One could not wear the same things too often, or one would be considered shabby.

To while away the time, during the hours she spent being pinned and fitted, Cassie asked Mrs Keeling, the seamstress, to tell her something about herself. The woman's initial reluctance to talk to a client was soon overcome by the genuine interest and understanding Miss Trent showed. Bit by bit, the seamstress was coaxed into revealing that she was a widow, the sole support of her four surviving children. They lived in an attic room in Garnett Lane, which was, she said vaguely, 'a coupla miles away'. She even one day let slip how much she was paid for the mammoth amount of sewing, all of it of a very high quality, which she had got through.

'Fourteen shillings a week for all this! But you're a skilled worker! You deserve far more than that!' Mentally subtracting the cost of the material from the enormous amounts charged by Mademoiselle Clunette for each completed garment, Cassie was shocked to realise how much profit the modiste was making on the transactions.

'That's only during the Season, miss, when there's a lot of work and a shortage of hands. It's less the rest of the time, and I have to do mourning then, which doesn't pay as well, and costs me more for candles.'

Cassie did not say anything, but decided she was going to find a way to help Mrs Keeling. If she had been going to get married, she would have hired her as a permanent sewing woman, but she was beginning to doubt she would ever marry. She had not, she was determined to tell herself, met a gentleman who made her heart even twitch, let alone flutter – neither in Lancashire nor in London. There was clearly something wrong with her.

Well, she would think of some other way to help the seamstress, because she would feel better if she did something useful while she was here in London. To be always thinking of one's own pleasure seemed a very unsatisfying way of life to her.

When the seamstress came to the house two days later, laboured of breath and clearly suffering from the influenza, Cassie could not stand by and see her struggle to continue working. She tried to send her straight home, but Mrs Keeling burst into tears and begged to be allowed to continue working, for her children's sake.

At another fitting an hour later, Cassie saw how the older woman swayed dizzily when bending to adjust the hem and decided that things had gone far enough.

'Mrs Keeling, you really are not fit to work. You must go home to bed until you're better.'

The seamstress burst into tears again, but allowed herself to be helped to a chair, sobbing that she would be all right if only she could rest for a few minutes.

'You need more than a few minutes' rest. Look, I'll *give* you two weeks' wages – it's nothing to me – but please do as I ask and go home.'

The sobbing became louder. 'She won't give me no more work if I let her down now! She won't! I know her!'

'Who won't?'

'Mrs Lambton – I mean Mademoiselle Clunette. Oh, miss, don't tell her I let her real name slip. She'll murder me!'

At this inopportune moment, Mademoiselle herself walked in, an apparition of restrained elegance in dark brown silk, with a matching pelisse, the whole surmounted by an enormous poke bonnet tastefully embellished by beige feathers and silk flowers in exactly the same shade of beige. She was accompanied by Lady Berrinden and they were animatedly discussing the rest of Miss Trent's toilettes. Both women fell silent in shock at the sight of the weeping seamstress.

'Has *cette femme* been annoying you, Mademoiselle?' demanded the modiste, who was the first to recover.

'In a manner of speaking, yes,' replied Cassie, trying to think of the best approach to take.

'You . . . get out!' hissed Mademoiselle Clunette in far from genteel tones, then resumed her exaggerated French accent as she turned back to Lady Berrinden. 'I am sorree, *madame*. I do not permit that one of my women should annoy a *cliente comme vous*.'

'No! No! You quite mistake my meaning!' Cassie forced a smile to her face. 'It's Mrs Keeling's devotion to her job that is annoying me.'

The modiste looked at her in astonishment. '*Plaît-il, Mademoiselle?*'

'Mrs Keeling is obviously suffering from the influenza, but she refuses to go home.'

'If that woman has the influenza, she must leave the house at once,' announced Lady Berrinden, taking a step backwards and retreating to the door, just to be safe. 'I cannot take the risk of it spreading to my servants.' She would have died rather than admit it, but she had a great fear of contracting the influenza. She had once been laid low by this dreadful scourge and had had to keep to her bed for several weeks, dependent upon others for all her needs. Never again did she intend to suffer that indignity.

At that moment Mrs Keeling gave a gasp and slid to the floor in a faint. Cassie stepped forward, concern on her face. Mademoiselle Clunette joined her, clucking in annoyance.

Lady Berrinden held her handkerchief to her nose. 'Come away immediately, Cassandra!'

She was not obeyed. Cassie cut off the modiste's abject apologies for the inconvenience they were being caused. 'I have been more than satisfied with Mrs Keeling's work, and shall be happy to pay her wages myself until she is fit to return to your employment.'

After a moment's pause, during which Edith Lambton reflected cynically that Keeling had struck it lucky here, and decided that it would do no harm and cost her nothing to humour Miss Trent. 'I comprehend fully and deeply admire, *mademoiselle*, your so-kind desire to 'elp those *moins fortunés* than yourself.'

'I was sure you would,' said Cassie. 'Mrs Keeling's work is exquisite and does full justice to your clever designs. She cannot, after all, be blamed for feeling ill. Now, if you would help me out of this dress, I shall see she gets home safely.'

Lady Berrinden, handkerchief still in position in front of her face, had been listening in mounting indignation to this exchange. 'Cassandra, come away at *once!*' She glared at the modiste. 'Kindly remove this person from my house instantly, *mademoiselle!*'

'*Certainement,* milady.'

'I'm afraid I can't leave, because there is no one but me to help Mrs Keeling,' said Cassie, coolly ignoring her aunt's order. 'She's a widow and has only four small children at home.'

Lady Berrinden, purple with indignation, swept majestically away from the risk of contamination, tossing over her shoulder, 'I shall speak to you later, Cassandra!'

Her niece didn't even hear the words. She summoned Mary Ann and asked her to make sure Mrs Keeling was given a cup of strong, sweet tea. Then, before going to change her clothes, she also ensured that Mademoiselle Clunette would remain her ally. 'It might be best, my dear Mademoiselle, if you were to go to my aunt now and tell her that you will have another seamstress here as soon as possible. I'm sure I can rely on you to find work for Mrs Keeling when she's better. I myself will be needing several more garments made and I prefer her work to that of anyone else.'

'I understand you *parfaitement*, Miss Trent.' The modiste, who had already decided to increase her charges in order to compensate for all this extra trouble, went off at once to try to soothe an influential client whose custom she did not wish to lose, any more than she wished to offend Miss Trent, who was far richer than her aunt, judging by the lavish way she ordered clothes, as well as being pretty enough to provide a walking advertisement for Mademoiselle Clunette's skill.

The modiste's attentions were balm to Amelia Berrinden, after the brazen way her niece had actually dared to defy her, and she even went so far as to confide how difficult it was to introduce such a nobody to the ton. And one from the North, too.

'But if anyone can do that, it's you, milady,' Mademoiselle murmured. 'Such an honour to serve you, for no lady can be more respected in the ton.'

A setback occurred, however, when the butler made the mistake of ushering in Mr Giffard while the modiste was still closeted with her ladyship. Mademoiselle immediately began to curtsey her way out. Simeon, unsure of his welcome, remained next to the still-open door, and the whole incident coincided with Cassie's descent from the second floor. An angry flush suffused Lady Berrinden's face as she realised her niece and maid were supporting the unfortunate Mrs Keeling between them.

When his innate courtesy impelled Simeon to go to their aid, his hostess rushed across to the doorway to call after him, 'Pray do not expose yourself to such risks, my dear Simeon. That woman has the influenza.'

The looks she cast at her niece would have sent Lord Berrinden scurrying to take refuge in his club and would have made her daughters turn pale with terror. Cassie did not even notice.

At that moment, Mrs Keeling fainted again and Simeon Giffard stepped forward just in time to catch her, calling to the butler, still hovering in the vicinity, to lend a hand. Together the two men carried the woman to a sofa on the landing.

'Don't just stand there, Meckworth!' snapped Simeon. 'Fetch her a glass of brandy!'

He turned to Cassie. 'How may I help you further, Miss Trent?'

She barely spared him a glance. 'I can manage perfectly well, thank you, Mr Giffard. I intend to take Mrs Keeling home, for I must find out for myself whether her children are old enough to cope adequately during their mother's illness.'

'Then you must permit me to accompany you and render you whatever assistance is necessary,' he insisted.

This time she did stop and look at him. '*You?*'

He drew himself up. 'Why not me? You clearly need help. I'm only sorry that I didn't come here in my own carriage, for that would have made our task far easier. Perhaps her ladyship will let us take hers?'

'*Take my carriage?* Impossible! I would not dare to use it myself afterwards! You must be mad to risk touching her, Simeon!' Lady Berrinden clapped one hand to her brow. 'Meckworth! Send for my maid at once. I am about to have the palpitations!' She then tottered strategically back into the drawing-room.

Cassie had hardly noticed her aunt, for she knew herself to be in the wrong for the way she had spoken, and after a brief fight with herself, felt impelled to apologise. 'I do beg your pardon, Mr Giffard. I didn't mean to be so rude. I was a little distracted.'

'Meckworth, please call us a hackney carriage,' Simeon ordered. 'And make sure that it's a clean one.'

'Yes, sir.' The butler's expression was wooden, but, as he later told the housekeeper over a restorative glass of port, he had never been so demeaned in all his years of serving the Quality, and what the world was coming to when a man in his position was forced to run round after a sewing-woman, he feared to contemplate!

It took the hackney carriage a little over fifteen minutes to wind its way through the traffic and reach Garnett Lane, which turned out to be a malodorous alley about twenty yards long, heaped high with refuse of all kinds and bearing no resemblance whatsoever to a lane. The carriage had to stop at the end, as the street was too narrow for it.

'What a terrible place for children to live!' declared Cassie, looking round in disapproval. 'It's as bad as anything I've ever seen.'

'I think it would be best if you stayed in the cab, Miss Trent.' Simeon eyed the piles of refuse lying around in disgust and tried to ignore the smells.

'Why? Do you think I'm afraid of a little dirt? I've often visited our operatives when they've been ill. Though our town's drains are better than these, I must say.'

'But there will be rats and other vermin. And you'll get your clothes dirty.'

During all this time, the seamstress had been slumped in a corner, her eyes closed. Now she opened them and groaned.

'Come, Mr Giffard,' Cassie said bracingly, 'this poor woman must be got to her bed. What does it matter if I get my hem dirty in the process? I dare say I have a dozen other dresses. And I'm not afraid of a rat or two.'

'Would you just help me lift her out, sir?' asked Mary Ann.

Simeon was scowling. 'Upon your own head be it, then, Miss Trent!' He turned to the maid. 'Leave her to me. It'll be easier if I carry her.' He got out of the carriage and with Cassie's help, took the seamstress in his arms. Then he followed the maid up the narrow rickety staircase to the attics.

Well, no one could accuse Mr Giffard of being a weakling, thought Cassie, making up the tail of the procession and smiling at a couple of urchins who were hovering nearby. It took a strong man to carry a woman so easily. From behind, he reminded her of her father, who had also been tall, and noted for his strength and endurance. But, of course, her father had not been so odiously arrogant – or so handsome, either, she had to admit.

Mrs Keeling and her four children lived in one attic room, which was fairly clean, considering its situation, but sparsely furnished. Simeon laid the sick woman down on the mattress which they all seemed to share and watched as Cassie spoke quietly to the eldest child, a girl of eight. To her Cassie entrusted a sum of money in small change, with instructions to send out for more fuel and to buy some nourishing food from a cookshop. Here Mary Ann intervened.

'I think it'd be best, Miss Cassie, if I stayed here for an hour or two and helped them. That little lass is a bit young yet to manage everything on her own. How would that be, Betty? Will you let me help you see to your mother?'

The little girl, overawed by the company, particularly Mr Giffard, nodded and sidled over to stand by her mother, who was lying with her eyes closed and an expression of acute pain on her face.

'Sorry, miss,' she muttered. 'Me head hurts. I can't think proper.'

'Don't try to do anything, Mrs Keeling,' Cassie said firmly. 'We shall make all the arrangements. Your only task now is to rest and get better. I've arranged everything with Mademoiselle and as soon as you're better there will be work for you. In the meantime, I'll make sure you have enough money to feed your family.'

Tears were rolling down the sick woman's pale cheeks. 'So kind!' she murmured. 'Can't thank you enough.'

'You'll thank me best by getting well again. Now – Mary Ann will send for a soothing draught from the nearest apothecary, because I know how the influenza makes one's head ache.' She signalled to Simeon and led the way out.

Mary Ann came to the doorway. 'You'd better work out how to deal with your aunt when you get back, Miss Cassie.'

Simeon was amazed at the way both women exchanged a smile, as if Lady Berrinden was a subject of amusement to them, and was even more amazed when Cassie hugged her maid.

'Are you sure you don't mind staying on, Mary Ann?'

'A-course I don't! But I'd be grateful if you'd send that there hackney back for me, miss. I don't fancy walking home alone through this neighbourhood, and that's a fact.'

Here Simeon intervened. 'I shall come back for you myself, Mary Ann, and on the way, I'll stop at an apothecary's for something to help this poor woman.'

'Thank you, sir. That's very kind of you – very kind indeed. But now you'd best get my mistress back to her aunt or we'll never hear the last of this.'

He smiled and nodded acceptance of this charge.

Cassie allowed him to escort her back to the hackney. 'I'm sorry to take up your time like this, Mr Giffard.'

'It's been my pleasure and privilege to help you, Miss Trent.'

She could not help smiling slightly at that. 'Not exactly a pleasure, surely?'

He relaxed a little. 'Not exactly, but it doesn't matter. Are you much given to philanthropic acts?'

'I couldn't stand by and see her lose her job because she was ill.'

His voice was sincere, his eyes warm on her face. 'I very much admire the way you've helped that poor woman.'

Cassie turned a bright peony red at a compliment from such an unexpected source and tried to cover up her embarrassment by making light of it. 'Well, Mrs Keeling has worked hard for me. She's made most of my clothes, you know. Where would we ladies be without our fine gowns?'

'Do you know, I had not formed the impression that you cared all that much for high fashion – or that your concern for Mrs Keeling was based upon your need for her services!'

Really, why could he not let the matter drop? Cassie thought. 'I've done very little. And – and I don't care to be complimented for doing my duty.'

He smiled. 'This is, I think, the first time I've seen you looking flustered.'

She looked up, her gaze meeting his. 'Well, how ungentlemanly of you to say that!'

He laughed at her indignation and caught hold of her hand, raising it to his lips. 'Cry pax, Miss Trent!'

She pulled her hand away, surprised at the warmth coursing through her from it. 'Pax it is, then.' But her eyes had begun to twinkle and when she glanced sideways, she saw that he was still smiling warmly at her – which made her look hastily elsewhere.

As the hackney slowed down to let a dray turn off the road, she gave a sudden chuckle.

'May I be permitted to share your amusement, Miss Trent?'

'I've just realised how angry my aunt will be at my riding

back alone with you in a closed carriage. Oh dear, I'll never be able to soothe her down now!'

He was smiling too. None knew better than he how fussy Lady Berrinden was about the proprieties, because his mother was exactly the same. 'Just why did you come to London, Miss Trent?' he asked suddenly, for he had been wondering about this for a while. 'You don't really seem to care for the life of a lady of fashion.' Nor did she seem to be looking for a husband, if he read the signs aright – and he'd had a lot of experience with those who were hunting husbands.

'I came because it was my mother's dying wish that I have a London Season, just as she once did.' She sighed. 'It seems a great waste of time to me, but it's what she wanted—' Cassie broke off uncertainly, not having meant to confide that information to anyone in London, let alone the arrogant Mr Giffard. 'I expect you find it foolish of me – after all, this is your world – but I don't really feel to fit into it and I don't want to devote my whole life to the social round. My aunt thinks only of making a suitable match for me, but I do not intend to marry just for the sake of it, let alone marry someone who is interested only in my fortune.'

This confirmed his own thoughts and why her words should give him pleasure, he could not quite work out. 'But you might meet someone you wish to marry.'

'I might. I haven't done so far, though. Either at home or here in London. I think I'm destined to remain a spinster.'

When she gave another of those little chuckles, he could not help thinking how attractive her laughter was.

'My aunt says I'm too hard to please and too opinionated,' she murmured. 'Perhaps she's right.'

So much for poor Albert's chances, he thought.

Perhaps the enforced intimacy of the carriage had made her relax; perhaps it was the need to confide in someone, for not even Susannah could understand her feelings on this.

85

'And yet, there is the problem of what to do with myself.'
Cassie hesitated.

'Yes?'

'Well, you see, although I love Uncle Joshua and all my
family in Bardsley, after my mother died, I found it very
painful to live there. And when I go back, I shan't quite
know what to do with my time. A single lady is so much
more restricted in what is proper than one living with her
widowed mother. You see, I can't help in the mills like
Will does – it wouldn't be suitable and, quite frankly, I
don't enjoy the noise and dirt – but I must have something
worthwhile to fill my days. Oh, how I wish women's lives
were not so limited!'

'I'd never thought of it that way. The ladies of my
acquaintance seem only to care about getting married and
raising their families.'

'Well,' she was smiling again, 'I'm not so unusual as that!
I love children and I would indeed like to marry if I could
meet someone whom I could love, as my parents loved each
other. But that's very rare, I think.'

'Very rare indeed!' He had not seen it often among his
acquaintances, that was certain.

There was silence for a moment, then he said quietly,
'Thank you for honouring me with your confidences, Miss
Trent. You can be sure I shall respect them. I, too, have
felt a similar lack of direction at times. But I'm fortunate
to have Stovely Chase.'

'Your home?'

'Yes. It's very beautiful – well, I think so, anyway.
And it's a great responsibility. So many people's lives
depend upon the owner – their livelihoods, their housing,
everything. An estate like mine is something worth devoting
one's life to, something to pass on to one's children. Or at
least, it seems so to me.'

They were silent for a few moments, but it was a more
comfortable silence than was usual between them.

'I hope,' he said after a while, 'now that we understand one another a little, we may become better friends. If I can be of any further help to you, with Mrs Keeling or with anything else, you have only to ask me.'

So far she had felt no embarrassment at the close quarters they were sharing, but as she looked across at him, it felt as if all the air had disappeared from the carriage. It must be his offer of friendship which had filled her with this tingling warmth, for she'd guess he was not a man who made friends easily. And she'd be happy to call herself his friend for, in this mood, she liked Mr Giffard very well indeed.

When she glanced at him again, she felt her cheeks go warm, for she was suddenly aware of everything about him, the lean, good-looking face, the way his dark hair tumbled over his forehead, the grey eyes steady on hers.

He leaned forward as if to speak, but to her great relief – or was it disappointment? – the carriage drew up in front of the Berrindens' tall, narrow town house and the moment of closeness was lost.

It was the aloof member of the London ton who helped her down and insisted on accompanying her inside, though his expression was perhaps not quite as distant as usual, and he did exchange smiles with her when informed by the butler that her ladyship and Miss Susannah were in the small parlour.

'I'll come up and make my apologies to Lady Berrinden,' he said calmly.

'She said she wasn't at home to callers, sir.'

'She'll be at home to me, Meckworth. I have a message for her from my mother.'

When they were both shown into the small parlour, Lady Berrinden turned a stony gaze upon them. 'I see you have returned safely, at least, Cassandra.' For once she did not smile at Simeon, merely acknowledging his presence with a regal inclination of her head.

Susannah, hands clasped tightly in her lap, was looking very ill at ease.

'We've performed our charitable act,' Simeon said lightly, 'and are now back to apologise for abandoning you.'

He smoothed down her ladyship's still-ruffled feathers, praising Cassie's actions lavishly and congratulating an astounded Lady Berrinden on her niece's great sense of Christian charity.

From her place beside her aunt, Cassie flashed him a glance of compounded amusement and gratitude, which he acknowledged by a slight softening of the eyes, without her ladyship even becoming aware of the exchange.

The final seal on Lady Berrinden's change of mood was Mr Giffard's disclosure that he had come to see her originally because he was the bearer of an invitation from his mother, who wanted the Berrinden family to spend Sunday with her at Stovely Chase, stay the night and then return to London on the Monday. 'My mother knows it's the height of the Season and you must be inundated with invitations, but she's feeling a little better lately and would welcome the chance to see her old friends.'

Rightly divining that this was setting the scene for a proposal of marriage, Lady Berrinden instantly accepted on behalf of her family, but cast a doubtful glance at her niece, whom she could hardly leave alone in London, and yet who would be a considerable encumbrance if her suspicions were correct.

'Miss Trent is, of course, included in the invitation,' he said smoothly. 'I think you might enjoy a visit to the country-side, Miss Trent, after the beauties of Garnett Lane.'

How could Susannah *not* feel attracted to him when he smiled like that, Cassie wondered, but her cousin was not even looking in his direction, just staring down at her hands.

After Mr Giffard had left, Lady Berrinden immediately began making plans for the journey, which was all of twenty-five miles, and issuing a series of instructions to her daughter about what Susannah was to wear. She confined her reprimand to Cassie to an acid request that in future her niece kindly leave menials and their affairs to those whose responsibility it was to look after them.

After that, the escapade was scarcely mentioned, beyond her ladyship once or twice expressing a hope that Cassandra had not taken the influenza because of her quixotic behaviour, and voicing several fervent wishes that she would have nothing to blush for in her niece's conduct at Stovely Chase.

The next day, when they were chatting over a pot of tea, Susannah said thoughtfully, 'I can't understand why Mama is making such a fuss about a short visit to Stovely. We are forever staying with them there, and it's always the same. To tell you the truth, my dear Cassie, it won't be at all interesting. Mama will gossip with Mrs Giffard, Papa will retire to the library and fall asleep,' she giggled, 'as he always does! And Simeon will take us riding or driving round his precious estate. I think Stovely Chase is the only thing in the world he cares about. He's always making improvements and conducting agricultural experiments. It's too tedious for words! And the house is so dark and old-fashioned! I'd simply hate to live there! I always feel as if I'm shut up in a dungeon when we visit.'

'Well I'm looking forward to seeing it.' Cassie stirred her tea vigorously. How was it possible for Susannah to remain so blind to her mother's hopes? Not to mention Mr Giffard's attentions? She debated warning her cousin about what might lie in store, but decided it was not her place to do so and, anyway, she was already in her aunt's black books. She compromised by dropping a hint. 'Well, everything will be in fine order for his wife, then. He's bound to marry one day, after all. If he loves Stovely so much, he'll want an heir for it, won't he?'

Susannah wrinkled her nose. 'I pity anyone he marries. Simeon can be very stern and aloof sometimes. He and my brother are very much alike in that. They will both make uncomfortable husbands.'

With this statement, Cassie could not agree. She thought Mr Giffard might make a better husband than most, if he really cared for someone. The trouble was, she was almost certain that he did not care for Susannah. Well, that was not her concern. She was just glad she was a Trent and had not been brought up to think marriage a mere business arrangement.

'My brother is so unlike your cousin.' Susannah sighed at the thought of Will. 'Mr Trent is so friendly and easy to talk to, whilst Richard,' she pulled a face, 'takes after my mother, I'm afraid.'

This final remark sent Cassie back to her room feeling worried. Surely Susannah wasn't still thinking about Will?

What a shock it would be to her pretty cousin if – no *when* – Simeon Giffard asked her to marry him. Would Susannah dare say no? It didn't seem likely. Poor Susannah!

And poor Mr Giffard, too! What an unsuitable pair they would make! Cassie couldn't decide which of them would be the unhappier.

And why was she worrying about Mr Giffard? It was Susannah who mattered, Susannah was her cousin and such a dear girl. Only – Simeon Giffard had a kindly and responsible side to his nature, even if he did not always show this to the world. And he did not deserve to be unhappy, either.

Six

Sunday morning saw an imposing cavalcade set out from Bransham Gardens at the sedate pace deemed suitable by her ladyship. First came a travelling chaise, in which Lady Berrinden and her family sat in state. This was followed by another carriage, in which sat Lord Berrinden's valet, Lady Berrinden's dresser and Susannah's maid, who was to look after both young ladies on such a short visit. A third vehicle carried the luggage, of which there was a surprising amount for a mere one night's stay.

Even three hours of sitting facing her aunt did not take away Cassie's pleasure in the scenery, which was very unlike the moors around Bardsley. Her involuntary exclamations of delight at particularly fine vistas did much to restore her to her aunt's favour.

'I fancy you will be equally delighted with Stovely Chase,' Lady Berrinden informed her niece graciously. 'Such an elegant residence! Such beautiful grounds!'

'Good shootin', too. Giffard keeps his woods well stocked,' Lord Berrinden contributed.

Having set off at the almost unheard-of hour of seven o'clock in the morning – an early start which, Lady Berrinden informed them, they would not begrudge her dearest Flora – they arrived just before ten. Stovely Chase was not the gracious palladian residence Cassie had some-how expected, but a large, sprawling building, extended and added to by generations of Giffards. Its lack of symmetry and unmatched bricks and architectural styles had been considerably softened by a luxuriant growth of ivy, and it was surrounded by carefully tended gardens.

An imposing flight of shallow stone steps led up to the front door, which opened even before their carriage drew to a halt to disclose Simeon Giffard waiting to greet them in person.

'Dearest Simeon is ever the gracious host!' cooed Lady Berrinden. 'Cassie, allow your cousin to get out first, if you please. Henry, where have you put my reticule?'

'Eh?'

'Oh, there it is, just by you, Cassie! However did it get there? Please pass it to me before you get out.' This blatant ploy to give Susannah and Simeon some time together did not seem to bear much fruit, for Cassie noticed that they barely opened their mouths as they stood waiting for the rest of the party. Surely, if he was intending to propose to Susannah, he should not be standing there like a stuffed dummy, she thought in exasperation, but telling her how happy he was to see her. Cassie would expect that sort of greeting if she were thinking of marrying someone. Which she wasn't, of course. Certainly not. Well, not yet.

When her ladyship had been helped from the carriage by a footman, she turned to mount the stairs without waiting for her niece and husband to join them. Simeon and Susannah had perforce to accompany her inside the house and leave Lord Berrinden to escort his niece.

Cassie was all agog to meet her hostess, whose praises Lady Berrinden had been singing ever since they received the invitation. She had expected someone very grand, but was disappointed to find that Flora Giffard, sitting waiting for them in the Great Hall with her companion, Miss Canley, was an emaciated lady, whose twisted arthritic hands and sallow complexion testified to her genuine ill-health. However, her behaviour betrayed as elevated a view of her own consequence as Lady Berrinden's did.

She was attired in a rustling black silk dress, with a high

neck and long sleeves. Upon her sparse grey locks was a delicate cap of white lace, which unfortunately only emphasised the sallowness of her complexion. She obviously had a weakness for jewellery, because her person was embellished with so many necklaces, bracelets and brooches that she positively jangled as her companion helped her up. Miss Canley, who was wearing a very plain gown, stayed behind her, hands folded, as if she wished to be regarded as another piece of furniture.

Their hostess greeted her 'dearest Amelia' and her 'dear, dear Susannah' with enthusiasm, showed a calm indifference to Lord Berrinden, who had fallen silent as soon as they entered the house, and displayed the barest civility towards Cassie.

Simeon sighed and stepped into the breach to introduce Miss Canley and inquire of Cassie how the journey had been. His mother had already complained at length about the necessity for inviting this Miss Trent person, for she never forgot an old scandal, or forgave those involved.

'To be entertaining – *and in my own home* – the daughter of a woman who eloped with a person who made his living by trade is not something I can face with equanimity,' she had complained. 'And I'm surprised you even ask it of me.'

Simeon hoped he had managed to plant the idea in her mind that Amelia Berrinden was nobly carrying out her duty to her family by sponsoring her niece and should receive the support of her friends in this charitable enterprise. He was only moderately confident that his mother would not be openly rude to Miss Trent and was ready to intervene, if necessary.

Since Cassie was not dependent upon Mrs Giffard's goodwill, she did not let this cool reception bother her. She was quite ready to be amused by her hostess, whose manners were very exaggerated and fussy, and was only sorry she could not share that amusement with someone like her cousin Will.

Flora gestured towards the stairs, at the bottom of which the housekeeper stood waiting. 'Perhaps you'd like to go up to your rooms and then join me in the garden room? I've had light refreshments set out there, not that I can eat much, not with my troubles. But the room has a charming view over some beautiful rose gardens, which you might enjoy.' She sounded dubious about that, however.

Lady Berrinden pressed her hand. 'How kind of you to take all this trouble, my dearest Flora.'

When they came down again to a late breakfast, Cassie found that the garden room was indeed charming, but since Flora had placed Susannah next to Simeon, and Cassie on her own at the other end of the table, it was difficult for her to hold a worthwhile conversation. She concentrated on her food, then suddenly realised that everyone else was waiting for her.

Mrs Giffard cleared her throat. 'If you've all finished – oh, you are still eating, are you, Miss Trent? Do not let us hurry you. Some people do suffer from excessive appetites.'

Simeon frowned at his mother and muttered something, but she ignored him

With her hostess staring down the table at her and her aunt looking disapproving, Cassie laid down her knife and fork. 'I've quite finished, thank you, Mrs Giffard.'

'Then we can get ready for church. I never miss it – if I'm well enough to attend, that is. It's *so* important to contemplate one's own mortality on the Lord's Day. And there are some charming gravestones in the church yard.'

Cassie blinked at this, met Simeon's eyes and looked hastily away. He seemed both irritated and embarrassed, but surely that was a gleam of amusement in his eyes as well. After that, she kept her eyes resolutely down, so that her aunt would not see how comical she found her hostess. What a pity Mary Ann had not come with them, so that she could share the tale with her later!

*　　*　　*

They were driven into the village in state in two carriages, with a coachman and a footman on each. Lord and Lady Berrinden accompanied their hostess and her companion in the first vehicle, whilst Simeon escorted the young ladies in the second. As the church was only half a mile beyond the gatehouse, this journey did not take long.

Cassie sighed as she looked out at the beauty of the park and the fine spring weather. She would have much preferred to walk. And how could Susannah say the woods at Stovely were dark and gloomy? Their lush green beauty graced every vista that unfolded and promised a wealth of shady walks later in the day. She turned to her host impulsively. 'I think the grounds of Stovely Chase must be the most beautiful I've ever seen, Mr Giffard. No wonder you love it.'

'Do you really think so?' He could not hide his gratification.

'I wouldn't say so else.'

They smiled at one another, in accord again, then Susannah chimed in with, 'Yes, indeed! And such a fine day, too. Look at those pretty little clouds.'

The momentary rapport was lost as his smile faded and Cassie was surprised to feel disappointed about that.

'The village church is very old, and some parts date back to the eleventh century,' Mr Giffard said as the carriage slowed down outside it.

'That far end bears traces of a Norman style of architecture, does it not?' Cassie asked. 'I'd love to examine it properly, if that's not too much trouble?'

'It'd be no trouble at all. We're rather proud of our ancient church.'

'Oh, yes, indeed,' Susannah said. 'And that creeper on the wall is very pretty, too.'

Cassie tried to think of something which would show her cousin's remark in a better light, but could not. She had to admit to herself that although Susannah was a dear girl, she was not gifted with much intelligence, nor was she well educated. Cassie had not only had an excellent governess, whom she'd shared with Sarah, but had been turned loose among her father's books from an early age and he'd never been too busy to talk to her about what she was reading. Susannah seemed to have concentrated more on embroidery and her singing. Well, she did have a beautiful voice. It was just – sometimes Cassie longed for intelligent conversation, someone to tease her out of a blue mood or share a smile with her at life's silly little twists.

It was a relief to get out of the carriage and stand for a moment in the sunshine.

Simeon turned to the older members of the party, who were waiting for them on the church steps. 'Mother, Miss Trent is interested in architecture and would like to see over the church, so, with your and Lady Berrinden's permission, we shall stay behind for a little while after the service.'

Lady Berrinden raised no objections. Simeon Giffard could do no wrong in her eyes, and he was clearly pleased by her niece's interest.

Mrs Giffard also acquiesced, but turned to her friend and said, 'How conscientious a host my dear Simeon is, always ready to put himself out for his guests, no matter how unreasonable their demands.'

This made the conscientious host squirm with embarrassment and say pointedly, 'It is no trouble, Miss Trent, believe me.'

The service was brief and to the point, memorable only for the thin, out-of-tune singing of their hostess. Susannah winced visibly, Cassie felt a wild urge to giggle and Simeon stared fixedly at his hymn book.

After the older members of their party had left, he turned to his two younger guests. 'Let's start with the crusader's tomb. It's always been my favourite part of the church.'

The tomb lay against the side wall of the church, to the left of the altar. Cassie stepped forward eagerly, exclaiming in admiration at the delicate carving and the small dog lying asleep by its master's feet.

Susannah stood by her side and managed, 'Oh, it reminds me of a little dog I once had. I was so sad when she got lost in the woods and Mama said I couldn't have another.'

They moved on to the carved Elizabethan altar screen and Cassie listened raptly when Simeon told her how it had been preserved by an ancestor from desecration by the Roundhead iconoclasts by hiding it behind a false wall in the crypt.

'You're lucky to know so much about your family history!' she sighed. 'My mother used to talk to me about growing up at Fairleigh, but I've never even seen it.'

'Oh, we shall be going down there once the Season is over,' Susannah said blithely, seeming unaware of the sadness underlying her cousin's remark.

After a short pause, Simeon said, 'The rose window is an exact copy of the one destroyed by some over-zealous Roundheads. The same ancestor sketched it and commissioned another as soon as King Charles the Second came back to take his throne. She was a very clever woman. We have her diaries, if you'd care to see them sometime, Miss Trent?'

'I'd love that.'

So well did Simeon and Cassie get on as they wandered round the small, but exquisite church that she shared with him the joke of the crusader's tomb in her own church in Bardsley. 'It was counterfeited ten years ago at the expense of my uncle and several of the town's other leading citizens. They felt every church should have such a tomb, and they saw no incongruity in placing one in a brand-new red-brick edifice.'

Simeon chuckled at this, as she had known he would.

Susannah merely stared in bewilderment and asked, 'But is the tomb not well executed, then?'

Cassie saw Simeon's pained expression and sighed again for the unsuitable pair. She saw her gentle cousin become anxious, with no idea of why she had upset her host. After that, Susannah kept silent, doing little but endorse her companions' statements and comments, and watch their expressions worriedly as she did so, in case she inadvertently offended.

It was not until the church clock struck one that Cassie and Simeon were shocked into the realisation of how long they had been and also how they had neglected Susannah, who had dropped behind and not caught up with them again. Conscience-stricken, they hurried round to the front of the church, to find her chatting comfortably to the parson's wife and admiring the flower garden at the nearby parsonage.

'I do apologise for neglecting you, Susannah—' he began.

'It's my fault we got separated—' Cassie said at the same time and broke off to laugh, before giving her cousin a quick hug. 'I'm sure you'll forgive us, though.'

'Of course. Pray think no more of it. You were enjoying yourselves, and Mrs Greenby and I have had a comfortable cose together.'

As they drove back, Cassie wondered yet again why Simeon had decided to marry her cousin, for his attitude towards her was more that of a slightly weary older brother than a lover, and he could not help but find her conversation trite in the extreme. Cassie felt like giving him a shake and asking him to be more sensible about his future, but of course she could not interfere.

In fact, she really would have to stop worrying about it. This was not her world, and she could not expect people here to behave as her family did in Bardsley.

Luncheon was an exceedingly formal meal, served by a stately butler and two footmen – did they really employ two footmen at Stovely just to wait on one elderly lady? – at an enormous dining table, which would have been better, Cassie thought, if someone had removed a few of the leaves. Not only were the guests at least five feet away from one another, but a very ugly epergne, which formed the centrepiece, prevented any conversations from being conducted across the table.

Much of the conversation was devoted to the elegant house parties which Simeon would be able to hold 'once he was married'.

'I always think, Flora dear,' Amelia confided at one stage in a voice loud enough to be heard outside the house, 'that you can experience a sense of history here at Stovely, something we lack at Fairleigh, which is rather too modern for my taste.'

'It's dashed convenient, though,' his lordship said. 'Can't fault our plumbing, can you?'

His wife glared at him and changed the subject back to Stovely's attractions.

He blinked in surprise and addressed himself to his food.

Cassie watched, beginning to understand what Mr Darford had meant when he tried to explain Simeon to her. Indeed, it was a wonder the man had grown up so well, with a mother like that, or developed any sense of humour whatsoever. She sighed and followed her uncle's example, addressing herself to her plate.

After luncheon, the two older ladies both expressed an urgent need to retire to their chambers and rest, which the other members of the party correctly interpreted as a desire for a private gossip. Lord Berrinden, in response to a nudge from his wife, turned to Cassie. 'I dare say you'd like to see the library, my dear niece. It has a dashed lot of books in it.'

So the moment had come, had it? 'That would be delightful, Uncle Henry.'

Behind her she heard Simeon invite Susannah to walk with him around the rose gardens.

'They've recently been re-modelled, with arbours and paved walkways, and I think you'll enjoy them.'

Cassie saw her cousin shoot a startled look at her mama, saw the nod of approval from that authority, and turned with a sigh to follow her uncle.

As soon as they reached the library, Lord Berrinden confirmed his niece's suspicions. 'Herhum – hope you don't mind my bringing you in here, but you see, well, Giffard's asked permission to offer for Susannah, and Amelia, that is, *we* think it a very suitable match.'

He then settled himself in an armchair and waved his hand at the rows of books. 'You might as well read one while we wait. Bound to be somethin' with pictures in it, if you look around. Nice bindings, ain't they?' He then found himself a newspaper, shook it out to conceal his person and proceeded to fall asleep behind it.

Cassie selected a book about the antiquities of Greece, but had difficulty giving it her full attention and could not have said afterwards whether it had pictures or not.

On the other side of the house all was not going smoothly. Susannah, slightly uncomfortable at being alone with Simeon Giffard, but perfectly happy to admire the design of the new rose beds, flushed vividly when he took her hand. Gasping, she tried to pull it away.

'Susannah, you must be aware of the affection I feel for you.' The words he had rehearsed that morning came out stiffly and as she stared at him in shock, he felt her hand begin to tremble in his. He took a deep breath and continued, 'I have your parents' permission to ask you if you will do me the honour of becoming my wife.'

She gulped and her mouth fell open, but no words came from it.

As the awkward silence continued, he prompted her with, 'May I hope for your acceptance?' What was wrong with the girl? Why the hell was she staring at him like that?

'I – I am very flattered by your – by the honour you do

me,' Susannah whispered. 'I – I hadn't realised how you felt. It's such a sho. . . I mean, such a surprise!'

This wasn't surprise on her face, but sheer terror. Damn the girl! Why was she behaving in such a foolish, fluttery fashion? Surely she must have guessed what was going on? Since she clearly hadn't, he wondered savagely why Amelia Berrinden had not prepared her daughter to receive his offer?

An even more unwelcome suspicion crossed his mind as the terrified expression did not fade. 'May I hope that you do not, at least, look unfavourably upon my suit?'

'Oh, no – oh, I – Oh, no! It's just that – the surprise – I wasn't expecting . . .' Susannah clasped her hands together at her breast in an unconscious gesture of supplication.

'My dear, I shall be happy to wait for your answer until you have recovered from the surprise and had time to consider your feelings. Only let me assure you that I await your response with great eagerness.' Why was he speaking like a damned actor in a melodrama? He sounded stilted and false, even to his own ears. And why was she doing nothing to help him out of this awkwardness?

'Oh yes. Yes. Thank you. Greatly honoured.'

He offered her his arm and turned her firmly in the direction of the house. How stupid females were! All of them. How he wished it were not necessary to get married at all! Only for Stovely would he have done this. And to keep his promise to his mother, because a Giffard never broke his word.

Unaware that his expression was grim and that the shrinking girl on his arm was almost on the verge of fainting in terror, he led the way back into the house at a rapid pace. 'I'm sure you would like to retire to your room so that you can have time to consider matters.'

He bowed slightly and left her at the foot of the stairs, then stormed off to the library. 'Sir, I must express my dismay that you have not seen fit to prepare your daughter for my proposal!' he announced, almost before he was over the threshold. 'How could you allow me to—' He caught sight of Cassie and stopped short, feeling a flush warm his cheeks. Damn! What was she doing hiding in that alcove? 'Miss Trent!' He bowed slightly and scowled at her.

'I think you will wish to be private with my uncle, Mr Giffard,' she murmured and slipped out of the room, avoiding his eyes.

Lord Berrinden, who had been snoring gently in a chair, woke up with a start. 'Whassit? Oh, yes, um – er, congratulations, my dear boy. Congratulations!'

'Congratulations! On what, pray? *Your daughter,*' Simeon Giffard almost ground his teeth at the embarrassment of proposing to a young lady who had nearly fainted in terror at his offer, 'is not sure of her own mind. I would have *expected* either you or her mother to have prepared her to receive my offer!' He strode over to a small table, poured himself a glass of brandy and gulped some down.

Lord Berrinden jerked to his feet and backed towards the door. 'We'd better go and see Lady B., m'boy. Women handle these things best. Shy little thing, Suzie. Dare say you took her by surprise. Probably happy as a spring lamb in a meadow now she's had time to think about it!' He fled from the library, but his host did not follow.

Simeon Giffard swallowed another large mouthful of brandy, welcoming its fiery warmth. 'Hell and damnation! Why did I agree to do it?'

And why had Miss Trent looked so disapproving? What business was it of hers anyway? He did not need *her* approval for what he was doing.

As she passed Susannah's door, Cassie was brought to a halt by the sound of muffled weeping. She hesitated for a moment, then knocked and went in.

Susannah immediately flung herself into her cousin's

arms and began to pour out her dilemma. 'Mama will be so *angry* with me! Such a *shock!* Simeon looked so – so *furious!* As if he would devour me.' Here she stopped, her voice completely choked by sobs.

'You don't love him, then?' Cassie asked tentatively, to be answered by an eloquent shudder. 'Or – or at least – like him a little?'

Susannah looked at her numbly and tears rolled unheeded down her cheeks. 'He frightens me,' she whispered at last. 'Oh, not at parties, but when he gives someone a set-down – or when something displeases him. He's so c-cold! And I can't think why he would ever ask *me* to marry him. Why, I can't even talk to him without feeling foolish.' Her vehemence surprised Cassie.

'So you refused him?'

Susannah shook her head and the tears flowed afresh. 'I daren't! Mama must – she must *want* me to marry him, or she would never have brought me here or given permission for him to address me. Oh, Cassie, that must be why she was in such a good mood today. What am I to do?'

'You must tell him how you feel, Susannah, dear. It's the only way. They can't force you to marry a man you dislike. We're not living in the Middle Ages, you know.' But even as she spoke, she knew that there was little hope of her gentle cousin standing firm against anyone.

The door was flung open and Lady Berrinden stalked in. 'Kindly leave us alone!' she snapped at Cassie, who, after a compassionate glance at the drooping figure on the bed, left the room.

What went on behind the door that closed so firmly behind her, Cassie was not told, but by teatime, Susannah had recovered her composure enough to join the rest of the party. Within minutes, she had managed to convey to Simeon Giffard in a gasping undertone her acceptance of his proposal.

A touching scene took place at this news, with Flora

clasping Susannah to her withered bosom and declaring she could wish for no better daughter-in-law than her dearest Amelia's child, and Simeon bowing over Amelia Berrinden's firm white hand and assuring her he would take every care of her eldest daughter. No one but Cassie seemed to notice that, for a girl newly betrothed and presumably ecstatically happy, Susannah looked very wan and hardly opened her mouth all evening, least of all to her betrothed.

But Simeon did not fail to notice that Susannah jerked in shock every time he touched her and his expression grew steadily grimmer.

Sitting next to his lovely fiancée on a sofa, he told himself yet again that all women were insipid and that, if nothing else, in Susannah he would have a docile wife who would get on well with his mother. Anyway, it was done now and an honourable man could not withdraw his offer, so he would just have to charm her out of her nervousness. Now that he came to think of it, he and Richard had treated her in a rather cavalier fashion when they were all children. She probably still remembered that. He would teach her to like him, treat her with great tenderness. Surely she would soon learn to relax with him?

And why Miss Trent was still looking disapproving, he didn't know, and he'd thank her to mind her own business. He avoided her clear gaze from then on, for what could she know about the matter? This was how things were done in his world. A marriage was not made for love, but for the sake of the family. And if Miss Trent's parents really had loved one another so much, they were the exception rather than the rule, for he knew no marriages in his circles which were ecstatically happy. On the contrary.

Watching this charade, Cassie told herself bitterly that she had neither the right nor the power to intervene. The match seemed to delight everyone else, after all; it was only the bride who was reluctant!

One would have thought, however, that Simeon Giffard,

who had proved to be a man of some intelligence and compassion once one got to know him a little, would have been rather more perceptive about what was going on, and would not have wanted to force poor Susannah to marry him.

Well, Cassie promised herself grimly as the evening dragged on, her aunt had no power to coerce *her* into a loveless marriage! In a few months, she would be twenty-one and her own mistress. Until then, she not only had more willpower than her cousin, but more sense, too!

The following morning, Cassie managed to catch her cousin alone for a few minutes before breakfast.

Susannah, who looked as if she had slept very badly, waited until her maid had left the room, before blurting out, 'It's no use, Cassie! I'm not like you! I c-can't go against Mama's wishes!' She struggled against the tears she dared not shed and Cassie, unable to offer any other comfort, went and put her arms round her.

'It's all right, Suzie, I understand. And there could be worse fates than to become mistress of this house. Come and look at the view.' She drew the other girl over to the window. 'I think Stovely Chase is the most beautiful house I've ever seen. Don't you?'

As she was speaking, Lady Berrinden entered the room. It never occurred to her to knock on her daughters' bedroom doors, any more than it occurred to her to ask their opinions about the plans she made for them. She nodded approvingly at Cassie's words, saying bracingly, 'Yes, indeed! Susannah is a very lucky girl to be marrying Simeon Giffard. How happy she will be as mistress of Stovely Chase!' The expected 'Yes, Mama' was not forthcoming and she eyed her daughter searchingly. 'You look pale today, Susannah. Bring me your rouge.'

Numbly her daughter obeyed, and with a firm, steady hand, Lady Berrinden applied some colour to Susannah's cheeks. The effect was not good, but it was no worse than the pallor it replaced.

Cassie, who had mostly regarded her aunt with amusement until now, stood watching in disgust. What sort of a woman would force her daughter into a marriage with someone she feared? What sort of woman would not even notice that fear?

She followed the two of them downstairs and watched Susannah's nervous reception of the chaste kiss bestowed upon her cheek by her betrothed. She saw the satisfaction writ large upon the countenances of the two mothers and winced at her uncle's jovialities on the subject of marriage.

As for Simeon Giffard, she could hardly bring herself to be civil to him. Surely he could see what was happening and would do something about it? If he didn't, no one else would, and then two people would be unhappy for the rest of their lives.

But breakfast continued and he said nothing.

Nor did he meet her eyes once.

She had thought better of him. She really had.

Seven

The following day was again fine and sunny, a blushing, late spring morning that gave tantalizing hints of the glories of summer to come. The arching green of the trees, the beauty of the flowers and the singing of the birds formed a fitting backdrop to the architectural beauties of Stovely Chase, Cassie thought, as she took a turn on the terrace with her cousin, and waited for her aunt to decree how they would spend their time that day.

Since the visitors were not to leave for London until early afternoon, Simeon offered to take the young ladies for a walk around the lake to while away the morning.

Lady Berrinden nodded vigorously in approval.

Susannah strolled along between her cousin and her fiancé, a tight smile fixed on her face and her eyes devoid of expression. She seemed totally oblivious to the attractions of nature and was concentrating all her attention on what her betrothed was saying to her.

She would soon be uttering, 'Yes, Simeon,' as readily as she now said, 'Yes, Mama', Cassie thought angrily and had to take several deep breaths before she could speak calmly to either of them.

Fortunately, as the walk progressed, she was able to fill the awkward gaps in the conversation by expressing her sincere admiration for the lake and its sylvan setting – whatever she thought of its owner. Her remarks obviously pleased Simeon and she could see him begin to relax a little, but she still felt furious with him for being so blind.

107

How, she wondered, will he get on with his fiancée without myself or Lady Berrinden to smooth the conversational path? When Susannah is nervous, she becomes fluttery and utters meaningless exclamations, and with him she always seems nervous. I only hope that as she grows used to him, she will learn to feel more at ease. Strangely enough, Cassie had never felt nervous with him, and enjoyed his conversation very much.

But as she glanced sideways from time to time, she did not feel hopeful about the future. Her cousin was absolutely radiating apprehension. And anyway, Susannah had known Simeon since she was a child; if she were not used to him now, then she never would be.

While Simeon was delivering an enthusiastic monologue on the best way to landscape a lake (as if Susannah cared a fig for that!) Cassie dropped behind the other two. Her eyes fixed on the rippling surface of the lake and the swallows darting gracefully to and fro, she didn't see the tree root until she tripped over it. She cried out as a pain shot up her leg, but the cry was cut off as she fell awkwardly and struck her head on the path, losing consciousness for a few seconds.

She became dimly aware that the others had run back to help her, but the waves of pain made her feel so sick and dizzy that it was several moments before she could reply to their anxious inquiries.

'I'm sorry,' she managed at last, struggling to sit up, but finding herself quite unequal to the effort. She could only lie there and say helplessly, 'It's my leg. I think it may be broken.'

Susannah let out a little scream and began to sob.

Simeon Giffard said in a quiet, matter-of-fact voice, 'Lie still, Miss Trent and don't try to talk. I'm going to examine your leg. I have some experience of injuries. And Susannah, please be quiet. You're upsetting your cousin.'

At this Cassie heard a gasp, but at least the other girl

stopped sobbing. She felt a hand on her forehead, which was comforting, then a voice said, 'I need to check your ankle, Miss Trent.'

Susannah gave a little yelp of shock. 'Oh no! Simeon, you can't – I mean, it's not – not – Mama wouldn't like . . .'

Cassie saw her cousin falter to a halt under his scornful gaze. She wanted to reassure Susannah that she was all right, anything to stop her bleating on in that foolish way, but when she moved her leg inadvertently, pain lanced through her and only a groan came out.

'Would you rather, out of modesty, leave your cousin lying here in pain?' As he spoke, Simeon lifted Cassie's skirt and began gently examining her injured leg, asking her if she could move her toes and generally behaving with the air of one who really did know what he was about. She relaxed and let him do what he would, feeling safe in his capable hands.

When she glanced sideways again, she saw Susannah blushing furiously, presumably to see her cousin's limbs exposed to a man's gaze like that. Cassie had no sense of embarrassment because her leg hurt and it was all she could do to answer his questions without moaning.

At last he let go of her leg and she closed her eyes in relief. When she opened them again, it was to see him still bending over close to her, close enough to stroke the hair back from her brow in a gesture so soothing she even managed a half-smile.

'I don't think you've broken anything, Miss Trent, but I do think you've twisted your ankle badly and grazed your leg, as well as bumping your head. You've been very brave, but it must hurt a great deal.'

When he clasped her hand, she clutched him gratefully. Behind him, she was vaguely aware of Susannah wringing her hands and muttering, but could not seem to concentrate on her cousin, could only concentrate on him, on his strength and support, on the way her hand was tingling in his. And when he reached out with his other hand and again smoothed her hair from her brow, she found it suddenly difficult to breathe, difficult to think at all.

'Just lie still, Miss Trent,' he said softly. 'You need do nothing but recover. It was a bad fall, but your leg definitely isn't broken. I've seen enough accidents about the estate to know that, I promise you.'

So she closed her eyes, thankful for the opportunity to recover in peace. Birdsong had resumed around them. Or had it ever stopped? There was a faint rustling sound from a clump of dark green bushes near the path, as if a small animal were creeping through it. And his hand was still covering hers – warm, so very warm.

A piercing whisper disturbed the peace. 'Simeon!' Susannah's voice.

'Shh.'

'But Simeon—'

The hand left hers.

Cassie forced herself to open her eyes. 'The pain is . . . it's beginning to ease off a little now, Susannah.' But she could not help wincing as he pulled her skirt down and, when he picked up her shoe, she panicked. 'Please don't try to put that on again.'

'I won't.' He held the shoe out to Susannah, who took it from him and stood staring at it as if she didn't quite know what to do with it.

'You'll have to carry it back for Cassie.'

He'd used her Christian name, as if he were a friend. She liked that.

When he turned back to her, his gaze was concerned. 'How are you feeling now? Is the pain lessening?'

'Yes. A little.' She tried to move her head and winced. 'But I still feel dizzy. I'm sorry to be such a trouble. I think I must have hit my head as I fell, it hurts so much.'

'Yes. There's a bruise on your forehead. If you feel you

can bear it, we'll try to get you back to the house and then send for Dr Murray.'

She clutched his arm. 'Oh, please, no! I couldn't get up and walk yet!'

'There's no question of your walking. Susannah can go ahead to let people know what's happened.' The tone of his voice altered, becoming peremptory as he turned to his betrothed, 'Ask them to send the footmen to help me carry your cousin, Susannah – oh, and tell them to send for Dr Murray at once. At once, mind!'

Then he turned back to Cassie and his voice became gentle again. 'In a moment I'll pick you up and carry you back to the house, Miss Trent.'

'Not – not yet, please.' She looked up at him dubiously. 'And – and it's very kind of you to offer, but I'm too heavy, surely?'

'I'm not a weakling.' He noticed that Susannah hadn't moved and his voice became sharper. 'Are you still there? Pick up your cousin's bonnet, and hurry to the house!'

'Yes, Simeon.'

Cassie watched Susannah hurry off down the path and, pain or no pain, she couldn't help smiling wryly at this example of the new regime.

He looked down at her in surprise. 'Now what the devil are you smiling at?'

'Yes, *Simeon*,' she mocked.

'I don't see – oh, yes, I do!' He looked down at her, vainly trying to keep his face straight. 'Well, it's better than "Yes, Mama", isn't it? At least, I shall not bully her.'

The desire to smile suddenly left Cassie. 'You may think you won't bully her, but look how you ordered her around just now.'

'This is an emergency and she was simply standing there like a—' He broke off, annoyed that he had nearly said, 'like a fool' and knowing she had guessed that.

She looked at him and said frankly, 'Well, there'll be

other times when you get impatient, many of them. She's a dear girl, but she can be very indecisive. And personally, I would prefer an occasional "No, Simeon" or even a "No, Mama". It's not good for someone to live under a despot, even a benevolent one.'

His expression lost its warmth and he bent over her again, eyeing her closely. 'If you're ready, Miss Trent?'

'If you're sure you can manage.' She realised from his more formal mode of address that she had gone too far with her comments, but it was so difficult to see people you were fond of making mistakes. *Fond of?* She wasn't fond of Simeon Giffard. Well, she quite liked him now that she knew him better, but *fond?* No, certainly not!

With a rather grim expression on his face, he took off his coat and waistcoat, which were too tight-fitting to allow him any freedom of movement, and tossed them heedlessly on the ground, then bent down to pick her up. He seemed to find her weight no problem as he hefted her into the best position. 'It'd help if you put one arm round my neck.'

She complied, but reluctantly. With her arm round his shoulders, her cheek was nestling against his neck and his hair was tickling her face. It felt strange to be held so closely by a man. That must be why she was feeling so – disorientated. Or maybe it was the bump on the head.

No, it wasn't, she admitted to herself after a minute. It was him. He always had this unsettling effect on her.

She held on as he set off slowly towards the house. This was definitely not the same as hugging Will. Holding Simeon was very different indeed. She could feel the warmth of his body through the thin material of his shirt and was conscious of a faint odor of that same astringent cologne she had smelled on the day they had helped Mrs Keeling together. His heart was beating right next to her breast and she could see a pulse throbbing in time to it in his neck.

The chest against which she was pressed kept rising and falling, as the effort of carrying her made him take deeper breaths. She was so conscious of his breathing that she found herself trying to keep the same rhythm. It was as if those long, slow intakes of air were binding them both together, as if they were both keeping to some mysterious primordial rhythm.

And it felt so right, so natural.

After a while he stopped walking and set her down on a log, to give himself a rest. He stretched his arms and rotated his shoulders, looking so much the epitome of male strength and beauty that she had to blink and take a firm hold on herself. 'We could wait here for help, Mr Giffard.'

'Did I jolt you, Ca— Miss Trent?'

'No. No, of course not! You – you're carrying me very – er – well.' Oh heavens, her voice sounded as silly and gasping as Susannah's.

His eyes gleamed down at her. '*Merci du compliment,*' he mocked softly.

'Why are you laughing at me?' she asked, exasperation banishing the unaccustomed shyness.

'I'm not laughing, just smiling at your reaction to my holding you.' His eyes were gleaming with laughter. 'I don't bite, you know.'

'Well, you may have held a dozen women in your arms, but I've never been carried like that before.' He was still smiling at her and she felt so foolish, she snapped, 'In fact, I dare say you've had a great deal of practice at this sort of thing!'

'What, at rescuing damsels in distress? No, I'm afraid this is the first time. Unless you count Mrs Keeling?'

Her cheeks were burning. 'Don't be facetious!'

'Or do you mean holding women in my arms?'

She swallowed hard. She had indeed meant that.

'I'm no Lothario, you know.'

'And I'm no *Fair Penitent*, either,' she snapped back, referring to the play from which the character came. Anyway, he had no need to tell her that. She knew he was not a rake, for she had met some of the more rakish gentlemen doing the Season, and his manners were nothing like theirs. His eyes did not roam over women's bodies, nor did he press against you. And yet, if Simeon Giffard had wanted to become a rake, she was sure he'd have been highly successful, because he was a very attractive man – far too attractive for her peace of mind.

Glancing sideways, she spoke crisply, trying to dispel this strange mood. 'If you're ready, Mr Giffard, I'm happy to continue.' Sitting there with him studying her so carefully made her feel – flustered.

'I'm glad to see that you're recovering your spirit, Miss Trent, and my congratulations on being so well read. Now, may I pick you up again?' His voice was soft and his eyes were still dancing with laughter.

Scowling she held out her arms and allowed him to settle her against his chest. This time a strange quivering feeling settled in the pit of her stomach.

'Comfortable?'

The warmth of his breath fanned her cheek and she found it hard to breathe for a moment. 'No.'

'Liar!'

As always, she was very aware of the aura of power he radiated. It was this power, latent within him, that so repelled and frightened poor Susannah. It occurred to Cassie very forcibly that it would not have repelled her, indeed, she could never marry a weak man. She sighed and laid her head against him, because it hurt to hold it away from him. It felt so right to lean against him, so very right.

For all his teasing remarks, Simeon was just as aware of Cassie's body as she was of his, and aware, too, of the significance of their reactions to one another. As he looked down, he marveled at the length of her eyelashes, the softness of her skin, the beauty of her hair.

Under the layers of skirts and draperies which fashion dictated ladies wear lay an attractive body – he hadn't realised quite how attractive before, because she always suffered by comparison to her delicately built cousin. Tall and full-bosomed, not the fashionable fragile creature one was supposed to admire, Cassie had a ripely tantalising attraction that grew upon one slowly – and a very shapely pair of legs and ankles.

She would look even better as she grew older, he suddenly realised, which people said Lady Hamilton had done. He tried to suppress a disloyal image of a faded, older Susannah. His fiancée *would* fade, not improve with age, he was quite sure of that. Dear God, supposing she turned out as invalidish as his mother! For the first time, he felt a sympathy for his father, who had spent little time with his family and had taken refuge in his club more often than not. Perhaps that was what had led him to neglect the estate and gamble more than he could afford to lose, not to mention ill-treating his only son? No, his father had not cared for any of them.

When Cassie opened her eyes again, she kept her gaze down to avoid staring at Simeon's face, but as he stumbled on the uneven path, her arms tightened involuntarily around his neck and she looked up in alarm. For a long moment, their eyes met. Neither spoke, but each was intensely aware of the other, the warmth of skin upon skin, the faint sheen of perspiration on his face, the flush on hers, the scent of herbs in her hair, the slight roughness of his chin. Sensations ran together and swirled around them like an invisible mist, unseen but sensed so very vividly.

Simeon was panting again from the effort of carrying her, and they both seemed bound by his breaths, as if they were alone in the world, linked by the soft sounds he made and by the rise and fall of his powerful chest.

She wanted – oh, heavens, she wanted him to move his head just a fraction closer, wanted the softness of his lips on hers, wanted to kiss him back.

He opened his mouth to speak, his voice rough and

uncertain, 'Cassie, I—' He broke off to stare down at her in obvious shock, as if he too did not quite know what to say.

'Yes?' She heard her voice grow husky with invitation. She still wanted him to . . .

Then the spell was broken by Lady Berrinden's strident voice calling, 'There they are! See! Over there! Do hurry up!'

Cassie flushed vividly and dropped her eyes. Simeon muttered something under his breath and braced himself to greet their rescuers.

Apologising profusely to Mr Giffard for this trouble and inconvenience, loudly directing the two brawny footmen how to link their hands and carry Miss Trent, barely looking at her niece after the first angry glance, Lady Berrinden tried as usual to organise and dominate everything.

But Mr Giffard stubbornly refused to give up his burden and his footmen would no more have dreamed of disobeying him than Lady Berrinden's servants would have disobeyed her. It was he who carried Cassie into the house, taking her right up to her bedroom.

As he laid her gently on the bed, he ignored Lady Berrinden's icy disapproval of this breach of propriety to linger for a moment and say, 'I'm sorry about your injury, Miss Trent.'

'I'm sorry to have caused you so much trouble, Mr Giffard.'

Their eyes said what their lips dared not, that what they were sorry about was the interruption, that they had wanted to continue talking and being together.

What had he been going to say? she wondered dreamily. And would she really have let him kiss her?

As he stepped back, she watched his expression lose its warmth and his face fall into its normal cool lines, and she felt bereft, for the man she liked so much disappeared completely behind that mask. She knew perfectly well that she had no right to feel that way, but she could not help feeling troubled, moved, shaken to the core.

And she could not regret the encounter. Men and women did get attracted to one another. It was the first time it had happened to her, but at least it meant she wasn't a cold-hearted person, something she had rather feared. Next time she was attracted to a man, she only hoped he would be free to feel the same way. But she must guard against dwelling on Simeon Giffard. That way lay only trouble.

She watched him turn to Susannah's maid and say in cool, measured tones, 'Put a cold compress upon Miss Trent's ankle and keep changing it until the doctor arrives.'

She watched how cleverly he managed to shepherd everyone from the bedroom, even Lady Berrinden.

And she rejoiced that when he turned at the door, just for a moment the warmth was back in his face.

She knew it showed in hers, too. She could not prevent that, did not even want to!

'Try to rest, C— Miss Trent. I don't think the doctor will be long.'

Then he was gone. And she felt bereft all over again.

'Are you all right, miss?'

'Yes.' Sighing, Cassie closed her eyes, in no state to deal with the maid or anyone else just now. Even her own feelings were more than she could face, for she had felt an exhilaration in his arms that could not be mistaken, an exhilaration she had no right to feel. And would not allow herself to feel towards her cousin's fiancé again!

The rest of the party gathered downstairs to await the arrival of the doctor and discuss the incident. Only Susannah expressed any concern for her cousin, which for once won her an approving glance from Simeon.

All Lady Berrinden's thoughts and speculations were upon the inconvenience of the accident, and her only regrets were that her dearest Flora should have been given such a nasty shock and poor Simeon put to such inconvenience. She also expressed several times a worry that this might delay their return to London.

Flora Giffard, as was her way, made much play of how the accident had upset her and demanded first a glass of cordial to settle her nerves, then her special cologne to bathe her brow. Her companion hurried to fetch these and showed no signs of resenting the peremptory commands. Finally, Flora began to wonder aloud whether the doctor had not better attend to her before seeing Miss Trent, a suggestion heartily endorsed by her friend Amelia.

Simeon was used to his mother's selfishness and normally ignored it, but he was so disgusted by his future mother-in-law's behaviour, for he had previously thought her a woman of more sense and feeling, that, after listening to her for a few minutes, he interrupted to say severely, 'I can only be sorry that Miss Trent should have hurt herself while staying at Stovely. The fortitude with which she bore the pain is to be admired, whilst the trifling inconvenience to ourselves should be ignored. And if, Mother, you require any further attentions, may I suggest you retire to your room and let your maid and Miss Canley assist you. The doctor will, of course, visit Miss Trent first.'

This blunt speech arrested Lady Berrinden's flow of words and brought a peevish expression to his mother's sallow face. Susannah, however, dared to agree with him. 'Oh, yes, Simeon. Poor Cassie!'

Even this did not please him as it ought to have. The 'Yes, Simeon' with which she had prefaced her remark was too sharp a reminder of Miss Trent's critical amusement.

Fortunately, Dr Murray arrived just then and Simeon had an excuse to leave his guests and explain what had happened. Afterwards, he delayed his return to the drawing-room until the doctor had finished attending to Miss Trent.

But he could find no peace in his library, no escape from his thoughts. He was very attracted to the cousin of his fiancée, there was no denying that. And Cassie had responded to him, though of course, her reactions had been innocent and she had not been aware of what she had done to him – at least, he hoped she had not been aware.

A smile of wonderment crept across his face at the memory of that brief moment on the path. He had enjoyed holding her, no denying that. But then the smile faded and he scowled out of the window, seeing nothing of the scene outside – he had no *right* to enjoy it, no right at all to be attracted to her. He was engaged to Susannah now and he owed her his loyalty, even if he could not give her his love. She would make any man a charming wife. There wasn't an ounce of malice in her.

But she would bore him to tears! How would he stand that foolishness for a lifetime? How had he let his mother persuade him into this?

Eight

When the doctor came down to report to Lady Berrinden on his patient's injuries, Simeon joined them. Dr Murray spoke in his usual blunt manner, 'Your niece has sprained her ankle rather badly, I'm afraid, ma'am.'

'It is incorrect to address me as "ma'am". You should say "your ladyship".'

The look he gave her spoke volumes and he made no attempt to repair the omission when he continued, but instead addressed himself to Simeon. 'Miss Trent hit her head when she fell and has a touch of concussion. She needs to rest for a day or two, and she must keep her weight off that leg.'

Lady Berrinden was not to be ignored and raised her voice, 'My niece shall have every attention. We'll take her back to London straightaway.'

Dr Murray glared at her. 'Did you not hear what I said? She's got concussion, woman! She can't possibly travel yet. Not up to the jolting. She can go back on Wednesday, perhaps. Only if she's up to it, though.'

'Impossible!' Lady Berrinden declared.

'Why?' He turned to his host. 'You've got enough room to keep her here, Giffard, surely?'

'Of course we have.'

'That's all right, then.'

'But—'

The doctor glared at Lady Berrinden. 'Madam, I have

120

given you my professional opinion. Any other doctor would tell you the same thing. Kindly do me the favour of following my advice – unless you wish to imperil Miss Trent's recovery!'

She glared back at him, but he ignored her and turned back to address Simeon, 'I'll drop in to see her again on Tuesday afternoon. Nothing else I can do for her at the moment. Time's the great healer in these cases.' With a sketchy bow to the ladies, he was off.

Simeon escorted him to the door and the doctor's voice echoed down the hallway. 'Very upset. Feels she's being a nuisance. Given her a sleeping draught. Be all right for her to get up tomorrow and lie on a couch down here, as long as someone carries her down. She's not to walk on that foot yet. And don't let them upset her. She's a brave lassie.'

When Simeon returned to the sitting-room, his expression was coldly determined. 'Run up and sit with your cousin for a while, will you, Susannah? Assure her that she's causing *me* no trouble and my only concern is for her speedy recovery.'

After a frightened glance at her mother, who was looking thunderously angry, Susannah left the room.

'I trust, Lady Berrinden,' Simeon continued, 'that you will all accept our hospitality for the next few days.'

'Thank you, but that would be a little difficult. Apart from the fact that we haven't brought enough clothes, we're giving a dinner party ourselves on Tuesday and cannot easily cancel it.' She frowned at her husband, who had not said a word.

He realised with a start that she wanted him to agree with her. 'Oh, yes, dashed inconvenient, what?'

'My poor Amelia!' murmured Flora. 'How troublesome all this is for you!'

There was silence for a while, since each of them had things to think about – except for Lord Berrinden, who had suddenly noticed a large bird in the garden and was wondering if it was a wood pigeon and whether Giffard ever shot them for sport.

Amelia Berrinden looked around her thoughtfully. Perhaps this accident was a blessing in disguise. If Susannah spent some time with Simeon, she might lose her nervousness in his company. She had misjudged the girl there, and acknowledged to herself now that she should have prepared her daughter for the proposal. Really, Susannah could be a complete ninny at times! How could she not have realised why he continued to visit them, even though Richard was away? And as for Henry – she turned to frown at her husband, who was gaping out at the garden with his mouth slightly open – well, Henry was never the slightest use in delicate matters.

In the end, it was agreed over a late luncheon that Susannah should also stay on at Stovely to keep her cousin company and that her maid should be sent back with some more clothes for the two young ladies.

After that, without bothering to visit their niece, Lord and Lady Berrinden left for London.

By late the following morning, Cassie had recovered enough to agree to Susannah's suggestion that the two footmen carry her downstairs to a small sitting-room which looked out towards the lake. Simeon was dealing with estate business and Mrs Giffard had not yet left her rooms. Her maid said that she rarely appeared until just before luncheon and Miss Canley usually went for long walks in the mornings. Apparently the effort of entertaining guests for two whole days, not to mention the shock of the accident and the sharp unfeeling way her son had spoken to her, had quite prostrated poor Mrs Giffard.

Susannah fussed over her cousin with such offers as: 'Are you sure you're all right?' And a little later, 'Shall I ring for a tea tray?'

She asked three times, 'Do you want more pillows?' and five times, 'Shall I read to you?'

'Stop fussing!' Cassie said at last through gritted teeth. 'It is only my ankle. My eyes are perfectly all right, and I still remember how to read to myself.'

'Oh. Oh, yes, of course. How silly of me!'

Which made Cassie feel guilty, as if she had kicked a kitten.

She had meant to deal coolly with Simeon Giffard, for she was aware that she had betrayed her reactions to his touch and was now rather embarrassed about that. But by the time he arrived, she was at screaming point and was so relieved to see him that she greeted him with a dazzling smile of welcome which made him pause by the door and blink in shock, then smile back at her.

Susannah greeted him with a nervous jerk and said hello in a breathy, nervous voice which made his lips tighten and set lines in his forehead.

But by the time they had settled to chat and Cassie had drawn him out about Stovely's history, Susannah had stopped fussing and his frown disappeared.

To the surprise of all three of them, the next few days passed very pleasantly. Simeon Giffard, at home in the house he loved, was a relaxed and courteous host. His mother, relapsing into her invalidish habits now that she had achieved her objective, joined them briefly for luncheon, rested in her rooms for most of the afternoon and retired to bed immediately after dinner. Her companion only appeared when she was there.

Although she was affable enough to her future daughter-in-law, Mrs Giffard was never more than distantly civil to Miss Trent, but Cassie did not let that worry her.

As for Susannah, it was the first time she had been away from her mother's domination since she came out and, after an uncertain start, she blossomed like a flower in the sun, for no one snapped at her or criticised her – indeed, both her companions listened to what she had to say with every sign of interest and enjoyment. She began to think it might not be so bad to be married to Simeon, after all.

Cassie, too, enjoyed the reprieve. Finding a well-stocked library, she was able to indulge in hours of quiet reading, lying on a *chaise-longue* by a window overlooking the lake. Susannah, who was not bookish, would stitch away at some embroidery she was finishing for Mrs Giffard, or try to sketch the view from the terrace. She had some small talent as an artist and produced a neat water colour of Stovely which she bestowed upon her cousin as a memento of their stay.

To everyone's relief, Dr Murray forbade his patient to leave Stovely until Friday.

The weather continued to smile on them, with a series of sunny spring days, which brought out a host of flowers in the beautiful gardens.

Cassie watched with relief as Susannah continued to relax with Simeon. In the evenings, they all played childish card games together, or they sang to Susannah's accompaniment, or, better still, they persuaded her to sing to them. This she was happy to do, for she only grew shy before large audiences or with people she did not know.

Cassie and Simeon found no difficulty in chatting quietly together while Susannah played the piano or leafed through the piles of music. He was, Cassie thought, a man of sense under that cool exterior – except when it came to choosing a wife!

Even Simeon was beginning to hope that life with Susannah might be quite tolerable after all. He did not admit to himself that it was Cassie's conversation he was enjoying, and her skill that kept their encounters so harmonious, but he did decide that she was an intelligent woman, as well as an attractive one, and would make some man a good wife one day. Albert could count himself fortunate indeed if she accepted him.

Then, on the Thursday night, Cassie was woken by something. She lay in the darkness, listening. There! It sounded like – it was – Susannah was weeping in the next bedroom. Cassie lay in bed for a moment or two, trying to gather her senses and wondering what could have happened. Her cousin had seemed happy enough when left to say goodnight to her fiancé.

The sobbing continued unabated, so Cassie sighed and got up. Lighting a candle, she limped into the next room to see if she could help. 'Suzie, dear, what on earth is the matter? Can I do anything?'

Susannah's voice was muffled. 'No! No one can!'

'Tell me what's wrong, anyway.'

'He – Simeon – he kissed me – on the mouth – and he wouldn't stop! It was dreadful! I thought I should choke. And when I – when I tried to pull away, he became angry. He said the least I could do was to learn to be an – an obedient, if not a willing wife. I thought I should *die!*'

Cassie was perplexed. 'But you goose, it's only to be expected that he'll want to kiss you. Now surely—'

'You don't understand!' Susannah covered her face with her hands. 'Cassie, I hate it when he touches me. I could bear getting married to him, if only he wouldn't touch me. He's always frightened me when he grabbed hold of me. He's so big! So strong! Even when he was a boy, I used to run away and hide from him. And – and he saw how I hated it tonight – and – oh, he was absolutely furious! I nearly fainted when he kissed me again, so roughly. Cassie, I c-can't pretend when he touches me!'

There was a moment's silence. 'Then you must tell your mother you can't marry him.'

'I can't do that either.' Susannah's voice was a despairing whisper. 'I know I'm a coward. You don't have to tell me that, Cassie! But she frightens me even more than he does.'

'Perhaps your father . . . ?'

Susannah sniffed. 'Papa can do nothing, for he's as afraid of her as I am. Oh, what am I going to do, Cassie? I think I shall kill myself if I have to marry Simeon!'

'Nonsense!'

Susannah hiccuped to a stop, in shock at this bracing treatment. 'But Cassie—'

'If you feel that desperate, I shall think of some way to help you. I don't know exactly what yet, but I shall think of something, you may depend upon that!'

'There's nothing you can do. There's nothing *anyone* can do!'

'Oh, isn't there! We shall see about that!' Cassie sat by the bed, stroking Susannah's hair and murmuring meaningless endearments until her cousin fell asleep, then she limped back to her bedroom. Such a muddle! Useless, of course, to expect Susannah to stand up to her mother. Equally useless to expect her to be anything but unhappy with Simeon Giffard!

She lay awake for over an hour, pondering the problem, for she could not bear to stand idle and see two lives destroyed. Once, she smiled as she realised that her Trent cousins would have immediately recognised her determination to do something about a problem. That same determination had led all three of them into trouble many a time. Her mother would have been suspicious, too. 'Cassie, you're plotting something,' she would have said at once.

And Susannah's maid did stare suspiciously at her in the morning and say, 'You're up to something, my lass!'

'Oh, pooh! I'm just feeling better, that's all!'

'Tell that to the poor mad King!' retorted the maid.

That night at Stovely, Cassie was not the only one to lie awake worrying. In another bedroom an equally wakeful Simeon Giffard was lying scowling in the darkness that seemed as black as his future. He had seen the expression on Susannah's face when he kissed her. It was more than a young girl's timidity. It was – well, he could not deny it – it was *revulsion!* Why on earth, then, had she accepted his proposal?

Lying there alone, he let out a bitter laugh. The answer was obvious. Her mother. He had been a fool to be taken in by Lady Berrinden, a fool to have heeded his own mother, too. He should have followed his instincts and not let anyone persuade him to propose marriage to someone he did not care about – even for the sake of Stovely. Shy young girl, indeed! Susannah was not shy of him; she could not bear him to touch her!

He remembered her cousin, lying in his arms and staring at him with those large brown eyes. *She* had not found him repulsive. That moment between them had underlined the difference between a woman who found you attractive and a woman who did not. Oh, yes! And the difference was enormous.

The blame for this tangle was not all his, though. Susannah must share some of it, too. If only she had shown a little more spirit, stood up to her mother! But no! As Cassie Trent had not hesitated to point out in that damned impertinent way she had, Susannah could not manage to say, 'No, Mama' in small things, let alone refuse to do Lady Berrinden's bidding in such an important matter.

He thumped the pillow, then thumped it again for good measure. Damn all women! And damn you too, Cassie Trent, with your scornful brown eyes. Who are you to judge anyone?

He was trapped now, with no escape possible, for Lady Berrinden had wasted no time in having an announcement of the engagement placed in the newspapers. In a mood of deep depression, he got up, poured himself a large brandy and sat scowling into the empty grate by the light of one badly trimmed candle.

What sort of a life would it be with a wife who could not

bear him to touch her? He should break off the betrothal now, before both their lives were ruined. But a gentleman could not, in honour, draw back from an engagement. It was the grossest of insults to offer a lady.

And besides, a Giffard never broke his word. That had been drummed into him since birth. The brandy sank deeper in the decanter. Well, he would have to go through with it now, but once he had set up his nursery, he would not bother his wife with his attentions, that was sure. There were enough willing women around to take care of a man's needs. He would be discreet, of course.

But somehow the thought of taking a mistress did not comfort him in the slightest. He did not want to be discreet about anything. If a man had a wife, he should not need to find other women.

Several brandies later, he stumbled over to the bed, flung himself upon the tangle of fine damask counterpane and fell into an uneasy sleep. But even this was haunted by a pale phantom which said, 'Yes, Simeon', 'Yes, Simeon', until he thought he would strangle it, while a pair of brown eyes hung in the air above looking down at him scornfully.

The next day, Susannah was composed enough to bid her fiancé a polite farewell and thank him for his hospitality. Simeon kissed her very briefly on a hand that quivered at his touch and assure her mendaciously that it had been a great pleasure to have her at Stovely. He would look forward to seeing her and Miss Trent again in town.

He knows, thought Cassie, watching this comedy being enacted. She betrayed herself last night and he knows exactly how she feels. But what's he going to do about it? She sniffed in annoyance. Nothing, obviously. No gentleman jilts a lady.

Well, I shan't allow him to sacrifice himself for his noble principles. And I shan't allow my aunt to sacrifice Susannah, either. You had to make some attempt to set things right if you cared about people, as she cared about Susannah, and – she stared at him in shock as he waved farewell – about Simeon, too. He would not be a happy man if he were to marry her cousin. And she did not want to see him sad and unfulfilled.

Nine

S imeon Giffard did nothing to terminate his engagement. It would have been against every canon of his upbringing and he couldn't – he just could not! – bring himself to embarrass and insult Susannah in that way. And when he dreamed of Cassie Trent, he told himself firmly that his response to her had been an aberration and these feelings, this fleeting attraction between them, would soon pass.

Thanks to Lady Berrinden's announcement, congratulations had begun to pour in even before the two young women returned to London. Like a mechanical doll, Susannah wrote replies to these, spoke to her well-wishers and did whatever else her mother decreed. But she avoided tête-à-têtes with her cousin, to Cassie's distress.

It was going to be hard to help someone who didn't even try to help herself, but Cassie was increasingly determined to find a way. If she didn't, two people were going to be very unhappy indeed.

A party to celebrate the engagement was planned, and was given within a week of their return to London. Susannah and Simeon stood next to Lady Berrinden to receive the guests. Romantically minded persons sighed over the picture they presented, he so tall and darkly handsome, she so dainty and ethereally fair. One or two of the more perceptive people wondered why Susannah smiled so little and why Giffard was not showing any sign of happiness. But then, they reminded themselves, he had always been very reserved, a cold fish, in fact. Took after his mother in that.

Lady Berrinden went round telling everyone how dearest Simeon had swept Susannah off her feet. Behind her back, her friends told one another that Amelia had been throwing her daughter in Giffard's path all Season and now she'd caught him, though why she had succeeded where so many with equally beautiful daughters had failed, they could not quite work out.

Cassie sat at the side of the room one night with Albert Darford, since her ankle, although much improved, was still preventing her from dancing. She stared at Susannah, who was dancing with Simeon. Her cousin's body was stiff, her eyes firmly fixed on his waistcoat. Cassie sighed. In spite of her resolves, her glance slid to his face and she saw that he was staring to one side of Susannah's head. Neither of them had spoken the whole time they were dancing.

Albert followed her gaze. 'They don't look exactly overjoyed, do they?'

'Not exactly!'

'Oh, come, Miss Trent, you can speak frankly to me! We both know how unsuited they are.' His lazy, good-humoured face was, for once, absolutely serious. 'Most people look at the pedigrees and decide it'll be a good match, but I tell you, Miss Trent, it's the worst thing old Simeon has ever done. Not got anything against your cousin – in fact, she's a very nice girl – but couldn't think of a worse wife for him.'

'Or a worse husband for her! There must be *something* we can do about it. We can't just stand by and let them ruin their whole lives.'

He shook his head. 'There's nothing we can do. If you think Simeon will jilt a girl, especially a nice girl like your cousin, well, you don't know him. All the Giffards pride themselves on keeping their word, whatever the cost.'

'And there's no chance of Susannah crying off, either; she's too afraid of her mother!' Cassie looked around her at the brightly lit room, with its groups of smiling people, and shook her head. How false all this gaiety was! How insincere the lively conversations! But whatever the obstacles, she was still determined to help her cousin.

After the engagement party, it began to be noticed that Miss Trent and Albert Darford were seeing rather a lot of each other, and were chatting together in corners with the ease of people who are on very comfortable terms. Rumours began to spread of an impending engagement in that quarter.

Albert, who had still not made up his mind whether to launch into matrimony, which he had carefully avoided for the last ten of his thirty years, did nothing to scotch the rumours, but neither did he make any attempt to woo Cassie formally. It was enough, for the moment, to enjoy the novel sensation of making friends with a woman, of simply enjoying her company and her refreshingly different views on life.

Lady Berrinden went round looking like a cat that had swallowed a bucket of cream. Never had her family found her so easy to live with! Never had she spoken so caressingly to her children! She began to make plans for the coming-out of her second daughter, Marianne, in two years' time. Of course, Marianne did not have Susannah's looks, so she could not be expected to make as good a match, but she was pretty enough, when properly dressed, and as biddable as her elder sister. She must be persuaded to practice the pianoforte more rigorously, however. She had a good ear for music, though her voice was nothing like as strong as Susannah's, but she wouldn't shine with her present standard of performance.

Then there was Richard. He was presently travelling in Europe, which was such a foolish thing to do and why he had insisted on going, Amelia would never understand, for she had told him straight that he was not even to think of travelling in countries which had so recently known the ravages of warfare. But he had gone his own sweet way regardless. He was even worse than his father, who could also be as stubborn as a mule. Henry had started drinking heavily again whenever he was out of her sight and was making a fool of himself regularly at his club.

When Richard returned, they must find a suitable bride for him. She had several girls in mind, all from good families, of course, but, more important, all with respectable fortunes of their own. She and her son might disagree about the benefits of foreign travel, but they were as one in their desire to restore the family fortunes.

So much did Lady Berrinden allow herself to become immersed in dreams of further triumphs that she failed to notice the strain on Susannah's face, or the fact that her eldest daughter was becoming daily thinner and had quite lost the roses in her cheeks.

In desperation, Cassie approached her uncle and begged him to intercede. 'Susannah doesn't love Simeon Giffard. She doesn't want to marry him.'

He wriggled uneasily and looked over his shoulder. 'Nonsense. Said yes, didn't she?'

'That was my aunt's doing. You know it was.'

'Women are always the ones who arrange these matches. It's Amelia's business, not mine, to marry off the girls. And she knows what she's about. Very astute woman, your aunt.'

'Uncle Henry, Susannah is *afraid* of Mr Giffard.'

'Nerves, just nerves. Innocent as a new-born lamb. She'll be all right once they've tied the knot – settle down, make a good wife, all that sort of thing. Always been a nervous sort of girl. Never given us a minute's trouble, though. It'll be all right, you'll see.' After that, he refused point-blank to discuss the matter again.

Cassie tried several times to talk to Susannah, but her cousin just said, 'It's no good. I can't defy Mama. And I – I'm getting quite used to the idea of marrying Simeon now.'

133

After that, she too refused to talk about it to Cassie, though her dark-circled eyes still spoke of sleepless nights.

Then, very suddenly, Lady Berrinden's idyll was broken by a stiffly worded note from Richard Berrinden's valet, carried across Europe at considerable expense by a special messenger. His master was desperately ill in a town called Freiburg in Bavaria. Lord and Lady Berrinden should come at once, if they wanted to see their son and heir alive.

This letter threw Lady Berrinden into a panic. Although she would never have admitted it, Richard was her darling, her first-born, her only surviving son. He was the one who most closely resembled her, the one upon whom she could rely, as she never could rely on Henry. For once, her calmness and self-control deserted her. She wept in her husband's arms and begged him to take her immediately to her son.

When she grew calmer, she realised what a dilemma this had placed them in. 'We must go, for I cannot trust foreigners to care for Richard properly, nor can I rest till I see him myself. But what are we to do about the girls?'

'Eh? What about the girls?'

'Marianne and Charmian can go down to Fairleigh while we're away. Cousin Fanny and the governess will be there to look after them. But what about Susannah and Cassie?'

'Go to the country, too?' he asked cautiously.

'Don't be stupid, Henry!'

'Stay here in London, then?'

'Of course they can't stay in London on their own! Susannah and Simeon need someone responsible to chaperone them.' And someone had to make sure Susannah did nothing foolish. Really, Lady Berrinden had so much to bear! And no one was properly grateful to her for what she did for them! 'Besides, there's Cassie's future to think of. Albert Darford is just coming along nicely. He needs encouraging or he'll slip off the hook.'

'Albert and Cassie?' He shook his head, certain of himself for once. 'No, no, my love. That hare won't run.'

'*Won't run?* They're together every time we go anywhere, sitting in corners, chatting like old friends. The match will do very well, I tell you. And she can be grateful to find herself a husband like Albert.'

'Not what I meant.' He struggled for words. 'What I mean is, they're good friends, yes, but nothing else.' He saw the scorn on her face and added emphatically, 'A man don't marry his friend. Take my word for it.'

'We shall see about that.'

He opened his mouth to protest, looked at her grim expression and closed it again. But he knew he was right. Whatever she said, Albert was not the marrying sort.

'In the meantime, Henry, we have a problem to solve. I suppose we shall just have to send them down to Fairleigh with the others.'

She toyed for a few minutes with the idea of leaving Henry at home and making do with Cousin Clarence as an escort for herself. But no, that wouldn't work, either! Clarence was a poor traveller, and Henry, whatever his other faults, was an excellent traveller. Besides, although he was Susannah's father, he would have no idea how to handle her. As well leave the gardener in charge as him! No, they would have to send the two girls down to Fairleigh with the others, after all.

She had no sooner decided this than further doubts shook her. Supposing Simeon decided to stay at Stovely and visit Fairleigh regularly? Undoubtedly it was his lovemaking that had frightened Susannah and there would be far more chances for him to pay her those sorts of attentions with only Cousin Fanny in charge. Did the silly child not realise that his interest in such things would decline once the couple had set up their nursery?

She sent Henry to make the travel arrangements, told his valet to pack his clothes and whisked into her bedroom to sort out her own arrangements. But she could not help worrying about what would happen while they were away.

It was Cassandra, of all people, who furnished her aunt with a better solution. She had received a letter from that lumpish cousin of hers (Lady Berrinden shuddered at the memory of Will's homely face and provincial tailoring.) He was apparently about to get engaged and wished Cassandra to return to the North and attend the family's celebrations.

Normally, Lady Berrinden would have vetoed that idea without a second thought, but it suddenly occurred to her that this might be the solution to all her problems. 'I think,' she said graciously, 'that it would be very proper for you to attend your cousin's engagement party, Cassandra. After all, they are your only family on your father's side.'

'Oh, do you really think so, Aunt Amelia? I won't go, if you don't think it right, but I must admit that I'd love to be there.'

'The – er – the young lady in question . . . ?'

'Oh, she's from a family in the next town – very rich. They're millowners too.'

Lady Berrinden repressed a shudder. 'Yes. I see. Very fitting. The only thing is – what am I to do with Susannah?'

'Susannah?' Cassie opened her eyes wide, trying to look as innocent as possible. Her aunt was more likely to take to an idea if she thought of it herself.

'Yes, Susannah. Why is everyone so *stupid* this morning! I cannot take Susannah with us to Freiburg. I shall have no time to chaperone her properly and, in any case, she is not a good traveller. The other girls are so much younger, not out yet, so she'll have no one to keep her company in the country.' She looked hopefully at her niece.

'Oh. I see. Well, if you like, she could come with me. My Aunt Lucy would be happy to have her. She adores visitors.' Cassie hoped her expression looked innocent. It didn't feel innocent from the inside, but you just had to do the best you could in an emergency – and Susannah's unhappiness was definitely an emergency as far as she was concerned.

Lady Berrinden pretended to think this offer over. 'Hmm. Well, it might be the best solution, given the circumstances. If you're quite sure your aunt will not mind.' A stay in an outlandish place, and with such vulgar people too, ought to show her ninny of a daughter upon which side her bread was buttered.

Then they encountered a further problem. Lady Berrinden would in no way countenance the two girls travelling so far without a gentleman escort.

Matters were at an impasse when Simeon Giffard called round. No sooner had he been informed of Richard's illness and the girls' projected visit to the North, than he volunteered his services as escort. 'I can visit my Cousin James at Moorthorpe Grange at the same time.'

Fortunately for Cassie's plotting, Lady Berrinden, who had completely forgotten that Simeon had relatives in Bardsley, missed this last remark.

'Oh, no!' exclaimed Cassie involuntarily. His presence was the last thing they needed. She wanted to get Susannah away from him, not throw her into his company. 'I mean,' she amended hastily, seeing her aunt's affronted expression, 'we couldn't think of troubling you, Mr Giffard.'

'It would be no trouble at all, Miss Trent,' he replied with a small bow. 'Indeed, it would give me great pleasure to escort you both.'

'Susannah, my dear,' chided Lady Berrinden archly, 'you must show a little gratitude to dear Simeon for his kind offer. It will not do for you to be taking him for granted *before* you are married!'

'Yes, Mama.'

Simeon winced, caught another scornful glance from Miss Trent, mentally damned her impertinence, then listened with a show of polite interest as Susannah mouthed a few phrases expressing her gratitude. If only he need not . . . but no, he must not think of that!

Before Cassie could think of a way out of this dilemma, she was tossed into a new one as the butler opened the door and announced, 'Mr Trent, m'lady.'

Simeon stared across the room in surprise, because, unless he was very much mistaken, that was panic he saw upon Cassie's face. It was almost instantly erased and replaced by a smile, but he knew he had not been mistaken. He watched suspiciously as she flew across the room and cast herself into Will's arms in a hoydenish way that made her aunt hiss in disgust and glare at her.

Cassie whispered urgently in Will's ear, 'Don't look surprised! You've just got engaged to be married!' Then she held him at arms' length. 'Oh, Will, how kind of you to come all the way down to London so that you can accompany us back to Bardsley!'

Apart from a slight intake of breath, Will managed not to show his surprise. Knowing his cousin and her scrapes of old, he steeled himself to meet the next shock, as she nipped his fingers in warning.

'I wouldn't have missed your engagement party for worlds!' she gushed.

She was behaving in a manner so unlike herself that Will was amazed the others did not become suspicious. His face wooden, he responded with a faint, 'Oh, yes?' and waited to be enlightened further. To whom had he become engaged? And what mischief was Cassie up to?

Only Simeon Giffard noticed the by-play of squeezes and whispers and began to suspect that the news of his own engagement had come as a complete surprise to Mr Trent. Intrigued, he watched the two of them more closely. This would bear further investigation. Maybe – he did not dare allow himself to consider that 'maybe'. Not yet.

For once, Cassie did not notice Simeon's interest, though she was usually only too aware of what he was doing. She was busy expanding her tale and preventing Will from saying anything that would ruin her plans.

Her cousin responded nobly and assured them all that he would like nothing better than to escort Cassie and Susannah up to Bardsley – and, yes, the very next day would suit him.

Then there was a pregnant silence as they all turned to Lady Berrinden and waited for her response.

'We're all very grateful to you, Mr Trent, and we accept your kind offer.'

'Oh – er – it's my pleasure, your ladyship.'

Susannah did not allow herself to gaze at Will for long, but she did study his face for a moment or two and decide that he was looking well. Being engaged obviously suited him. She sighed at how little it suited her, then brightened marginally at the thought of how pleasant it would be to leave London for a while, and spend time in such delightful company, for she was sure all dear Cassie's relatives would be as charming as Mr Trent.

Simeon Giffard took his leave a little later, looking thoughtful.

Since Cassie was still babbling on interminably, Lady Berrinden suggested wearily that her niece take Mr Trent into the breakfast parlour and continue the discussion there. 'And Susannah, would you kindly go and set the maids to packing your sisters' and your own things?'

'Yes, Mama.'

'And would somebody *please* see if Henry has spoken to the coachman yet about our journey to Freiburg?'

'I'll do that as well, Mama.' Susannah hurried away, feeling better than she had for quite a while, but also feeling guilty at how pleasant the prospect of some time away from her fiancé seemed. Perhaps in Bardsley she would have time to become accustomed to her new status.

Once safely out of her aunt's presence, Cassie collapsed into a chair and fanned her flushed face. 'Oh, my goodness! I thought it was all over when you were announced just then, Will. I nearly died! How clever of you to catch on so quickly to what I was doing?'

He looked at her suspiciously. 'I'm not sure I have caught on fully yet. How do you think I felt when I heard I was engaged to be married?' He grinned at her. 'A bit sudden, isn't it? Do I know the lady?'

'Oh, Will, it was the only thing I could think of on the spur of the moment as an excuse for going to stay in Bardsley.' The laughter vanished from her face and she pulled him down on the sofa next to her, her voice low and for his ears only. 'The thing is, my aunt's made Susannah get engaged to Simeon Giffard.'

There was a moment's silence, then he managed to say, 'Seems a pleasant enough fellow.'

'He's not. No, that's not fair. He can be very, um, nice.' A sudden memory of the way he had carried her made her catch her breath for a moment, but she dismissed that memory firmly, as she had learned to do over the past few days. 'The important thing is he's not the right man for Susannah. She can't even bear him to touch her, but she's so terrified of her mother that she didn't dare refuse him.'

'Is that why she looks so . . . so . . .' It was the first thing he had noticed, for of course his eyes had been drawn to Susannah the moment he entered the room.

'Yes. She's quite worn down by it all, poor thing. We must help her.'

'Cassie, love, this isn't the sort of thing that even you can interfere with.'

She jerked backwards and scowled at him. 'Oh, isn't it? I suppose you think I should just stand by and let them all bully her to death, then?'

'But Giffard must love her or he wouldn't have asked her to marry him! It's for *him* to look after her now.'

'Well, he doesn't love her! That's what's so awful. He just wants a suitable wife.'

'Oh.'

'So you will help me to do something about it, won't you?'

Will ran one hand through his unruly hair. 'If I can, I will. But I can't see how it will help your cousin for me to pretend that I'm engaged, dashed if I can, Cassie.'

'I made that up to give us an excuse to get away to Bardsley. I haven't worked out a proper plan for breaking off Susannah's engagement yet, but I shall once we're safe in the North, you see if I don't!'

He shook his head and a reluctant grin lit up his face. 'Never thought I'd let myself be dragged into one of your scrapes again, love!' The memory of Susannah's pale unhappy face made the smile fade and he added quietly, 'If you think it'll help for me to pretend I'm engaged – if you think of anything I can do to help Miss Berrinden, then you have only to ask.'

'Oh, Will!' She planted a kiss on his cheek. 'You're the *best* cousin a girl could have!'

There was a knock on the door and Susannah entered. 'Mama says would Mr Trent like to stay to luncheon, and then he can arrange all the details of the journey? She and Papa are to set off this afternoon for Freiburg.' She spoke listlessly, and if anything further was needed to convince Will that he should help, it was the sight of her looking wan and hopeless, when he remembered all too clearly the image of radiant young beauty that he had carried in his heart ever since his last visit to London.

They set off for the north the next day in a hired post-chaise and four, with Mary Ann and a huge pile of luggage following in a similar vehicle, for Cassie said there would not be room to house Susannah's maid.

Susannah started to look better as soon as the chaise

pulled away from Bransham Gardens – or so it seemed to Cassie.

Will thought the same thing and set himself to entertaining Susannah, making her smile, coaxing her to eat, for she looked as fragile as a bird. He was unaware that he betrayed his feelings every time he looked at her – not to her, but to his cousin – and that this had given Cassie a new worry.

The same night, in the inn bedroom they were sharing (on Lady Berrinden's express orders) Cassie confessed to Susannah the deception she had practised to gain permission for them to go to Bardsley. After the first shock, Susannah shed a few tears and admitted that it was indeed a great relief to get away for a while. But she could not be persuaded that there was any way out of the engagement, so Cassie let the matter drop.

Will was much more successful in cheering Susannah up. In fact, watching the skilful way he handled her, his cousin began to wonder whether he would not make an excellent husband for a timid girl, whatever the alleged differences in their social status. There was something very solid and comforting about Will. She herself had loved him dearly all her life, from when she'd been very small and he'd mended her toys, to her first grown-up dinner, when he'd soothed her nerves beforehand and kept up her spirits by winking at her occasionally across the table.

She looked at him now as he sat in the jolting carriage explaining something to Susannah, breathing on the window to make it go misty and drawing little diagrams on it. Even his kindest friend would not call him good-looking. Of no more than medium height, he was sturdily built, with a fresh complexion and spiky reddish-brown hair which would never lie flat, let alone hold a style. His eyes were perhaps his best feature, being a bright blue, but his lashes were of a sandy colour, and there were already laughter lines at the corners of his eyelids. He had a nondescript, lumpy nose and a wide generous mouth.

With a faint feeling of surprise, she noted that he was more fashionably dressed than ever before, in a blue frock coat, with a roll collar, over a striped waistcoat, and with a pair of the latest style of pantaloons strapped neatly under his shoes. It must be the business trips to London, she decided, which were giving him a little more style.

Will could have told her that there had been no real need for this business trip. He had just felt that he must see Susannah one last time before she married Giffard. He knew it was hopeless to care about her, for her parents would never have looked favourably upon his suit but, somehow, he had not been able to stay away.

They had to travel gently because of Susannah and it was three days before they arrived in Bardsley. Cassie had not realised just how unsightly the town was until she had seen other places and now its ugliness came as a shock. A picture of Stovely Chase rose unbidden in her mind, to be quickly dismissed. There were few places in England like Stovely, she reminded herself as the carriage rolled along by the river Bard in the deepening dusk.

The river looked pretty enough in this light, but it was filthy with the effluent from the mills and manufactories, and it gave off an unpleasant smell. They drove past narrow streets of mean houses through to the better part of the town, with Susannah exclaiming at what she saw, Will explaining things and Cassie silent in her corner of the chaise.

Then they arrived at the Trent home, and it was a hurly-burly of explanations and hugs. Aunt Lucy met them in the hall and shouted to 'our Sarah' to come and see who Will had brought back with him. Sarah ran down the stairs and fell upon Cassie, hugging her fiercely and twirling her round. Someone noticed that Susannah was standing shyly in a corner of the hall, and she too was drawn into the circle. Aunt Lucy claimed the privilege of a kiss and Sarah declared she was not to be left out, since she was 'almost a cousin'.

After that the family swept off into a large untidy sitting-room. Aunt Lucy demurred a little about the choice of room, mentioning the front parlour, but she was argued down by her children and her niece.

'Do you want Susannah to feel like a visitor?' demanded Will, in mock indignation.

'I wouldn't feel as if I were at home, if I had to sit in the parlour,' declared Cassie. 'This is the best room in the house, Aunt Lucy.'

Susannah's wondering gaze took in the untidiness. A sewing box lay open on the floor, with half its contents spread around it. The whole surface of a side table was covered by magazines, some open, and there were books and an embroidery frame on top of the battered piano – in fact, total confusion everywhere. She had never seen a room like it in all her well-ordered life. In Lady Berrinden's house, comfort was sacrificed to elegance, and a rigid tidiness prevailed. Here, none of the chairs matched, the carpet was worn and the curtains had seen better days. But no one sat upright and made meaningless conversation; instead, they sprawled on the large, comfortable chairs and interrupted one another at will.

Within two days Susannah felt at home enough to practise a duet with Sarah, untangle Aunt Lucy's embroidery silks for her, and tease Will about his spiky hair, which was a family joke. She began to regain her appetite, too, and stopped jumping at sudden noises.

For Cassie, however, the homecoming was a mixed blessing. It was wonderful to be with her 'real' family again, for although she had grown fond of Susannah, she had never felt close to Lord and Lady Berrinden. But it was heartbreaking to be back in Bardsley and know her mother was not there.

That loss was still so sharp that it took her two days to pluck up the courage to go and see her former home, going there alone, with only Mary Ann to keep her company.

She enjoyed the walk across town, for she was stopped and warmly greeted by several women, wives of senior operatives in the Trent mills. They enquired about her stay in London as if it had been the moon, and told her all their news, who had died, whose daughter had got wed and who had had another baby.

As they walked along the grey streets, Cassie said suddenly, 'It's very different from London, isn't it, Mary Ann?'

'Aye. Different from *your* London, Miss Cassie. Some of it's not all that different to Garnett Lane, though.'

'I'd forgotten how ugly Bardsley was.'

Mary Ann stared around in some surprise. 'I suppose it is.'

Dirty barefoot children dodged in and out of lines of ragged washing in the side streets, erupting occasionally into the main street to steal rides on the tails of passing carts and drays. Women shrilled at other people's children to clear off or at their own offspring to come home this minute. Over it all, smoke drifted, from the new steam engines that were thudding in the Trent mills, from the dye works that coloured the river and from the small round chimney-pots of the myriad terraced dwellings. There was not a tree in sight, not an inch of garden to be seen in this part of town.

They arrived at Cassie's old home and she had to take a few deep breaths to keep her composure. How odd, she thought, to ring the doorbell and have to wait for someone to answer it! Shuffling footsteps came down the hallway and an unsteady hand fumbled with the handle. An old man peered out, then his rheumy eyes lit up as he recognised Cassie and threw the door wide open, calling excitedly, 'Our Ellen! Our Ellen! It's Miss Cassie! Come quick!'

Ellen came pounding up the back stairs, to clasp Cassie to her ample bosom. 'Eh, Miss! We heard you was back. Welcome home! Shut that door, our Dad, an' go an' push the kettle over the fire!'

'How are you all?' asked Cassie, a lump in her throat.

'Oh, we're champion, miss, but it's been a bit quiet without you. Eh, but let me look at you! Well! Well! Fine as a duchess, you look, fine as a duchess!' She fingered the delicate muslin reverently, then clasped Cassie's hand in hers, her face working and tears in her eyes. 'Eh miss,' she said huskily, 'it's good to see you, that it is!'

After a while, Cassie interrupted the flow of talk. 'I'll just have a wander round by myself. You go with Ellen, Mary Ann. I'll come down and have a cup of tea with you in the kitchen later.'

Upstairs she wandered round aimlessly, sat for a while in her mother's bedroom, then dried her eyes and said fiercely, 'Maudlin nonsense! You fool, what did you expect to find here?'

By the time she joined Mary Ann and Ellen in the kitchen, she was determinedly cheerful, a pretence she kept up all the way back to her Aunt Lucy's house, but which didn't fool Mary Ann in the slightest. But it did prevent her maid from commenting.

Ten

S usannah settled happily in Bardsley. The Trents were so
warm and friendly, and as for Will – well, she thought
him quite the most comfortable man she had ever met. You
never had to worry about whether you had said the right
thing to him; you could just say what you wanted. And
not only was he kind and interesting, but he also took the
trouble to explain things to her.

If only Simeon were more like Will! If only – In the
privacy of her bedchamber, she blushed guiltily and blinked
away a tear. That could never be, so she must just make the
most of her days here, then she would at least have some
wonderful memories to help her through the difficulties of
her marriage. More tears fell and would not be held back,
but she did not dare allow herself to weep and redden her
eyes. No one must know about her feelings. *No one at all!*

She was fascinated by everything she saw in the town.
'It's so different from Fairleigh,' she told Cassie one day.
'Just imagine a damp climate being an advantage!' She
had already experienced for herself how often it rained in
Bardsley. 'And the steam engines! How exciting to think
that one engine can turn so many spindles!'

'You've been talking to Will again,' teased Cassie.

Susannah blushed. 'Yes. He – he said he would show
me the whole process for producing cotton thread.' Mama
would not approve of this at all, but Mama was far away
in Germany by now, and surely for a little time, Susannah
could allow herself to be happy?

On the Sunday after their arrival, they all went to church. Much interest was shown by the congregation in the Trents' London visitor, and they were not disappointed. Susannah, free from her mother's dominance and clad in soft blue and white muslin with a fine silk shawl and a delicious new high-poke bonnet, was a sight worth seeing.

It was clear to Cassie that Will Trent thought so. She had never seen him look at a female like that before. She watched her two cousins ruefully. It was one thing to speculate that a man like him would make a good husband for a shy girl like Susannah; it was another thing entirely to promote a match that could bring nothing but trouble. Cassie was not faint-hearted, but even she shuddered at the thought what Lady Berrinden might say about it.

And there was Simeon Giffard to consider, too. How was she to dispose of him in a kindly manner? He did not deserve the humiliation of being jilted, even if he was an arrogant wretch at times. Oh, it made her head ache just to think of it! In fact, it was aching now.

After the service, Aunt Lucy introduced Susannah to all her special friends in Bardsley. Cassie was disappointed that the Moorthorpe Grange party were not there that day, because she would have liked to meet them. Sarah had been full of tales of her new friends.

Will stood in the sunshine and watched all this gossiping impatiently. What on earth could Sarah find to talk about to the parson's daughter for so long? And why did his father want to discuss cotton prices on a Sunday, when he'd been going on about nothing else all week? It was quite half an hour before the family could get away, and they only made the move then because Will urged them to it.

'Well,' said Aunt Lucy, 'I don't know what's got into you today, our Will. I disremember when I've seen you in such a twitchy mood! Whatever will Mrs Soper think of you, interrupting her like that?'

'I'm *not* in a twitchy mood, Mother! But I told you, I've

arranged to show Miss Berrinden round the mill, and there won't be time before luncheon if we don't get back now.'

'There'll be plenty of time this afternoon.'

'No, there won't. The men will be coming in to check the machinery later. They'll be making a racket and raising a lot of dust.'

'I don't know what you two want to go looking at those nasty machines for at all, I really don't! You won't find them anything special, Susannah, that I can tell you! You want to leave such things to the men. They seem to like getting themselves dirty. You never saw such a boy as our Will was for getting himself mucked up! If I've had to scrub him down once, I've had to do it a score of times. Not to mention tearing his breeches. He's torn the seats out of more pairs of breeches than you've had bonnets.'

By the time they got home, Will was stiff with embarrassment at his mother's revelations about his childhood peccadilloes, and Susannah was having a hard time not to burst out laughing at the expression on his face.

Joshua Trent vanished the moment they got back to the house. Cassie declined to accompany them round the mill, because her headache had grown worse. Aunt Lucy, looking at her niece's heavy eyes, said it wouldn't surprise her if Cassie hadn't got a cold coming on. She sent her straight up to her bedroom and bustled off to the kitchen with a promise of concocting her own special hot lemon and honey drink, a sovereign remedy for head colds.

'Right, then,' said Will. 'Let's go. Are you ready, Sarah?'

'Goodness, no! I've seen inside the mill only too often, thank you very much. I've no intention of ruining my favourite dress in all that dirt. Are you sure you really want to go, Susannah? Don't let our Will push you into it.'

'Well, yes. I would like to see it, actually. If it's not too much trouble for you, Mr Trent?'

'Will. We've agreed that you'll call me Will, since you're almost a cousin.'

'Will, then.' She blushed as she said it. One thing to whisper his name in the privacy of her bedchamber, quite another to say it in front of a room full of people.

'I'd better lend you one of my old dresses,' said Sarah, frowning. 'That ruching round the hem of yours will pick up all the dirt and fluff.'

Susannah changed quickly and put on a stouter pair of shoes. Mama would be furious at her making this tour of the mill alone with a gentleman. But as the gentleman in question was Will Trent, she had no qualms. She would trust herself to him any time. And besides, he could almost be classed as a relative, though none of her relatives was half as nice. She tripped blithely across the yard, her hand resting lightly on his arm, her eyes bright with anticipation.

They were let into the mill by the old watchman, and it was everything Susannah had expected, an echoing cavern of a place, with rows and rows of huge machines, whose purpose she couldn't even begin to guess. Suitably impressed by their size and complexity, she tried to follow Will's careful explanation of how the raw cotton fluff was cleaned, carded and then spun into thread. Her attention was so firmly fixed on Will that she did not notice the step at the end of one of the rows, missed her footing and fell awkwardly. As she banged her arm on the edge of a machine, she cried out in shock and pain.

Will leaped forward to pick her up, cradling her in his arms. 'Susannah! My darling, are you all right?' The words were out before he knew it and they looked at one another in consternation. 'I'm sorry. I forgot myself.' Then he saw the blood on her arm and forgot himself completely.

'Oh, my little love! You *are* hurt! Let me see!'

Useless to protest, to say it was nothing, with the blood trickling down her arm and staining Sarah's dress. Will picked her up and carried her into a little office nearby, where bandages were kept for just such emergencies. Neither of them thought of calling for Aunt Lucy's help.

Tenderly he bathed the wound, which was fortunately not deep, and bandaged it with soft white linen. Then he sat back and looked at her. 'Can you forgive me? I had no right – I shouldn't have said what I did.'

'Oh, please,' she whispered, eyes downcast. A tear ran slowly down her cheek and he stretched out a finger to wipe it away. Before either of them could think what they were doing, he had gathered her into his arms. She nestled there, fitting naturally into the curve of his arms and chest, feeling completely at home.

'I love you too, Will,' she confessed. 'I know I shouldn't, but I do!' Somehow she had no shyness with him.

His eyes lit up and he held her at arm's length to study her face. 'Are you sure?'

'Oh, yes.'

He whirled her suddenly round the little office, laughing exultantly. Then, as he looked at her, the exultation faded, to be replaced by a warm expression, all his love showing in his face. 'Aye, I know it's a mess, love, and I'm the last person your family would want you to marry, but we'll come through it somehow! I didn't think that a person like you *could* fall in love with a rough fellow like me. Now that I know you love me, well, I'll *make* the rest come right, you see if I don't!'

'Oh, Will, if only we could . . .' She stretched out her hand and he took it in his.

'We'll find some way . . .'

She shook her head and spoke painfully. 'There's nothing we can do. You forget that I – I've promised to marry Simeon Giffard. And I can't – I just can't face him and Mama. I know I'm a coward, but they . . . I just can't defy them.' Her voice tailed away and her eyes filled with tears.

He sat down next to her on the edge of the table and wiped the tears away. 'No, love, I wouldn't ask you to do that,' he said softly. 'She's a real dragon, your mother. She fair terrifies me as well.'

That made her smile through her tears. 'Oh, Will, I don't believe you. You never showed any signs of nervousness, not even the first time you came to the house.'

'And me shaking in my shoes!'

'You are a tease! You never did! You even gave Simeon a set-down.'

'They're only people, Simeon and your mother. And he doesn't seem a bad sort of fellow if you stand up to him.'

She shook her head, her eyes filling with tears again. 'He f-frightens me.'

Will patted her hand and then kept hold of it, kissing the fingertips one by one. 'Well, you just leave it to me. I'll find a way out of this mess for both of us. Only mind, you're not going to marry Giffard.'

'Mama will never let me—'

'Then I'll not send you back for your mother to bully. Look, love, it's not the sort of thing I like, but if necessary, we could make a runaway match of it. Would you do that – if we had to? Would you trust me to look after you?'

'Yes, Will. Oh, *yes!*' She stared at him, hope suddenly creeping into her heart. Was it really possible to get free of her engagement to Simeon Giffard?

He had to kiss her again to seal the bargain and it was a while before they moved apart. Eventually, he took out his watch. 'It's nearly time for luncheon, my darling. Here, let me tidy your hair.'

When they were ready, she looked at him with troubled eyes. 'We shall have to tell Cassie. I can't lie to her. She's been so kind to me.'

'If I know her, she's already got a fair idea of how we feel. She's no fool, our Cassie isn't.'

And indeed, when Susannah crept into her cousin's room that afternoon, to confess to the invalid that she was in love with Will and he with her, Cassie showed no sign of surprise.

'I could see how it was between you. But oh, Suzie, I never meant this to happen. It's going to cause so much trouble. I only brought you to Bardsley to get you away from your mother for a while, to give us time to think of a way out of your engagement. Your mother will never agree to Will as a husband for you.'

Susannah fiddled with the counterpane. 'He – . . . he says he'll find a way – even if we have to make a runaway match of it.'

'Would you really do that?'

'Oh, yes! I had begun to love Will long before this visit, so you mustn't blame yourself.' Her eyes were softly glowing. 'I used to dream about him, and think about how much I liked being with him. I used to wish Simeon were more like him.'

'They're as different as chalk and cheese.'

'I know.'

They were both silent for a moment, then Cassie smiled. 'Well, if you're quite sure of your feelings . . .'

'Very sure.'

'We'll work something out.'

'That's what Will said.'

'Yes, but it's not going to be easy. It's how to get you free of your other engagement that worries me. Simeon Giffard won't take kindly to being jilted, nor does he deserve to be made a fool of.'

'Jilted!' Susannah exclaimed. 'Oh, I never meant to *jilt* anyone. What will people think of me?' She looked quite stricken. After a moment she said painfully, 'Cassie, do you – do you suppose Simeon – well, do you suppose he loves me? That he'll be very hurt if I . . .?'

'I'm absolutely certain he doesn't love you. He merely sees you as a suitable wife.'

'Yes. That's what I thought. And I'm not a suitable wife, not for him, anyway. I seem to irritate him all the time.'

'You should have stood up to him more. No one really likes to get their own way all the time.'

'I'm not – I can't . . .'

'I know, love.'

And there matters stood for the next few days, while Cassie nursed her cold, Aunt Lucy cosseted and dosed her, and the others popped in and out to cheer her up.

Not until Cassie was better did Will tell his family about himself and Susannah, for he wanted her support.

'Well, you're old enough to know your own mind, I suppose,' said Uncle Joshua, 'but Susannah had better get rid of that other fellow before you announce your engagement. Scandal's bad for business.'

Aunt Lucy shed a few tears. 'To think of my Will wanting to set up as a married man. And as for this Mr Giffard, well, I have no pity for him. I've no time for fancy London gentlemen, who've never done an honest day's toil in their lives and who look down their noses at people like us.'

She opened her arms and clasped Susannah to her bosom, and they both shed some more tears together. 'Just let them try to take you away from my Will! They'll have his mother to reckon with, if they do!'

Cassie was very quiet. She felt a responsibility to sort out this tangle. Only how would they ever persuade Lady Berrinden to let her daughter marry a mere millowner when she could have had a Giffard?

That night, in the darkness of her bedchamber, Cassie faced up to the other side of this awkward situation. Unlike her cousin, she was very attracted to Simeon Giffard – and had even wondered if he felt something for her. There had been a moment in the cab coming back from Garnett Lane when something had seemed to flow between them – and another moment, after she had hurt her ankle at Stovely and he was carrying her back to the house. She wondered if he would have said something if they had not been interrupted.

No, of course he would not have done. By then he had offered for Susannah.

But now – if Susannah withdrew from the engagement . . . No, he still would not want Cassie. Like Will, she was not good enough to marry into one of the leading families in the ton.

She wished her mother had not arranged for her to have this Season. No, she didn't! What she really wished for was quite impossible, and she had better make up her mind to that once and for all, and concentrate her efforts on helping Susannah and Will.

But rack her brain as she might, she could not think how to do it.

Eleven

When Cassie was better, she decided to go for a ride on the moors. She wanted some time alone to think about her future, and in the big untidy family house someone was always around. It seemed obvious that her Berrinden relatives would not want her to stay with them in London after Susannah's engagement to Simeon Giffard was broken off, especially if Will then made an offer for her cousin.

Since Cassie's own horse was still in London, she hired one from the livery stables and let it be assumed that a groom from there would be accompanying her, because she knew Aunt Lucy would be horrified if her niece went riding without an escort. She felt a little guilty about that, but it could not be helped and what people did not know could not hurt them. Besides, she was hardly likely to meet any of her aunt's friends up on the moors!

The afternoon was cool but fine, and the rain that had threatened that morning was holding off. Cassie rode along quite happily for a while, forgetting all her worries in the pleasure of taking deep breaths of the bracing moorland air and feasting her eyes on the gently rolling landscape. She loved it up here away from the smoky little town. She and her father had often gone walking across the tops, stopping for a drink of milk at a farm or egging each other on to jump over the little streams that criss-crossed the Pennine hills. She turned to look down at Bardsley, a huddle of smoke-blackened buildings in the valley below her, then she stared out across the starkness of the moors. This place was not nearly as pretty as Hertfordshire and . . .

Why did she always keep comparing places to Stovely Chase? Annoyed with herself, she banished Simeon Giffard's home firmly from her mind, and did her best to banish him, too, but was not successful.

Lost in thought, she rode up one of her favourite tracks, which led eventually to Moorthorpe Grange. She would turn off long before she got there, of course, because she had not yet met the new owners.

When she saw someone riding towards her, she did not at first worry, then, as the figure came closer, she stared at it in dismay. It looked like – it couldn't be – no, she was imagining things. *But it was!* Simeon Giffard was approaching from the direction of the Grange! She reined in, but too late. He had seen her and was cantering along the track to join her.

'Good day, Miss Trent. This is an unexpected pleasure.'

'What are *you* doing here in the north?' she exclaimed before she could prevent herself.

He raised his eyebrows at her tone. 'I'm staying with my relatives at Moorthorpe Grange, of course, and am on my way to visit Susannah. I trust your aunt won't mind my calling on her?'

'Oh. Er – of course not.' But Cassie could well imagine the shock his appearance would give her timid cousin and her heart sank. She also had a very good idea what sort of a confrontation there would be if Mr Giffard met Aunt Lucy, who was more famous for her blunt tongue than for her tact, and who could be a very lioness in defence of her children.

Anger welled up in Cassie. His coming would spoil everything. At all costs she must keep him away from Susannah. It took a huge effort for her to speak calmly, but she managed it. 'I'm afraid it would be a wasted journey today. Susannah isn't at home.' It would have to be a runaway marriage for her cousins, after all, she decided, running rapidly through the possibilities in her mind.

'Then I shall call and simply leave my card. I wish you a pleasant ride, Miss Trent.'

When he made to turn his horse, she detained him with a gesture. 'I – we didn't know that you were thinking of coming to Bardsley,' she said casually – well, she *hoped* her manner sounded casual – as she desperately tried to work out a way to prevent him from visiting the house.

'It suited me to take advantage of a long-standing invitation to visit Moorthorpe Grange.'

Cassie swallowed hard. *Suited him!* Did he care so much for Susannah, then? She had not thought so, but if he did, she must have been entirely mistaken about his reactions to herself. Never mind that. Her feelings did not matter. What mattered was Susannah, who was so tender-hearted she would never pluck up the courage to jilt someone – especially if she thought he loved her.

There was no help for it: at all costs Mr Giffard must be prevented from calling and Cassie was the only one who could do that. She continued to play for time as she examined and discarded ideas. 'It must have been a very sudden decision, your coming here, I mean?'

'Yes. I only arrived yesterday.'

'I hope you had a pleasant journey?'

'No, as a matter of fact, I didn't. One of the horses went lame.' He inclined his head and turned again to leave.

'Wait!' She tried to look as if she had just had a pleasant idea. 'I'm on my way to meet Susannah and Sarah for a – a picnic. The others went in the gig, but I felt like a ride. There'll be plenty of food and we should be happy to have your company. Why don't you join us?'

'Well . . .' Simeon hesitated, frowning at her and then looking up at the sky, which was clouding over rapidly.

She could see the suspicion on his face. No wonder! This was not at all the sort of day for an excursion. She met his gaze with eyes as wide and innocent as she could make them, hardly daring even to blink.

'I don't wish to intrude upon your picnic party,' he said after a moment. 'And I'd like to leave my card at your aunt's house as a matter of courtesy. I can always ride over to see Susannah tomorrow.'

Panic filled Cassie. If he called at the house now, he would not only find Susannah at home, but her own lies would be exposed. 'As you please, but if you wish to speak privately to my cousin, you'll have more chance at a picnic than in a house full of people.' Ah, she had caught his attention with that! The details of the plan began to take shape in her mind. If she could keep him away from Bardsley for a while and get a message back to the mill, Will could take Susannah away. After all, he had said he was prepared to elope, if necessary, and now there was no other way out of this impasse.

She eyed Simeon Giffard surreptitiously. She had forgotten how large and masterful he was. He would be angry with her when he found out what she had done, very angry indeed, but she had never flinched from her duty. 'Do join us!' she urged.

'If you're sure I'm not intruding,' he replied, at his most cool and reserved.

She could not quite understand the expression on his face, but at least the first part of her plan was working. 'Lovely! It's this way.' Wheeling her horse, she galloped off along the moorland track, setting a cracking pace and effectively preventing conversation, apart from a few brief exchanges about the scenery.

About a mile further on, she crossed the main road to Yorkshire and stopped for a moment at a small farm, where she knew the family. 'Would you mind if I called here briefly? Their little son is ill. I won't delay you for more than a few moments, I promise.'

She slid from the horse's back before he could help her,

gave him her reins and left him outside. When she glanced back, he was frowning and walking both their horses up and down. Oh heavens, was he starting to suspect something?

Once inside the house she promised the sturdy eight-year-old son a shilling if he would take the short cut into town and bear a message to Trent's Mill as soon as possible. Paper was found, a scratchy quill pen and some lumpy ink. She scrawled a quick warning to Will, making several ink blots in her haste. After she had folded it, she pressed a clumsy blob of sealing wax on the join and wrote URGENT in large letters on the outside. She did not feel happy with how she had worded her message, but time was pressing.

When she went outside, she let Simeon help her up into the saddle, and felt the warm imprint of his hands on her waist for far longer than was reasonable afterwards. You fool! she told herself. Stop imagining things. It's only you who feels like this. He is quite indifferent to you.

The next stage of her plan meant keeping him away from Bardsley for as long as possible, preferably for several hours. Since he did not know the countryside, she led him by a roundabout route towards one of the higher peaks, assuring him this was to be their rendezvous for the picnic, and that a much shorter road approached it from the other side. He was beginning to look at her with open suspicion on his face, but thank heavens he did not challenge her actions. When it was necessary to converse, she managed to babble on brightly about the scenery, life in Bardsley compared to life in London, anything at all to fill the heavy silence. He must think her an absolute fool, but that could not be helped.

She was relieved when they reached the place she had in mind, because he had twice asked her if she was quite sure she knew the way, and his frown had become very pronounced. They dismounted near a few stunted trees and as they tied up their horses, she made great play of blowing her nose.

'You'd never think there was a road so close, would you?'

she asked gaily, leading the way down towards a little dell where a few stunted trees, sheltered from the harsh scouring of the wind, had managed to survive.

'No, you wouldn't.'

'Oh, bother!' She stopped suddenly. 'I've dropped my handkerchief. Wait here. I won't be a moment.' And giving him no time to volunteer to retrieve the handkerchief for her, she turned and ran back.

Her plan had been to ride off with his horse and leave him to make his own way back but, at the last minute, her conscience would not allow this. He might get lost on the moors and that could be dangerous. So she untied both horses and chased them away, her heart thumping with nervousness in case he came back and managed to catch them.

At first the two animals were puzzled, reluctant to move, so she threw a few stones at them, muttering, '*Will* you go away, you stupid creatures!' As they galloped off, her own horse in the lead, no doubt heading for its nice cosy stable, she heaved a sigh of relief.

'What the *devil* are you doing?' a voice thundered behind her just as the horses vanished from sight.

'Oh! You came after me,' she said rather unnecessarily, quaking inside at the anger on his face, for all her resolution to stand firm. Taking a deep breath to steady her nerves, she looked him in the eyes. 'I – I owe you an explanation, Mr Giffard.' She was pleased that her voice was not wobbling. Well, not much. 'And – and since it's likely to take a while, perhaps we could sit down on these rocks?'

As she turned to lead the way, his hand shot out to grasp her arm. 'Miss Trent,' he snapped, 'your explanation had better be nothing short of miraculous!'

He released her and when she went to sit down, he stood in front of her, one hand on his hip, his eyes on her face.

It was even more difficult to explain than she had expected. To tell him that his fiancée had had to be coerced into agreeing to marry him was a task which would have tried the most accomplished diplomat. If anything, his anger increased as she faltered out the tale of Susannah's cowardice, for such it certainly was.

'This only shows that she does not wish to marry me, which I had already guessed,' he grated out, as she faltered to a stop. 'It in no way explains your damned idiotic behaviour this afternoon!'

'I wanted to – to keep you out of the way, so that Susannah could escape,' she stammered, quailing at the fury on his face. 'I sent a message back to Will from the farm.'

'*Escape!* What in hell's name did you think I was going to do to her?'

'Shout at her, as you're shouting at me now! And – and *bully* her! You'd probably also inform her mother – and if Susannah once gets back in Lady Berrinden's clutches, she'll not dare do anything but marry you!'

'I can assure you, Miss Trent, that I have never bullied anyone in my life, and I would *never* force an unwilling lady to marry me! Your quixotic interference was totally uncalled for!' He began pacing up and down, throwing words at her. 'Indeed, I think you must have run mad today!'

'Well, I'm not afraid to help those I love,' she muttered, but already she was having doubts about what she had done and was not looking forward to the long walk back.

'How can it help *anyone* for you to get us lost on the moors?' he roared, having stopped pacing for a moment to glare at her.

'It'll give Will and Susannah time to escape.'

He snorted in disgust. 'You've been reading too many gothic tales, Miss Trent.'

'Lord and Lady Berrinden will never let Susannah marry Will,' she flung back at him, 'and I wouldn't put it past Lady Berrinden to find a way to *force* you to marry Susannah. If not, then she'll find someone else from the ton for my cousin to marry, someone equally unsuitable for a girl so gentle. With a mother like her, Susannah stands almost no chance of happiness.'

He folded his arms and looked down his nose at her. 'Meaning, I collect, that—' He broke off abruptly as a few drops of rain splashed against their faces, then, by unspoken consent, they moved to the shelter of the stunted trees.

'Oh, dear! I hadn't thought of it raining so soon!' exclaimed Cassie, staring anxiously at the leaden sky.

'You should have ridden off and left me,' he said flippantly, then turned back towards her. 'And why ever didn't you? You must have known I'd be furious. Why *did* you stay? Weren't you afraid I might *bully* you, as I do Susannah?'

She flushed at the scorn in his voice. 'I didn't want you to get lost on the moors. You don't know them and I do.'

'So you sentenced yourself to a long walk back as well as me. I suppose I ought to feel grateful, but I don't! If it weren't for your irresponsible and *totally irrational* behaviour, we should neither of us be in this fix.' He turned to survey the stark moors, which stretched in all directions with not a single sign of habitation. 'I only hope you know where we are.'

'Of course I do!'

He let out a snort which sounded more like disbelief.

'There really is a shorter way back,' she offered.

'Then I pray that you will remember it!'

By this time the rain was falling in earnest and the trees had begun to drip on them.

'I think we had better make a move, Miss Trent. I can see no break in the clouds and there's no real shelter here.' He swept her a mocking bow. 'Pray lead the way! Rescue me from danger! Guide me to safety!'

Head held high, she marched out from the dell, heading across the moors towards a path she had used before with her father, which would mean a much shorter walk back, –

though it would still take them two or three hours, at least. Her anger carried her along briskly at first, but she soon had to slow her pace. Not only was it raining steadily, but beneath her feet tussocks of coarse grass alternated with marshy flats, making it difficult to walk until they reached the other path. She tried to carry the tail of her riding habit in her hand, to keep it from trailing, but dropped it once or twice and it was soon as sodden as the rest of her clothing.

Little streams with eroded banks added to the difficulties and several times she had to accept Mr Giffard's hand to help her across one. That made her breath catch in her throat and made him stare sideways at her.

Once, he kept hold of her hand in its thin leather glove, commenting, 'You're cold, as well as wet.'

She managed to say, 'I shall not melt,' but it was hard to speak calmly with him touching her and what she really wanted was to cling to his hand.

With an ironical inclination of the head, he let go.

She started walking again, hoping he had not noticed her reaction to his touch. Oh, what a fool she was, hankering after a man who was not in the least bit interested in her!

They passed an occasional group of trees, twisted by the wind, but in the rain and with lowering clouds above them, it was a desolate landscape indeed. After a while the rain dwindled to a misty drizzle and the wind fell, but by that time they were very wet indeed.

Cassie was wearing riding boots, which added to the difficulty of walking, and the tail of her skirt was growing heavier as it became soaked with rain. However, she couldn't very well complain about the difficulties when all this was her fault. She still felt it had been necessary to do something, but she was beginning to wonder if she hadn't been rather too enthusiastic in putting such a distance between them and Bardsley.

And what if, after all her trouble, that boy had let her

down? What if Will did not get the note and help Susannah to escape?

'I think we'd better stop and rest for a moment,' drawled the sarcastic voice behind her, 'then we can do something about that riding habit of yours. I hope it's not your favourite garment, because I fear we shall have to cut the bottom off.'

She stopped and looked up at him. She was panting slightly and the rain was running down her face, but she brushed it away impatiently. 'Do you have a pocket knife?'

'Yes. But this is going to ruin your habit.'

She stood there motionless as he handed her his hat and knelt to hack at the skirt. 'Oh, that! That's the least of my worries!'

He looked up. 'And what, if one might ask, is the chief of your worries?'

'Why, to get you back safely,' she answered in surprise, then gaped at him as he abandoned her skirt and stood up, roaring with laughter, then, as he looked sideways at her, starting all over again.

'Well, I'm glad to see you've recovered your sense of humour,' she remarked stiffly.

It was a few moments before he had control of himself again. 'Not my sense of humour, my sense of the ridiculous! Miss Trent . . .'

His smile this time was quite genuine, the sort of smile that would make any lady's heart beat faster – including, she found, her own.

'. . . do you often take such wild notions into your head?'

She smiled back at him reluctantly. 'Not *very* often.'

As he knelt again to finish cutting off the bottom of her skirt, she looked down at the sleek dark head bent over, just within reach of her hand. She had raised that hand to stroke his hair before she realised what she was doing, but managed to pull it back in time. Had she gone mad? What had got into her today?

He stood up and draped the length of material he had cut off around her shoulders a couple of times like a narrow cape. 'It's wet, but it may help hold the warmth in.'

As she looked up at him, her breath caught in her throat and for a moment neither of them moved, then he drew in a sharp breath and took a quick step backwards, replacing his hat and waving one hand. 'Lead on then, fair captor!' But the biting sarcasm was gone from his voice.

Feeling suddenly shy, she set off again.

The next hour was spent in a tacit truce, with both of them saving their breath to get over the rough terrain as quickly as possible. Their progress was far slower than Cassie had expected and the ankle she had sprained at Stovely was now aching furiously. She said nothing, trying not to slow them down.

When they paused for another rest, however, it was noticeably darker and heavy black clouds had massed in the sky above them. In fact, the moors themselves looked dark and threatening. She had never felt so far from other habitations when she had ridden here or walked with her father on sunny days, but everything seemed different today. Different and threatening.

He reached out to stop her for a moment. 'I hesitate to add to your worries, Miss Trent, but a mist is forming.'

She tried not to shiver, but her hands and feet were numb with cold, and he looked thoroughly chilled as well. She was also feeling horribly guilty that she had caused this predicament. 'Yes. I'd noticed. These mists can come down quickly, so I – I think we'd better try to find some sort of shelter and – and stay put for the time being. There are rocky outcrops ahead. One could fall down a cliff and hurt oneself. All the locals tell you to stay where you are if a mist comes down.'

'Yes.'

He looked really anxious now and no wonder. She, too, was seriously concerned about their safety.

166

He pointed over to their left at a square-shaped huddle of stones. 'That looks like some sort of man-made construction.'

'I think you could be right.' She closed her eyes for a moment in sheer relief, then turned to him and tried to smile.

'We must leave the path again and the going will be even more difficult. Let me help you.' He held out one hand to her and she put her own into it before she realised what she was doing. His hand was warm and strong, and he was a great help over the rough terrain, but she was so conscious of his touch, even through the thin leather of her gloves, that it made her nervous. Once she almost fell, and he put out his other hand to hold her safe until she had regained her balance. That set her pulse beating even more furiously.

'Thank you.' She was sure her cheeks must be bright red from the warmth that suffused them. But she did not try to take her hand away. And he did not try to pull his away, either.

They found what Cassie recognised as a shepherd's shelter, a low structure only slightly higher than Simeon's head. It was about ten feet square, with a slate roof and dirt floor. It had no windows, just an ill-fitting door, which was creaking to and fro in the rising wind.

'Not the most luxurious of accommodation,' she remarked, trying for a light touch.

'No.' He pushed open the door and ducked his head to stare inside. 'At least the roof seems to be watertight.' He ushered her in and began to poke around.

'What are you doing?'

'Looking for kindling. We need to light a fire. We're both soaked to the skin and shivering. Someone must use this place occasionally. See.' He pointed to a few pieces of half-burnt wood on a crude hearth in a corner, a faded and torn blanket hanging from a rough hook and some frayed pieces of rope. There were even a couple of old-fashioned horn beakers lying on the long piece of stone which formed a mantelpiece. An oblong slab of rock about six feet long was set like a seat in front of the fireplace.

Without wasting any more words, he began to collect wisps of dried grass from corner crevices inside the hut, piling them up and surmounting the small heap with a few tiny twigs and splinters of wood. 'The chimney is as roughly constructed as the rest of the hut, but it should serve to carry away the smoke. We need to get warm as quickly as possible.' He pulled out his knife. 'I have a flint on this which is supposed to be able to start a fire. I managed it once or twice when I was a lad. Let's hope I can still do it.'

It took several minutes of hard work with the flint before the grass caught light, and the tiny flame flickered out almost immediately. By that time Cassie was being racked by violent fits of shivering which she could not control. His expression grim, he set to work again. They both heaved an audible sigh of relief when the little pile of grass and twigs finally caught fire. Carefully he built it up with slightly larger pieces of wood.

When it was blazing nicely, Cassie crouched beside him to hold her hands out to the warmth. 'This is wonderful.'

He stood up again. 'We need to find some more wood in case the mist settles and we have to spend the night here. Those few pieces won't be enough.'

'Spend the night here! But . . .' She fell silent, as the full implications of this began to sink in.

'Exactly. I was beginning to wonder when it would occur to you that in saving your cousin from a monster like myself, you had jeopardised your own good name.'

She flushed, but looked him in the eye. 'I can assure you, Mr Giffard, that I shall not mind that. It's Susannah's happiness which matters most to me.'

He stared back at her, holding her motionless with the sheer power of his gaze. 'Well, *I* mind it very much, Miss

Trent, because you have jeopardised *my* good name as well
as your own!'

'Oh!' Another shiver took her by surprise. She was so
cold she could not think at all clearly.

He studied her, frowning. 'You really ought to get out of
those wet clothes.'

She tried to speak lightly. 'We both ought to do that. But
it's hardly possible.'

He went across to pick up the blanket. 'You could wrap
yourself in this.'

'Definitely not!' But if she had not clamped her mouth
shut, her teeth would have been chattering.

His expression was determined. 'This is not the time for
false modesty, so either you get out of your clothes and into
that blanket while I'm gathering some more wood, or I'll
undress you myself.'

'I shall come out and help you. After all, it's my fault
we're here. That'll warm me up, I'm sure.'

A firm hand pushed her down on the piece of rock. 'Miss
Trent, you have had quite enough of your own way today!
Oblige me by resting that ankle, which you have been
favouring for the past hour.'

'Oh. I – I didn't think you'd noticed.'

'I couldn't help noticing.' His tone became more gentle.
'Is it hurting very much?'

'A little. But I can hardly complain. It's my fault we're
here, after all.' She brushed a lock of hair back, then as more
wet hair tumbled out of its pins, shook the whole mass loose
and tried to wring some of the water out of it .

He gave her a strange look. 'No. You wouldn't complain.
Now, are you going to get out of those clothes or am I going
to take them off for you?'

The silence seemed endless. The image of him doing that
should have shocked her, but it didn't. She knew men and
women touched one another's bodies, because her mother
had once tried to explain what happened between husband

and wife – but no man had ever touched Cassie like that. Only – she found now that she would not mind Simeon caressing her, she had wanted to touch him herself earlier. Her face flamed and her voice was low and husky as she said pleadingly, 'I can't. It wouldn't be right.'

He picked up the blanket and tossed it at her. 'It wouldn't be right to die of cold, either. Your health is my main concern now, so if you don't do it, I will.' Then he went out.

She stared at the door. He didn't mean that. Did he?

She couldn't do it. Could she?

But as another violent shiver shook her, she admitted to herself that if she didn't get out of the clothes, she would find it very hard to get warm.

With one eye on the door, she began to unbutton her jacket, but in spite of the fire, her fingers were so cold, she had trouble pushing the buttons through the holes, and when he came in, she had only half finished.

He looked at her.

'I was trying to get undressed,' she protested hastily, 'only my fingers are c-cold and clumsy.'

He dropped the wood near the fire, put a couple of pieces on it, then turned back to her. 'Let me help you, Cassie.'

Numbly she took a step forward, standing next to him, with the fire warming one side of her body and making steam rise from the damp material. Her other side felt icy, however, because of the wet fabric clinging to her.

He bent over the row of small buttons on her jacket and undid them for her, and though his fingers fumbled and hesitated, they did not feel as cold as hers. Then he undid the buttons of the shirt she wore beneath the habit, fashioned like a man's shirt, but with a stock that tied around her neck. When he had finished, he took a deep, ragged breath and stepped backwards, averting his eyes. Looking down, she saw with a shock that the fine lawn of the chemise beneath it was so wet as to be almost transparent.

Muttering something under his breath he turned his back on her and busied himself tying two pieces of rope together to form a clothes line over the fire. 'Hurry up,' he said in a half-strangled voice when she did not move.

Hurriedly she slipped out of the rest of her clothes and wrapped the blanket around herself. Although it covered her fully, she did not feel covered. She felt naked and vulnerable. 'I – I'm ready.'

He turned and nodded. 'I'll wring out your clothes and hang them on the line.' A smile briefly softened his face. 'I've seen women's underclothes before, you know.'

'Yes.' But no man had seen her like this before.

As he hung up her things, she began to worry about him. 'You're cold as well,' she blurted out. 'What are you going to do about yourself?'

'Nothing until I've brought in a lot more wood. Fortunately for us, there's a pile behind the hut, probably dumped there for the use of the shepherds. There's also a barrel of rainwater. I'll fetch you a drink as well before I settle.'

He went outside, stopping for a moment to blow out his breath and try to gather his wits together. Her body was as beautiful as he'd thought, with firm breasts thrusting up under the fine material. And she hadn't been wearing corsets, so had felt soft and yielding against his hands. The thought of her being naked beneath that thin blanket was having a marked effect on his own body, an effect he hoped she hadn't noticed. In a burst of strenuous activity, he dragged some of the drier pieces of wood out from the bottom of the pile and carried enough of them inside the hut to last the night, warming himself up somewhat by the activity, though his clothes were still soaking.

'The mist is very thick now,' he announced as he came in with a final load and wedged the door shut behind him. 'One can see for scarcely ten paces. We were lucky to find this hut.'

As he squatted in front of the fire and held his hands out

to the blaze, she could smell the damp wool of his jacket and the equally damp leather of his boots, but the firelight, which was now their only illumination, was not enough to show the expression on his face as clearly as she would have liked. In spite of the warmth of the flames he was shivering.

'You need to get out of your wet clothes, too,' she reminded him.

'There are not two blankets.'

'No. But – you could take off nearly everything, could you not? Leave on your – your drawers. That would help. Your shirt would soon dry.'

He saw her fiery blush, but knew she was right. 'No false modesty,' he'd said to her earlier. The same must apply to him. He could only hope his body would not betray him again and embarrass them both. He did not think he had ever been as thoroughly soaked in his whole life as he was today – or felt as cold.

As Simeon stepped to one side and began stripping off his clothes, Cassie kept her gaze firmly on the fire. When he moved to hang his shirt on the line, however, clad only in short linen drawers, she could not help staring at his body. Well muscled and with no chest hair, his skin gleamed in the firelight. She had seen pictures of Greek statues, men wearing no clothes at all, and had studied them with furtive interest, but they had not made her want to touch them as the sight of him did.

As he glanced quickly sideways, she tried to smile. 'It is . . . a difficult situation, isn't it?' she asked. Then she saw him shiver again and looked guiltily down at the blanket. It was so unfair for her to keep it when she was the cause of their troubles. 'It will not help if you catch your death of cold. Why do you not come and sit close to me? That will at least keep one side of you warmer.'

'Are you sure you don't mind?'

'Yes.' Her voice was just a whisper.

He finished hanging up his clothes and came to sit beside

her. After a slight hesitation, he moved closer and put one arm round her shoulders, pressing against the warmth of her body and letting out a sigh.

But he was still shivering, though he tried to hide this, and the door was so ill-fitting that gusts of cold damp air were finding their way inside. 'It's I who should be putting an arm round you,' she braved herself to say and before he could object, she wriggled round and managed to put one blanket-covered arm round his shoulders without revealing her own body. With a tired sigh, he allowed her to do this.

For a long time they sat there quietly, sharing the warmth of their bodies. He took no liberties, made no advances, and yet the naked flesh of his shoulder beneath her hand filled her with longing. Her mother had once told her that a woman longed for the man she loved to touch her, and wanted to touch him in return – that this was a perfectly natural and enjoyable thing. Not until now had Cassie truly understood that. She wanted him to touch her very much, as well.

When the silence grew too heavy, she blurted out, 'I'm sorry. I still feel I had to try to protect Susannah, but I'm truly sorry it's turned out like this.' Without thinking, she stretched her other hand towards him and he held it in both his for a moment.

When she tried to pull away, afraid of the blanket slipping, he would not let go. 'Cassandra Trent,' he murmured, his voice low and intimate, 'you are undoubtedly the most infuriating woman I have ever met in my whole life, but I could not wish for anyone more courageous to share an adventure with. Most women would have long ago been in hysterics.' A pause, then his voice softened, and he added, 'There is no one quite like you.'

His words made a warm feeling settle in her breast. For a moment, as they stared at one another, she thought he was going to kiss her, hoped for it. But he took a deep breath and moved his head backwards a little, then broke the spell by saying crisply, 'Tell me about yourself and your family.'

She felt disappointed – and was angry with herself for that. Clearly he did not feel as attracted to her as she did to him, not even now. He just found her odd. And infuriating. To cover her confusion, she began to talk about her life in Bardsley. From that, he led her on to talk of the mill and how the Trents had made their fortune partly from the spinning of cotton.

In turn, she tried to draw him out, but was less successful, for he had no brothers or sisters, only distant cousins and of course his mother, about whom he seemed reluctant to talk. Well, having met Flora Giffard, Cassie could easily understand that, so she turned the conversation instead to Stovely Chase, about which he spoke affectionately – its history, its beauties and his plans for its continued restoration.

After a while, he stood up to feel her chemise and turn it round so that the damp parts faced the fire. 'It's nearly dry now.'

Once or twice, he went to look quickly out of the door, but reported each time that the mist was just as thick. When he came back he was shivering again, and when she held out one hand, he sat down and pressed himself against her.

Was it just the cold or did he want to be near her?

Though nothing had really happened between them, not even a kiss, the tension inside Cassie was mounting, a tension such as she had never experienced before. She continued to feel very aware of his body – its strength, its masculine beauty. And of her own, which was tingling with longing for him. She was also aware of his eyes on her and her own increasing reluctance to meet them. She found it difficult to breathe evenly.

When her chemise and one of her petticoats were dry, he stood up and turned his back while she put them on hurriedly. After that she insisted on sharing the blanket

174

with him properly, flinging it round their shoulders like a cape and wriggling till they were both sitting on the bottom edge of it. By the time they got comfortable again, his arm was round her and she was nestled against him, her head against his bare chest. It felt so good that she never wanted to move away.

When Simeon got up to put on his dry shirt, he also made another trip to the door to stare outside, but it was fully dark now. He returned to sit down beside her and as she offered the blanket, he pulled it round them with a wry smile. 'I think it's time to discuss our situation, don't you, Cassie?'

'Yes, I do. It's – it's well, a bit awkward,' she admitted.

He looked sideways at her, met her eyes briefly, then looked away again. 'It's more than *awkward*. By morning, we shall be irrevocably compromised in the eyes of society, even if I have not touched you.'

'But—'

His voice grew sharper. 'And don't tell me again that you count the world well lost for your cousin Susannah! You're too intelligent to underestimate the extreme seriousness of our situation!'

Cassie swallowed and her reply was a mere scrape of sound. 'Yes. It is serious, Simeon.' She found she liked using his first name.

'In fact, there's only one thing we *can* do now.' He stared straight ahead as he added without any trace of emotion, 'Get married.'

She had guessed what he was going to say, but disappointment raced like acid along her veins. Not like this! she wanted to plead. Don't propose to me as if it's only a business arrangement. 'That's surely not necessary,' she managed when she could control her voice.

'Of course it is. You know it is!'

'But we hardly know one another and – and you don't

175

even like me! Why, only a short time ago you said I was the most infuriating woman you'd ever met.'

He looked at her in surprise, then a slow smile curved the corners of his lips. 'I don't *dislike* you, Cassie! And I don't think you dislike me, either.'

She did not contradict that, could not. 'And what's more, you've been engaged to my cousin for a month! You still are! So you can't offer me marriage?'

'I can't offer it formally yet, but I wish to assure you that I intend to offer you the protection of my name – afterwards. I hope,' he paused and the silence seemed to go on for a long time, 'that you'll accept – for both our sakes.'

She stared down at the folds of her petticoat, not knowing what to say. If he had only said he loved her, or at least that he was growing fond of her, she would have accepted his offer on the spot. But he hadn't spoken of love. He had said only they *must* get married – which was something very different. She realised he was speaking again.

'I'm not going to pretend that the breaking of my engagement will cast me into despair. In fact, I shall be glad to have it ended. That's why I came to Bardsley, to talk to Susannah without her mother hovering over her, so that I could see how she really felt.'

'*What?* Oh, no! I thought you'd come here to fix your interest with her.'

'On the contrary.' His smile had vanished and he was frowning again. 'I apprehend that by now you expect Susannah and your cousin Will to have made a runaway match of it?'

'I hope so, for her sake.'

'Amelia Berrinden will never forgive them for that! But it's their business now, not mine.' After a pause his tone softened again and he repeated, 'I definitely don't dislike you, Cassie. Surely you know that?' Could she not see how she was affecting him, how difficult it was for him to keep his hands to himself?

She stared at him, clearly needing him to say more, so he told her the simple truth, 'If I hadn't been engaged, I would have shown an interest in – in getting to know you better.'

That made Cassie feel a little happier, yet she was still confused about her own answer. In spite of all the scandal this escapade would cause, she did not intend to marry him unless she felt they had some chance of happiness together.

'Even before we'd left Stovely, I was aware that Susannah found my attentions – unpleasant.' There was a moment's silence, then he was unable to keep the bitterness from his voice, 'But what could I do? In my world, Cassie, a gentleman does not cry off for no reason. If Susannah had told me then that she'd formed another attachment, I'd not have held her to our engagement, but she said nothing, so I thought she was – that she shrank from physical contact. Some women are like that, you know, but I don't think you are one of them.'

Cassie tried to hide her embarrassment at this by rushing into speech, 'Susannah wasn't in love with Will at that time, Simeon, well, not really, for they'd said nothing to each other. She just – she just didn't want to marry *you*.'

His voice was harsh. 'Yes. So I gather. Am I so repulsive?'

'No, of course you're not. Far from it—' She broke off again, glad it was too dark for him to see her confusion.

'So *you* do not find me repulsive?' His voice was even, expressionless almost. 'And I find *you* very attractive, Cassie.'

'Do you really?'

His voice was low as he added, almost to himself, 'I should not like to make the same mistake twice.' Then he looked at her and asked, softly, 'Don't you believe me?'

'I don't know what to think. Oh, how embarrassing all this is!' She pressed her hands to her hot cheeks.

When she still did not speak, he said, 'You know that polite society will be closed to you now if you don't marry me. Will the people in Bardsley be any kinder?'

'No.' Her voice was a mere whisper. She would rather he'd continued to speak about his feelings, for she hated the thought of him being constrained to offer her marriage. 'Need anyone know about – this?'

'Your family will already have called out a search party, so I should think the whole of Bardsley will know by now.'

'Oh. Yes, of course they will. Oh dear!' Her wits seemed to have scattered to the winds today.

'My cousins will be searching for me, as well, I've no doubt. So marriage it must be, Cassie. I see no other solution.'

Her main worry would not be held back any longer. 'But if you're *forced* into a marriage because you've compromised me, you'll surely wind up hating me.' She found the idea that he might grow to hate her extremely painful.

He stood up, pulling her to her feet with him and keeping her hands firmly clasped in his. 'Do you remember that moment on the path at Stovely, when I was carrying you back to the house?'

She nodded. She had thought of it many times, trying to understand her own reactions and feelings.

He let go of her hands and put one arm around her, then gently but firmly raised her chin so that she had to look him in the eye. 'This is what I wanted to do then.' Very slowly he bent his head and kissed her, kissed her long and hard, ignoring the inarticulate noise she made in her throat.

She could not help kissing him back, twining her arms round his neck and hoping he would say he loved her now.

But when he stopped kissing her, he said nothing. He was

178

breathing rather rapidly and simply held her close, so with a sigh she nestled against him. They were both so lightly clad she could feel the pounding of his heart against her breast and wondered if he could feel hers, which was beating equally rapidly.

After a moment or two, he moved his body into another position and looked down at her with a wry smile. 'I think you and I have a far better chance of a successful marriage than Susannah and I could ever have had. And I would *like* to marry you, Cassie. One doesn't have to fall desperately in love to be attracted to a woman, or to enjoy her company. Surely, we can build a reasonably happy life together?'

She leaned her head against him to hide her disappointment. It was not what she wanted to hear, but it was better than nothing, she supposed. But why had he stopped kissing her. She had wanted it to go on for much longer.

A little later, when they were sitting down again, he remarked, 'So it is decided. You will marry me.' It was a statement, not a question.

Their heavy outer garments took a long time to dry so they slept in their undergarments, wrapped in the blanket, with his arms round her. Occasionally he got up to put more wood on the fire. In spite of its blazing warmth, the hut was cold and draughts seemed to creep in on every side.

But as they lay together, Cassie thought dreamily how wonderful a man's body was, how strong and warm – and before she knew it, she had drifted into sleep again, feeling so very right in his arms.

Twelve

In the morning, Cassie experienced a moment's panic when she woke and found herself lying in a man's embrace. Simeon was awake already and was staring down at her, smiling slightly as she pulled away. She would have liked him to kiss her or at least give her a hug, but he stood up, making no attempt to touch her, so she had to do the same. It was still dim inside the hut, but as she was wearing only a petticoat with her shirt and chemise, she went to feel her other garments. They were dry again, but very crumpled.

His voice was as calm as if they were meeting at a breakfast party as he asked, 'Did you sleep well in the end, Cassie?'

She had to laugh. 'You know I didn't! And I don't suppose you did, either, Simeon. Oh, I'm so stiff!' She began to stretch her aching limbs, then realised that his eyes were lingering on her body and concentrated on finishing dressing. But he had seemed to approve of what he saw.

He put on his own clothes and went over to open the door and say, 'Fortunately, the mist has lifted. I'll leave you to – um, finish your toilette, Cassie, then we can leave.' He smiled at her as he added, 'Our adventure is nearly over.'

Although she was ravenously hungry, she wished the adventure might have continued for a little longer, for it had helped her get to know him better. That had not only deepened the attraction she felt for him, but it had also made her think they might deal very well together. They still needed more time to get to know one another properly, but she was already worrying about whether people would give them that once they returned. She doubted it. Young ladies were not allowed to spend time alone with gentlemen, even those to whom they were betrothed.

As she went behind the hut, she decided she could enjoy being married to a man who could take an escapade like this in his stride, even if he didn't love her as she loved him. But perhaps he might grow fond of her, at least. That was not too much to hope for, surely?

When they were ready to leave, he held out his hand and she took it without hesitation. The gesture seemed like a promise. And as they walked, they talked easily of this and that, like good friends. That seemed promising, too.

In just under an hour, they were looking down on the smoking chimneys and huddled terraces of Bardsley. They stopped to rest for a moment and tried to tidy themselves up, but nothing could conceal the ragged hem of Cassie's riding habit or make crumpled clothes smooth again.

'I shall never dare show my face in town again,' she said ruefully. 'I must look terrible. Whatever will people think?'

'You don't look terrible – you have beautiful hair, even when it's tangled,' his voice grew warm, 'in fact, especially when it's tangled.' He began to straighten her hair with his fingertips. Even this light touch made shivers run down her spine and when their gazes met, the world seemed to hesitate around them for a moment or two.

'Oh, Cassie!' he said softly. 'People will undoubtedly think the worst of us. They always do. I hope you won't let them hurt you.'

'No. I won't.' She smiled up at him, feeling that the rapport was building between them with every hour they spent together. As he smiled back, she said, 'Thank you for acting as lady's maid, kind sir!' When she sketched him a curtsey, he bowed gravely.

But perversely, she was caught by a sudden surge of anxiety and clutched his sleeve to stop him moving on again, asking urgently, 'Are you sure about this, Simeon? Really sure?'

'Oh, yes.' He reached out to take her hand and raised it to his lips. 'You will undoubtedly infuriate me, flout my wishes, scandalise my mother and goodness knows what else, but I am very certain of one important thing, Cassie Trent . . .'

When he paused, she asked instantly, 'What's that?'

'You will not bore me!' He pulled her towards him and silenced her protests with a kiss that made her tingle from head to toe. Then, as he had done the night before, he set her firmly away from him and took a few deep breaths.

She had to wonder if she'd shown herself too forward, betraying her enjoyment of his kisses like that. Perhaps he did not want a wife who . . . She shook her head. She did not understand the feelings which were shimmering through her body, but surely something which felt so wonderful could not be wrong?

He caught her hand and tugged her into motion. Looking up at him, she smiled and when he smiled back, joy began to bubble inside her. It would be all right between them, she was sure it would. They would make it right.

As she and Simeon walked through Bardsley, Cassie felt an urge to clutch his arm for support. The people they met stared at them in astonishment and one woman even exclaimed, 'Eh, Miss Cassie! Whatever's happened to you?'

'Riding accident,' said Cassie, feeling her face flaming. She hurried on as fast as she could, though her feet were aching and sore, tugging Simeon with her.

As they turned into the street where the Trents lived, they saw Will approaching the house from the opposite direction. He stopped dead at the sight of them, then ran towards them and gave her a bear hug. 'Cassie! Thank

God you're safe!' He looked at Simeon Giffard accusingly. 'What happened?'

Afraid the two men might quarrel, she rushed into speech. 'Did you get my message yesterday?'

'Aye,' said Will. 'And I gave the lad a shilling for you.'

'Will, where's Susannah? Why did you not take her away?'

'She's at home, where she belongs. With me here to protect her, I see no need for us to elope. What I want to know is what the hell *you* have been doing, staying out all night?' He scowled openly at Giffard as he spoke.

'So it was all in vain!' she exclaimed. 'Oh, Will, if you only knew what we've been through!'

'I can imagine,' he said grimly.

'Can you, Trent? Do tell us what it is that you can imagine?' There was a hint of menace in Simeon's voice, but at that moment they reached the door of the house, so when he got no answer, only a glare from Will, he turned to Cassie. 'I'll have to leave you now. Is there somewhere I can hire a gig to take me back to Moorclough Grange? My cousins must be imagining me injured or worse.'

'Aye, they are. They had searchers out yesterday and from first light today,' Will said. 'As we did for our Cassie.'

Simeon grimaced. 'Then I must reassure them as quickly as I can. I'll come and call on you this afternoon, if I may, Cassie.'

'Don't go yet!' she begged, clutching his sleeve. 'Come in for something to eat and get yourself warm first. We can send a message to your cousins but we need to discuss certain matters with my family. *Please*, Simeon!'

'Wouldn't you rather wait until later, when you've recovered?'

'No. I'd rather get it over with.'

He grinned at that unflattering comment, and she muttered, 'Well, you know what I mean. Do stay!'

Will watched this by-play in stunned silence. What on

earth had happened during the night to make them behave so familiarly with each other? If that fellow had been misbehaving with his cousin . . . His train of thought was interrupted by the opening of the house door.

Susannah shrieked and rushed out to fling her arms round her cousin. 'Oh, Cassie, you're safe! We were so *worried!*' Her voice tailed away as she realised who was standing next to her cousin. She gave a choking little cry and stood rooted to the spot, turning first white, then scarlet. 'Simeon!'

Sarah and Aunt Lucy, who had rushed out after her, moved to range themselves on either side of her defensively, scowling at Simeon.

Cassie took hold of his hand, and when he glanced at her quizzically, she realised he was waiting for her to give him a lead as to how he should behave.

'This is Simeon Giffard. We're both famished,' she announced cheerfully. 'We haven't eaten since luncheon yesterday and we're chilled through as well.'

As she had hoped, Aunt Lucy's motherly instincts immediately took over. Forgetting her hostility, she swept them into the house and within a very short space of time she had both of them wrapped in soft blankets and toasting themselves in front of a roaring fire. All Simeon's protests that he could not impose on her like this were brushed to one side. 'Time enough for explanations, Mr Giffard,' she declared majestically, 'when we have you warmed and fed. I know my Christian duty, even if you are a Samaritan – or do I mean a Philistine?'

He caught Cassie's eye and was nearly betrayed into laughing aloud at this point, after which he sat back, seeming to enjoy the experience, probably novel for him, of being cosseted. She could not imagine his mother cosseting anyone.

Sarah and Susannah had disappeared, but Will, informed by his mother that he now had no reason for spurning good food of a morning and would be doctored with her special physick if he did not eat a hearty meal, stayed with them.

Huge trays of food were brought up from the kitchen and both the wanderers fell to with an appetite that bore witness to their deprivations. Aunt Lucy hovered over them, pouring out cup after cup of tea, and urging more food upon them.

However, this respite came to an end when the maids had cleared away and Will said curtly, 'If you're feeling better now, Giffard, I should be glad of a few words with you in private.'

Simeon nodded.

Cassie held up one hand. 'We *all* need to have a talk, and since this trouble is mostly my fault, I don't intend to be excluded.' She looked challengingly across at both men.

'Look, Cassie, I think it'd be better if you left this to me,' Will said.

Aunt Lucy nodded vigorously.

'No!' Cassie looked at Simeon for support. 'This concerns me too closely.'

'If you prefer to be present, I shall discuss things in no other way,' he said at once.

She clicked her tongue in irritation at him, for his drawl was pronounced, the tone calculated to annoy. She saw Will's fists bunch for a moment, then as he growled in his throat, but sat down, she sighed in relief. She did not want two people she loved so much to be at each other's throats.

'I think we should also ask Susannah to join us, since this concerns her, too,' Simeon suggested.

When he looked at her, Cassie nodded her approval.

'I'll not have her bullied, mind!' warned Aunt Lucy.

'I am not, believe me, Mrs Trent, in the habit of bullying people.'

So Susannah was sent for and placed between Will and Aunt Lucy on a high-backed sofa. When she avoided Simeon's eyes and fiddled with her handkerchief, looking ready to burst into tears on the slightest provocation, Cassie could have shaken her.

'Now, it's about time you gave us a round tale of what happened to you last night. We've been out of our wits with worry.' Aunt Lucy looked accusingly at Mr Giffard as she said this.

'It's all my fault, not Simeon's.' Cassie launched into an explanation, trying to sound as if chasing away one's horses and causing two people to be lost on the moors all night was an everyday occurrence. 'You'd have thought I'd have grown out of my habit of getting into silly scrapes by now. Anyway, that's all there is to it, and – and all's well that ends well.' She spoke airily, but could see that Simeon was having great difficulty keeping his face straight, and Aunt Lucy did not seem in the slightest appeased by the explanation – in fact, was now bristling like an angry cat.

'*All there is to it!* You know better than that, I hope, Cassandra Trent! You spend the night alone with a strange man on the moors and then you say that's all there is to it! What would your mother have said? And what, pray, have *you* to say for yourself, Mr Giffard? Or do you intend to leave all the explanations to our Cassie?'

Four pairs of eyes swivelled round to focus on Simeon's somewhat dishevelled person. Three pairs were distinctly hostile, Cassie's were rueful, interested and amused, all at the same time. He could not help exchanging a quick smile with her before he began to sort matters out.

'There is a little more to it than that,' he admitted. 'But first, I need to settle something with you, Susannah.'

She gasped and clutched Will's arm for support.

'I believe that you were, shall we say *over-persuaded* into accepting my proposal of marriage? Please believe that I was quite unaware of this and deeply regret it. If it is your wish, I shall be happy to consider our engagement terminated.' She was now scarlet with embarrassment and he could not help feeling she deserved to be. If she had had any moral courage whatsoever, none of this need have happened. Then he exchanged another glance with Cassie and it occurred to him that not everything had been bad, that some parts of the previous night had, indeed, been distinctly enjoyable. Sleeping with Cassie Trent in his arms had felt – right. Kissing her had felt even better. In fact, he was looking forward to kissing her again – often – and having her in his bed.

He tried not to look disapproving as Susannah murmured something disjointed about kindness and regret, then shrank back between her two protectors. How would *she* have faced a night on the moors? In tears, probably. He realised they were all staring at him, so hurried into speech again.

'Now that my engagement to Susannah is over, it is my pleasure to inform you all that Cassie has done me the honour of agreeing to become my wife.' He bowed towards her as he finished and she nodded in agreement, an amused smile still on her lips.

'Well, it's certainly the right and proper thing to do,' admitted Aunt Lucy, 'and I respect you for that, at least, Mr Giffard. But I'd like to hear what our Cassie has to say about it all.'

'So would I,' said Will. 'I don't like to think of your rushing into a hasty marriage, love, and then living to regret it, just for fear of what people will say.'

Simeon glared at him. 'Such flattery quite overwhelms me. In fact, I have a great deal of respect and liking for your cousin Cassie, Mr Trent, and I shall be pleased and proud to call her my wife. Nor need you assume that she will live to regret marrying me. I have *every* intention of making her *extremely* happy!'

Will, Susannah and Aunt Lucy greeted this statement with a disbelieving silence, Cassie with a warmly encouraging smile.

Simeon waited, but as no one seemed to know what to say next, he rose to his feet. 'Now, I really must take my leave.

Not only do I owe it to my hosts to show them that I'm safe, but I must confess to being extremely tired. I also have a strong desire to get out of these sadly crumpled garments and into something more presentable.' He bowed to Susannah and Aunt Lucy from where he stood, but stepped over to Cassie and raised her hand to his lips, his eyes on hers. 'I'll see you tomorrow? I think I'll sleep for a long time once I get back'

She grinned. 'Yes, Simeon.'

'Minx!'

This interchange left the audience too stunned to make any further protests. When the front door had closed behind him, however, they began to bombard Cassie with questions, the gist of which was that she surely didn't want to marry that man, and, at the same time, she must do so, for the sake of her reputation.

In the end, she pleaded weariness, together with a desire for a hot bath and a long sleep, and made her escape.

But upstairs she had to face Mary Ann, and with her Cassie could not pretend. 'I know I acted like a fool, but please don't scold me any more. I'm going to marry Simeon, aren't I, so that should set everything straight again.'

'But do you *want* to marry him, lass?'

Cassie could feel herself blushing. 'Yes. Yes, I do, actually, Mary Ann. I – I like him very much.'

'Then there's no more to be said, is there?'

'Do you – shall you mind? You will stay with me, won't you? It'll mean living at Stovely, leaving Lancashire.'

The maid's expression softened. 'Of course I'll stay with you! Just you try to get rid of me! Didn't I promise your mother I'd look after you?'

'Yes, but – you haven't said what you really think about my marrying Simeon.'

Mary Ann came across and hugged her. 'Who can ever tell how such things will turn out, love? I think it may be all right. He's a proper man, at least. Kind, too.' And beyond that, she refused to be drawn.

When she came downstairs again late that afternoon, Cassie still had to face each of her relatives individually, except for Uncle Joshua, who said only that it was a lot of fuss about nothing and she must sort it out for herself. He was too busy to sit around gossiping. *Someone* had to attend to business, if Will was going to stay away from the mill on the slightest pretext.

Susannah was all sympathy. 'Such a horrid experience! And all for my sake.'

'I needn't have bothered. In fact, if we are to be frank, I made a complete fool of myself!'

'Well, I think you were very brave. I can't begin to tell you how much—'

Somehow her words grated on Cassie. 'Oh, pooh! I dare say it'll all work out very well in the end.'

'But to be out all night *with a man!* Were you not terrified out of your mind?'

Cassie chuckled. 'I promise you, my dear goose, that except for being hungry and a bit cold, it wasn't so very horrid. Simeon was a perfect gentleman – once we'd stopped quarrelling.' She hesitated, then added, 'I think we shall deal well together, actually. I very much enjoy his company.' She did not intend to admit to any deeper feelings about him, not to her cousins and certainly not to him, unless – she pushed that thought to the back of her mind and saw that Susannah was gazing at her round-eyed.

'You can't mean that!'

'I can and I do!' But nothing she said would persuade the younger girl that she was telling the truth, and her cousin continued to exude sympathy and gratitude at the slightest provocation, until Cassie was ready to scream at her.

Aunt Lucy's main worry was that Cassie would change

189

her mind about marrying Mr Giffard. 'For there's no denying, my dear, you are well and truly compromised, whether
he touched you or not, and if you say he didn't, I'm sure I
believe you, for you've never lied to me before! But I've had
that Mrs Borthwick round already while you were asleep,
pretending to be worried about your safety and asking if it
were true you'd been ravished. Of course I told her nothing,
except that you certainly hadn't been ravished, and I'd just
like to see anyone try, but the thing is, love, you *were* seen
coming back with him, and if you don't marry him, you'll
be ruined.'

'Well, I'm going to marry him, aren't I?'

'Yes, but how you can be happy with such a starched-up
creature, I don't know! My heart bleeds for you!'

Cassie lost all desire to smile. 'Your heart should bleed
for Simeon, not me. This scrape was all my fault in the
first place. In the circumstances, he was compelled to offer
for me.'

'Compelled! *Compelled!* He can just think himself lucky
to get a Trent! Not to mention your fortune, which is not
to be sniffed at!'

'I don't think he cares about that.'

'Of course he cares! A fortune is a fortune, and you won't
find him turning it down, or other people pitying him for
getting hold of it, I promise you!'

Later still, there was Will to face, and he was the
hardest of all to deal with. He waited until after dinner,
then asked if he could speak to Cassie alone. She sighed
and accompanied him into the front parlour, knowing she
could not get out of this.

He did not beat about the bush. 'I can't be happy with
what you're doing, Cassie.'

'What else can I do but marry him, Will? I acted without thinking and have landed him in trouble, as well as
myself. I can only respect him for the way he's behaved
towards me.'

190

'Respect, yes, but not marry!'

'You've been listening too much to what Susannah says about him. I think he and she bring out the worst in each other.'

'That's beside the way! And don't think to go side-tracking me, Cassie Trent! It's your *whole life* we're talking about here.'

She looked at him quizzically. 'What other choice do I have, Will?'

'It need not come to marriage, if you don't wish it. Whatever society may think of you, we shall still love and respect you. The gossip will die down in time. You've still got a family, you know. You're not on your own.'

She had to hug him for that. 'I know, but I think I would *prefer* to marry Simeon to becoming a social outcast.'

'You don't have to pretend with me, love.'

'Will, if you must know it, I find him a very attractive man!' she said in exasperation. 'I'm not like Susannah, afraid for him to touch me!'

'Oh, and how do you know that?'

'He kissed me. And I enjoyed it.'

'I'd like to black his eye for him! How dared he take advantage of you?'

'Will, he didn't force his attentions on me. I *wanted* him to kiss me – it nearly happened once before as well, just after he and Susannah—' She broke off, realising that relating this incident would not please Will, either. 'Anyway, what's wrong with enjoying being kissed by your future husband?' she ended defiantly. 'Don't you enjoy kissing Susannah?'

'That's not at all the same thing. Susannah and I love one another. It makes all the difference.'

She smiled. 'Well, I'm pretty certain Simeon enjoyed the kissing, too – so everything seems all right to me.' Besides, she did love him. Too much for her own peace of mind.

*   *   *

191

Strangely enough, Cassie slept soundly that night. No worries about the future haunted her dreams. It seemed that no sooner had she laid her head down than it was morning, and rather late in the morning at that, so that she had to hurry to get ready for breakfast.

Afterwards she had her aunt's permission to see Simeon on her own in the front parlour. Aunt Lucy had been very upset when she realised she had entertained an important visitor, on a crucial family occasion, in her untidy sitting-room, and she was determined to make a better impression upon him this time.

He arrived just after eleven in the Moorthorpe Grange carriage, as elegantly dressed as if he were paying a London call. However, Will intercepted him in the hall and insisted on speaking to him alone before this went any further.

Simeon met Cassie's gaze, shrugged and turned to follow Will into the front parlour.

Fuming, she rejoined Sarah and Susannah in the back room.

'Who does Will think he is, interfering like that? It's *me* who's marrying Simeon, not him! And as long as I'm happy about it, it needn't concern anyone else! I'm nearly twenty-one, after all!'

When she heard the parlour door open ten minutes later, she rushed out into the hallway, and stood there, arms akimbo. 'Well, have you two decided my fate, or am I to be allowed a say?'

Will ignored this challenge. 'I won't dress this up in fancy words, our Cassie, and it's no use your getting into a miff, because it has to be said. I've told Giffard, and I'm telling you now that I think you're very unwise to rush into this marriage. But as you're both so determined, there's nothing I can do about it.'

'No, there isn't. I'm not a child to be protected from life, Will. I'm quite grown up, now, thank you very much.'

'You're still my cousin, and I care about your happiness.'

She smiled at him, her anger abating a little. 'I know you do, love. But you won't change my mind.'

'Or mine,' Simeon added and gestured towards the parlour. 'May I speak to you alone now, Cassie?'

When the door had closed on the rest of the family, she stood there, looking up rather shyly at the man who was now her fiancé. 'I see you've recovered from your ordeal,' she commented, trying for a normal conversational tone and completely failing to hide the strange nervousness that had suddenly beset her.

Simeon bent to kiss her cheek and take her hand. 'And you. In fact, you look charming – as well as fully recovered.' He felt her hand shaking in his, so kept hold of it and led the way towards a very large, overstuffed sofa. 'Come and sit down, Cassie. Have your family been scolding you? My cousin and his wife have been quite unbearable. I had to threaten to move to an inn before they would stop trying to tell me what to do.'

She sighed with relief that he understood. 'Yes, they've all been on at me. In fact, they've hardly left me alone for a minute.' She felt dangerously close to tears and could not understand why, when she had been so calm in the face of all the problems of the previous day.

'Are you having second thoughts?' he asked, concern showing in his face. 'If so, you should tell me now, before this goes any further.'

'Not that, no, but I feel bewildered,' she said frankly, 'and ashamed, too. What a mess I've got you into! I'm so sorry, Simeon.'

'As I've said before, I'm not displeased with the situation. It was much worse before, with Susannah!'

'How can you wish to have a wife forced on you, though, and one who does such – such addle-brained things? Your cousins have probably told you nothing but the truth.' To her dismay, she felt a tear roll down her cheek. 'And I don't know why I'm behaving like this! I *never* cry!'

He had not seen her vulnerable in this way before and that made him feel protective. She had been so brave in the face of adversity, no tears, no complaints about the cold, no false modesty, either. He gathered her in his arms and, as she clung to him, he stroked her beautiful hair, feeling tenderness well up inside him.

After a while, when she had stopped weeping, he smiled down at her and brushed away a teardrop with one fingertip. 'If your cousin Will sees signs that you've been crying, he'll be after my blood. He's very fond of you and has made it plain that I'm to make you happy, or else I shall have him to answer to!'

She gave a shaky laugh. 'That's Will for you! He's always looked after me. He's been more like an elder brother than a cousin. I hope you don't mind too much about him and Susannah. I think he'll be just the person to make her happy.'

'As I am not! No, I don't mind at all. As a wife, she would have driven me to distraction in a month – a week, even. But you will believe, I hope, that I don't need Will's threats to make me do my best to look after you.'

'*I* might drive you to distraction, as well.'

As he took her by the shoulders and looked down into her eyes, his closeness made her catch her breath. He put up one hand to caress her cheek, a fleeting butterfly touch, but it made her breathing deepen, and she could not help wishing he would kiss her again, instead of talking.

'Cassie, please believe me when I say I'm very sure I want to marry you. I find you attractive and I enjoy your company, though I've no doubt that I shall get annoyed with you at times, especially if you make a habit of spending the night up on the moors with strange men.'

'Well, what a thing to say!' But he was smiling so broadly she found herself returning the smile.

He took her hands in his, drawing her closer. 'What about you? It seems to me that all the advantages of this marriage are on my side. I'd like *you* to reassure me that you're not unhappy about the prospect of becoming my wife.'

She hesitated over her choice of phrase. She did not dare reveal how much she wanted to marry him, how strongly she felt about him. Not yet, anyway. 'I'm not unhappy, believe me, Simeon. I – I've been a bit lost lately, since my parents died, and I've very much missed having a family and home of my own. Living with other people can be very wearing.' Something else suddenly occurred to her and she smiled mischievously. 'And I have an ulterior motive for marrying you.'

He stiffened. 'Oh? What?'

'I fell in love with Stovely Chase when we came to visit you. I can think of nowhere I'd rather live.'

His eyes lit up. 'Do you really mean that?'

'I wouldn't say it if I didn't mean it.'

He raised first one of her hands, then the other to his lips, and pressed a kiss on each. 'No, you wouldn't.'

She had to concentrate hard to continue breathing at all as his lips seemed to leave a lingering warmth on her hands. She wanted to pull his head towards her for a kiss, but of course, a lady could not do that. It was clear now, though, that the novels she had read did not nearly do justice to the strength of one's feelings when one was in love. She did allow herself to keep hold of his hand, however. And he didn't seem to mind, for he gave hers a quick squeeze.

'One of the things I like most about you, Cassie, is your honesty. And I'm delighted that you feel like that about my home. To me, Stovely is the most beautiful place on earth.'

When he let go of her hands, she felt she had to take a step backwards. Being too close to him scattered her wits to the four winds. 'I agree. I didn't realise how ugly Bardsley was until I'd seen your home. No wonder you love it so much! And – and I hope we have several children together, because I want a real family life again.' She blushed as she said this, but had decided that it had to be brought out into the open.

He stared at her in surprise, but he didn't seem displeased – on the contrary, he nodded agreement, so she blew her nose and said briskly, 'Well, then, if you're still of a mind to make an honest woman of me, Simeon Giffard, how shall we set about it?'

Thirteen

M eanwhile, in happy ignorance of what was happening in Bardsley, Lord and Lady Berrinden had rushed across Europe to rescue their only son. They found him weak, but recovering fast, thanks to the neglect of the local doctor who had little time for the English and who therefore had not meddled too much with nature.

Within a few days of his mother's arrival, Richard was out of bed, if somewhat shaky on his legs. A week later Lord Berrinden settled an astronomical bill without blinking, because he could not understand all that damned foreign money. He hated the messes served to him for food and was anxious to get back to civilisation, especially his club, because living in such close proximity to his wife, spending most of the day with her, was dashed difficult.

Two days after their return, Simeon called at Bransham Gardens and requested the honour of a few minutes' conversation alone with Lady Berrinden. He had considered keeping up the fiction that Lord Berrinden was head of the household and applying to him first, but had soon discarded that idea as a waste of time.

He thought as he shook hands how tired she looked, so did not waste her time on polite chit-chat. 'I'd better come straight to the point, your ladyship. Susannah and I have decided that we are not suited and wish to end our engagement.'

She gaped at him for a moment, then gasped, 'You cannot mean that!'

'I'm afraid I do.'

Her voice rose several tones. 'I won't allow it!'

'There's nothing you can do about it. It's quite settled.'

She clutched her bosom, let out a piercing shriek and for the first time in her life, fell into a fit of hysterics.

The noise brought every servant within reach running to see what was wrong, and although Meckworth had the forethought to close the door on the gaping faces, the noise was still audible in the front part of the house. Richard pushed into the room and even Lord Berrinden came to investigate, but they both stood near her looking helpless.

It was left to Simeon to pat her hand and make soothing noises, then, when she pushed him away with every sign of loathing, he beckoned Richard over. Leaving them to it, he returned home, sure that she would not want him to witness her distress.

Richard remained with his mother, surprised at how long it took her to calm down, as she repeated what Simeon had said and begged her son to make them see sense. She looked so battered by the emotional storm that he insisted his father call in the family physician to attend her.

Dr Gilpin came down from her bedroom and declared that her ladyship was worn out by her travels and recent anxieties. 'I have not only prescribed complete rest, but have obliged her to take a sleeping draught. Whatever it is that has upset her and precipitated this attack must be dealt with by someone else.'

'Eh, what?' said his lordship. 'But we can't force the fellow to marry Suzie.'

Richard sighed. 'Shall I deal with it, Father?'

'Yes. Yes, that's the ticket. Giffard's your friend, after all. Go and find out what's happened, there's a good lad.' He went into the library and ordered a bottle of port, his usual solace in times of trouble, satisfied that his wife would not come and find him drinking.

Richard walked briskly round to Giffard House, determined to find out exactly what had happened between Simeon and Susannah, and, if possible, to mend the breach.

He was shown into the library, where he found his friend sitting frowning out of the window. 'Well, what's this I hear about you and Susannah having a falling out? Can't have that, can we?'

'It's more than a falling out, Richard. Susannah and I have decided we shall not suit.'

'Now look, old fellow, I know my sister. She's a shy little thing, but very biddable. It won't take much to bring her round again. Whatever bee she's taken into her bonnet . . . '

Simeon stared at his friend and for the first time saw a marked resemblance to Lady Berrinden. 'But I don't want to bring her round – and she doesn't want to be brought round, either.'

'But you must see that—'

'I must see nothing. The engagement is over.'

Richard brought out one of the best persuaders he could think of. 'Does your mother know about this?'

'Not yet. I'm going down to Stovely to inform her of the situation when I've done everything necessary here.'

'She'll throw a fit.'

'I dare say. But choosing a wife is my business, after all.' And he should never have allowed her to choose one for him.

Richard frowned and perched on the arm of a chair. 'Bit drastic, don't you think, ending the engagement? Won't look well for either of you. You haven't sent a notice to the papers yet, have you? Right then, surely you could give it another try?'

'Look, I care nothing for what gossips may say. I think it was a lot *more* drastic to force Susannah into agreeing to marry me in the first place.'

'*Force* her!'

'Yes, force! She tried to refuse me, you know, but your mother "brought her round", as you phrase it. However, the prospect of marrying me made her very unhappy and it did not please me, either, once I'd realised how she felt about me. I can only regret that I did not have the courage to break off the engagement there and then. Poor Susannah would have been saved a lot of unnecessary suffering.'

'But if you were to—'

'To put it bluntly, Richard, I don't want a wife who flinches when I touch her!'

There was silence, then, 'Oh. Bad as that, eh?'

Simeon flushed. 'Yes. She finds me physically frightening. And besides,' he took a deep breath, 'I was unable to say anything when I called, because of your mother's – um, indisposition, but your sister is in love, *deeply in love*, with William Trent, who will be calling upon your father as soon as convenient to ask for her hand in marriage.'

Richard stiffened. 'Well, if you think we'll let her throw herself away on a nobody like that, you're far and out! Dammit, the fellow's in trade!'

'I didn't think you'd consent easily, which is why I wanted to break the news to your mother first. If I feel you're about to try to coerce Susannah into another loveless arrangement, I shall go back north and help her and Trent to elope.'

Richard goggled at him. 'Have you run mad? Why on earth should you do that? If the engagement really is broken, Susannah's not your concern any more; she's the concern of her family!'

Simeon shrugged. 'I'm fond of her, I suppose. I've known her since she was a child, after all, and I'd like to see her happy. She *is* happy with Will Trent.' He saw that the other man was about to speak and held up one hand. 'Hear me out, Richard. You will, I suppose, take my word for it that they're deeply in love?'

'I suppose so. Rather vulgar, though, ain't it?'

'I don't consider it vulgar. But it may help you to grow accustomed to the idea if I tell you that William Trent is extremely well-heeled, worth five thousand a year, at least, even before he inherits the family fortune – which will probably increase that income tenfold.'

There was a long, low whistle of astonishment. 'You're joking!'

'No. We went into the family circumstances rather thoroughly, so that I could tell you exactly how he stood. It's not only cotton – the Trents have a finger in quite a few other pies as well.'

'I can't believe it!'

Simeon was delighted to see that his friend's expression had become thoughtful now, rather than hostile.

'Finally, you should know that Will Trent – whom I consider a rather decent fellow, by the way – is prepared not only to overlook the question of a dowry, but also to make a suitable settlement upon Susannah. And to do something for her sisters later. He is a very generous fellow and cares deeply about your sister.'

Another silence descended on the room as he waited for his friend to think matters through.

'Well, the money does put a slightly different complexion on things, I must admit,' Richard said finally. 'As you already know, our family's fortunes are not in good order, thanks to m'grandfather's gambling and m'father's complete lack of business sense.'

Simeon nodded. 'I know. I'm in rather the same boat. My own father died in the nick of time. Another couple of years and we'd have lost everything.'

Richard was looking thoughtful. 'You're absolutely sure of those figures – Trent's income, I mean?'

'Absolutely. If you can persuade your mother to put a good face on it, there are a lot of benefits to be gained from the connection. However, Will and Susannah are quite prepared to make a runaway match of it if your parents don't agree to the marriage. I'm sure Lady Berrinden would like *that* even less.'

'She won't like the connection, however rich Trent may be,' Richard said slowly. 'Bit high in the instep, m'mother.'

Simeon played his final card. 'She may look upon it more kindly when she knows that I'm about to marry into the same family myself. It's my pleasure to inform you that your cousin Cassandra has promised to become my wife.' He gritted his teeth and added, 'You'll no doubt hear from the gossips that I'm only marrying her because I compromised her. Well, I did – we were lost on the moors together overnight – but I'll tell you now that after spending time in her company, I came to the conclusion that I'd *like* to marry her. She's a fine woman.'

He looked Richard straight in the eyes. 'And if I don't despise your cousin's antecedents, I'm sure your mother will be able to come to terms with Will Trent – *and* with his fortune!'

Richard did not believe that Simeon meant what he said about wanting to marry Cassie, but he knew his friend had a strong sense of duty and loyalty, and would never admit that he had been forced into a distasteful marriage, so he did not challenge the statement. Besides, his cousin Cassandra was probably almost as full of juice as this Trent fellow.

He stood up. 'All right. I'll see what I can do. I'll send word to you once I've brought m'mother round. But I warn you, it won't be easy.'

In spite of the size of the Trent fortune, it took three days of persuasion to make Lady Berrinden accept the match. She several times described Simeon in Richard's hearing as 'a deceiving, perfidious dissembler' or 'that traitor to his ancestors' and at first she refused to have Susannah's name even mentioned in her presence.

It was only the discovery by Richard that Lord Berrinden

had mortgaged the family estate, unknown to anyone, to cover some gambling debts acquired at his club that made her ladyship accept the inevitable.

Once that had been settled, however, face-saving prevailed and to no one except her son and her long-suffering husband did Amelia Berrinden again bewail her eldest daughter's ingratitude.

Flora Giffard was even more horrified than her friend when informed that Simeon had broken off his engagement to Susannah. 'You can't do it!' she wailed.

'It's already done.'

'But you're a Giffard. Our family can trace its ancestry back to William the Conqueror.' Her voice rising, she clutched the arms of her chair as if the world were reeling around her. 'That young woman reeks of the shop! I forbid you to marry her, do you hear? Forbid it!'

'My mind is quite made up, Mama, and I've already sent off the announcement to *The Times*.'

'How can you do this to me?' She began to sob, clinging to him and wailing piteously, with an expertise perfected over many years.

For once he was not to be moved and when she began to build up for full hysterics, he handed her over to her companion and maid, and walked out, – though he was terrified that she would kill herself with this excess of fury. He could not, however, be held to ransom for the rest of his life by his mother's health. He had Cassie to think of now, and his own needs, too. The decision to give them precedence had removed a load from his mind. He would, of course, continue to do his best to care for his mother, but she must take some responsibility for her own actions as well.

When Miss Canley came down to report that she and the maid had got Flora calmed down, but said she feared his mother would never agree to the match, he simply replied, 'I'm thirty-three years old and don't need her permission.

However, I'm sorry for the trouble this will cause you, Cousin Jane.'

She gave him a faint smile. 'I'm quite used to that.'

It took Simeon several days and two visits from Dr Murray to make his mother realise that he was not going to change his mind. In the end, however, she agreed to keep up a public pretence of accepting *that conniving and unscrupulous female* in order not to add fuel to vulgar gossip.

'I wish to bring Cassie to visit Stovely,' he warned, 'and I will not have her exposed to any discourtesy from you.'

'*I* am a Giffard! I hope I know my manners better than that.'

'I also wish to give a small party for the neighbours, to introduce Cassie to them. Will you arrange that?'

Flora inclined her head.

'And I would like you to be present at the wedding, which will, of course, take place in Bardsley.'

She closed her eyes and shuddered. 'That I cannot promise. The journey would probably kill me.'

He had felt it his duty to invite her, but had expected her to refuse, and was glad of it.

The one thing she would not agree to was moving to the Dower House, and she lapsed into complete invalidism every time Simeon tried to discuss that.

As he knew it would take a while to renovate the place, he let the matter drop. His mother had her own wing and would not be with them all the time.

When he had left Stovely to meet his fiancée in London, Flora became very thoughtful. Her obstinate and pig-headed son was just as bad as his father and equally heedless of his responsibilities to the family. He was clearly not going to change his mind about marrying *that female*, so it was up to her to change it for him. She was not sure yet what she could do, but she would find something. No millowner's daughter was going to become châtelaine of Stovely if Flora Giffard could prevent it.

The scandal of Simeon Giffard breaking off his engagement to Susannah Berrinden was nothing compared to the spate of gossip caused by the subsequent announcement of his engagement to her cousin, Cassandra Mary Trent, of Bardsley, Lancashire. How had she managed to trap him like that? Imagine stealing your cousin's affianced husband? All the old tales of her mother's elopement were revived and most people decided that Miss Trent's personal fortune must be the attraction, for everyone knew that the Berrindens were not overflowing with worldly wealth nowadays.

Only Albert was sincerely happy for him. 'I guessed you were attracted to her,' he said. 'Well, more than attracted.'

Simeon was startled. 'You did?'

'Oh, yes.'

Simeon went away from that conversation thoughtful. He was, he admitted to himself, missing Cassie greatly. And was beginning to realise how fond of her he had become. He even dared indulge in the hope that she might have grown fond of him.

Two days later, another announcement in *The Times* revealed Susannah Berrinden's engagement to some Northern nobody of a millowner, another Trent, and polite society rocked on its foundations. What did these Trents have that made them able to attract members of the ton at will? Gossip immediately tripled the Trent fortune.

Too wise to her world's ways to pretend she was delighted with the match, Lady Berrinden smiled ruefully and confided in her friends that true love was not to be denied and she cared too much for her daughter's happiness to stand in her way. Her consolation, she sighed, was that although Mr Trent might be in trade, the family did come from quite respectable stock, and he was deeply in love with her daughter. He was also, she pulled a wry face, rich enough to keep the foolish girl in great comfort. She herself knew nothing about business matters, of course, but dear Simeon (and no one knew how much that term of affection cost her) had told them all about Mr Trent's financial situation. And who should know better than he, since his fiancée was a co-inheritor of the Trent fortune? Yes, indeed, a positive outbreak of romance, was it not?

Rumours about the real reasons for Simeon Giffard marrying Cassie Trent continued to circulate, however. No one gave any credence to the idea that he might be in love with Miss Trent. People knew him rather too well for that! A regular cold fish, Giffard, and always had been. It ran in the family.

Unfortunately, gossips in Bardsley lost no time in informing the world about how Simeon had spent that fateful night and with whom. In a few days, the news was all over the county of Lancashire; in two weeks, it had reached London. The scandal had been dying, but now it flared up again.

So Giffard had been compromised, had he? How the gossips tittered over that one! Well, there were a few people around who would not mind being compromised by a rich heiress. Some rumours even had it that Giffard had compromised the woman deliberately, for the sake of her fortune, and that Susannah Berrinden had been compelled to break off their engagement, for very shame.

For the first time in his life, Simeon found himself at the centre of a raging scandal. Loathing every minute of it, he hid behind a thorn hedge of reserve. Not even with his friend Albert Darford would he discuss the events that had led to his engagement.

At social events, any remark he considered impertinent made him bow and walk away, grim-faced. Once, he even walked out of a card party with a choice circle of friends, because wine had freed their tongues enough for them to tease him and demand a full explanation.

*   *   *

206

Arrangements now needed to be made for Susannah and Cassie to return to London. They were to be accompanied by Will, who would need to make a formal request to Lord Berrinden for permission to marry Susannah and also arrange the marriage settlements with the family lawyer.

Another month should see preparations complete, Lady Berrinden told her son, brandishing her smelling salts. Susannah must be married from Bransham Gardens, and after that she did not wish to see her eldest daughter again until she had recovered from the shock of such a misalliance – *if she ever did* – and had grown accustomed to being the mother of a mere Mrs Trent of Nowhere. As for Cassandra, presumably she would be married in Bardsley, and distasteful as it would be, the family would have to attend to avoid giving further cause for gossip.

Simeon wrote to tell Cassie that it was time for Susannah to return and face her mother. He also added that, in view of the rumours currently circulating in town, he felt it better for he and Cassie to publicly demonstrate a certain degree of affection in order to silence those with nothing better to do than spread tasteless and mendacious gossip.

Reading between the stiffly phrased lines, she guessed how much he was hating the furore surrounding their engagement. Well, she did not much like it either, and had been the butt of several offensive remarks, even in Bardsley. But there was nothing she could do about it, so she banished it resolutely from her mind and concentrated instead on her cousin. Susannah had nearly fainted at the mere idea of returning to London and facing her mother, and it had taken a lot of coaxing to persuade her to agree. Only the thought that she could not marry Will if she did not go back gave her the courage to leave Bardsley.

The three of them and Mary Ann arrived in town late in the afternoon on the first Friday in September. Simeon was waiting for them at Giffard House, and after they'd refreshed themselves, he and Will escorted the two young women to

Bransham Gardens, which was only a few streets away, for the ordeal of the reconciliation.

Poor Susannah was pale and trembling as she was helped from the carriage, but with Will's arm to clutch, and Simeon and Cassie forming a rearguard, she managed to stumble up the steps to the front door.

Richard met them in the hallway. 'So you're back, Susannah,' he remarked coldly. He then condescended to be introduced to his future brother-in-law. 'Ah, Trent!' He looked down his nose and did not offer to shake hands.

'How do, Berrinden,' said Will, winking at Cassie and exaggerating his Northern accent.

Richard winced visibly.

'And this is your cousin Cassie, now my fiancée,' said Simeon, taken with a sudden desire to laugh. He had not expected his old friend to be so pompous and unforgiving.

Richard inclined his head a fraction and bared his teeth in a smile which was more like a snarl. 'Cousin Cassandra.'

She did not even incline her head. 'Cousin Richard.' She had taken a strong dislike to him on sight, and could not imagine how this beefy, fish-eyed young man could possibly be the brother of gentle Susannah. Or the friend of Simeon. And although she hoped she was not betraying it, she too was dreading the next few weeks.

As Richard led them into the drawing-room where his mother was waiting for them, Mary Ann slipped out to the servants' quarters, where she refused point-blank to discuss what had happened in Bardsley.

Amelia Berrinden received the visitors coldly, but with none of the biting sarcasm for which she was famous. Indeed, she might have been greeting a stranger, rather than her eldest daughter, so cool and brief were her remarks.

Susannah, by now in floods of tears, humbly begged her mama's pardon and was told that it was granted, but the cheek she was allowed to kiss was cold and the kiss was not returned.

Bitterly disappointed at the way her beautiful daughter was throwing herself away upon a mere nobody, Lady Berrinden went through the forms of reconciliation, but when Simeon and Will had left, turned to her daughter and niece and said, still with that chill politeness, 'I assume you will wish to spend most of your time in your rooms, when we are not out together. You will both have a lot of preparations to make for the wedding. And Susannah, your sisters are rather busy just now, so I would prefer it if you did not disturb their lessons.'

'Mama—'

Her plea was ignored. 'Cassandra, given the gossip your behaviour has caused, and the way you have been compromised,' she shuddered, 'you will kindly make sure you are *never* alone with Mr Giffard again until you are married.'

'Yes, Aunt Amelia.'

'And now, please leave me. I have a headache.' Lady Berrinden closed her eyes and put one hand upon her brow.

Richard went to stare out of the window.

Cassie scowled at them both. How unkind they were! She helped Susannah up the stairs, then watched her cousin throw herself on her bed and begin to weep.

'You must not give way like this,' Cassie urged, patting her shoulder. 'You knew your mother would not be pleased with you.'

Susannah sat up and flung her arms round Cassie. 'I didn't think she would cut me out of her life – or keep me from my sisters.'

'No. Nor did I. And if I ever have any children, I'll make sure they know how much I love them, whatever they do.'

Susannah brightened a little. 'So shall I. Oh, I do hope they will look like Will.'

'Why don't you wash your face and put on a particularly pretty gown? After all, you promised Will you would keep as cheerful as possible.'

A dreamy expression came over Susannah's face at the thought of her beloved, and Cassie breathed a sigh of relief as she rang for her cousin's maid and went to her own room and Mary Ann's cheerful company.

After the two young women had left them, Richard and his mother sat on in gloomy silence in the drawing-room.

'I'm surprised at how pretty Cousin Cassandra is,' he said after a few minutes.

'Handsome is as handsome does!'

'Yes. And I must say I do not like her impertinent manners. Who does she think she is?'

'She is a scheming wretch and the sooner she is out of this house, the happier I shall be.' His mother waved her vinaigrette to and fro, but kept it carefully away from her nose.

'Can't figure out what Simeon sees in her.'

'Money. The lack of it can do strange things to people. However,' she sighed deeply, 'we must present a united front to the world about this. Only thus can we scotch that *odious* gossip.'

'Susannah seems dashed overset.'

'So she should be!' snapped his mother. 'Any warmer feelings I had towards her have been destroyed *forever!* She is an ungrateful viper!'

Richard was thoughtful as he changed for dinner. He had not liked to see his sister looking so very unhappy, and he had been surprised at how far his mother's anger and disappointment had carried her in her treatment of her daughter.

When he married, he rather thought he might persuade his parents to retire to the country estate, where his father couldn't incur any more gambling debts. And he would persuade his father to turn over all the business side of things to him immediately, before the family was completely ruined. *He* did not wish to be obliged to marry a large

210

fortune, whether he liked the woman or not, as Simeon clearly had to. That was the only explanation he could find for his friend's behaviour. The financial situation of the Giffards must be far worse than anyone had realised.

The day after the arrival of the two young ladies in London, the Berrindens' lawyer spent the morning with Mr Trent. He then went round to Bransham Gardens to verify that the marriage settlements he had tentatively drawn up were acceptable to the family.

When Lady Berrinden perused the details of the financial settlements proposed and saw further proof of exactly how rich the Trents were, her cup of gall overflowed. Her ungrateful wretch of a daughter was going to be even more wealthy than she had expected! 'There is,' she declared afterwards, *'no justice in the world!* That man is as rich as Croesus.'

'Seems a dashed good thing to me,' his lordship commented unwisely.

'*Good thing!* How can you *ever* say that, Henry?'

'Well, he's not only full of juice, but he's being very generous with it.'

'I am deeply thankful that I am not myself of such a mercenary nature, and I would be grateful if *you* would stop saying such things, because it is *not* and never could be, a good thing for someone of our birth and breeding to sink into the ranks of trade!'

'Well, it don't hurt to have a fistful of the readies,' muttered Lord Berrinden mutinously.

Thereafter he tried to moderate his joy when his wife was there, but continued to feel delighted that his little Suzie would be able to live as high as she liked. To his mind, such wealth could only reflect credit on the family, whatever Amelia said, though of course he did not go so far as to contradict her openly.

And whatever Richard said about him stopping going to

his club, Henry Berrinden fully intended to resume his visits there once the wedding was over. Why should he not? Little Suzie had repaired the family fortunes and he would drink to that any time. What was the world coming to if a fellow couldn't take a hand of cards with his friends? He rang the bell and sent for another decanter of port.

Within two hours he was completely befuddled and when his wife sent Richard to look for him, was discovered sound asleep on the floor of his dressing-room.

'Let him stay there, then!' snapped her ladyship. 'It is no more than he deserves. *He* is partly responsible for this disaster, for being so stupid as to bring his niece to this house in the first place.'

Preparations for Susannah's wedding went on apace, for Lady Berrinden wished to waste no time in ridding her household of such a hideous example of the undeserved rewards of filial disobedience. She kept the younger girls strictly segregated from Susannah and Cassandra, in order to avoid further contamination, though they would have to act as attendants to their sister if tongues were not to have further cause to wag. And she made it a point of honour to ensure that Cassie and Simeon were never alone together, engaged or not.

The ceremonies were to be held two weeks apart, with Susannah and Will marrying first in London, then Simeon and Cassie getting married in Bardsley. Before that there was a visit to be made to Stovely, since Flora refused point-blank to travel to the North to be present at the wedding, nor would she contemplate a trip to London.

In Bransham Gardens, Richard and Cassie continued to grate on each other's nerves. When she answered his sneering remarks sharply, he did not hesitate to retaliate with oblique references to why Simeon was marrying her and the depth of obligation she should feel towards such an honourable man. She was too proud to let him see how much this hurt, but it did hurt greatly. She found that she could not even discuss her feelings about Simeon with Mary Ann, because this was too important to her, too close to her heart.

Since she was not allowed a single opportunity to be alone with her betrothed, she could only cling to her memories of their night together and hope that once all this fuss was over, the two of them would settle down amicably together at Stovely. There was so much she longed to know about him. And she also wanted to know what was going to happen about his mother, but it seemed crass to ask him this with other people there, especially her aunt. It would sound as if she wanted to throw Flora out of her home.

Lord Berrinden spent as much time as he dared at his club, taking refuge there whenever he could sneak out of the house, and bribing its doorkeeper not to give him away to his son. Cassie did not blame him. The atmosphere in his home was, to say the least, uneasy. Her aunt alternated between awe-inspiring dignity and sheer bad temper; Susannah was often discovered weeping in corners, and Cassie had to acknowledge the correctness of her uncle's remark that she herself had 'come over dashed absent-minded all of a sudden, except when you're snapping Richard's nose off.'

She was paying dearly for her foolishness – and so was Simeon, who had been very stiff with everyone since their return to London. Would he hold that against her after they were married? She prayed not. In the meantime, it was an effort each morning to leave her bedchamber and go down to face her aunt and Cousin Richard over the breakfast table, an effort Susannah did not always feel equal to.

Fourteen

The party to celebrate her son's engagement and introduce Cassie would, Flora decreed, just involve the neighbours and a few close friends and relatives from further afield. Fortunately, it was almost full moon, so apart from the Berrindens none of the guests would need to stay the night, a thing Flora loathed.

Secretly, she made plans to do more than introduce Miss Trent. With the intention of showing *that female* in her true colours and freeing her son from this ridiculous engagement, she wrote to some neighbours, the Earl and Countess of Elmsworth, whom she had not seen for a long time, but whom she considered her friends still, since they were the only people in the district of superior rank to the Giffards. She knew that they had their own problems and offered her help in solving them, enclosing a sealed note for their son, Viscount Summersby, with the one inviting them.

For days, Jane Canley was kept busy writing invitations, planning the supper menu and arranging for extra help from the village.

So much fuss was made about the preparations for this festivity that Simeon soon began to regret pressing for it. 'If it's too much trouble for you, Mother, we can cancel the party. Everyone knows you're not in good health and they'll understand.'

'No one shall ever accuse *me* of failing to do my duty,' declared Flora, wiping away an imaginary tear, 'and when my only son decides to take a wife, however much I deprecate his choice of partner,' she shuddered theatrically, 'I know that I must play my part. I do not even begrudge giving up the company of Jane so that she may assist in the preparations.'

It seemed to him that Jane was being ruthlessly taken advantage of and was working far too hard, but when he apologised to her, she became flustered and backed away from him in a flurry of phrases such as, 'only obeying orders' and 'not to be blamed if things do not go as expected'. If he had been less busy, less angry about the gossip that was still going the rounds about himself and Cassie, he might have taken the trouble to ask Jane to explain these strange comments, but he simply did not have the time.

He grew tired of his mother's attitude towards his intended wife and one night said firmly, 'I'm very grateful that you're giving this party, Mother, but I don't like to hear you refer to Cassie so scornfully and I would be hurt, as well as upset, if you said such things to others. As you get to know her better, I'm sure you'll come to like Cassie and appreciate her.'

She patted his hand. 'My poor, loyal boy! Perhaps people will make allowances for her. Our friends will perfectly understand that you were *compelled* to offer – you were ever the soul of honour, my dearest! – though I will always believe that she *schemed* to catch you and I shall *never* be able to trust her, even if she is rich. But what is money, after all, when we have an honoured line that spans the centuries, which is why I console myself with the thought that we shall overcome this blot upon the escutcheon, and in time her name will fade from memory, though *what* sort of children she will produce, I dread to think. You must be sure to engage the strictest of governesses, to counteract any plebeian tendencies in your offspring, and . . . and . . .' She lost her thread at last, broke off and frowned. 'Dear me, what was I saying?'

'The party. We were discussing the party,' he said through gritted teeth, 'and the strain it will be upon you.' He tried once more to reason with her. 'Mother, you're seeing problems where there are none. But if you don't feel you can receive Cassie with complacency, then we must cancel the party and I shall—'

'Dearest one, when have you ever known *me* to be uncivil? I, at least, was raised a gentlewoman. It is *that female's* manners about which you should be worrying. I felt last time that she was very pushy, positively *flaunting* her wealth. Who is to know what she will say or do this time? But I shall be on my guard, fear not! Vigilance shall be my watchword!'

He had never been able to handle her, any more than his father had, and with the worry of her health on top of everything else, he had allowed her too much leeway. Giving up the attempt to discuss his fiancée, he placed his hope in the fact that his mother was always cold and correct in company, and would reserve such diatribes against her future daughter-in-law for private utterance. He would need to warn Cassie to pay no attention to what was said when guests were not present, and to assure her that nothing was ever good enough for Flora Giffard.

Hoping to prevent his mother throwing the sort of tantrum which the doctor had warned him might be fatal, he bit his tongue more than once, for Cassie's sake. It would look so much better for her if his mother was seen to accept his future bride.

The Berrindens arrived at Stovely the day before the party, and were received in the garden room by Flora, resplendent in the blackest of crepes, embellished by all the family jewels she could hang around her scrawny neck or otherwise attach to her person. As they entered, she made great play with a black-edged lace handkerchief. She had never come out of mourning for her husband, not because she had been devoted to him, for they had rarely spent any time together after the first year or two and he had treated her abominably, but because it saved her so much trouble in choosing clothes.

'My dearest Amelia! I knew you would not fail me!' she cried, clasping her hands as near to her withered bosom as the necklaces would permit.

'What else are friends for in times of trouble?' Lady Berrinden sat down beside her on the sofa, and they stared at Cassie in joint disapproval.

Normally, Cassie would have found the situation amusing and ignored such remarks but, lately, she seemed to have quite lost her sense of humour. Indeed, she was sick and tired of all the fuss and would be glad to get the wedding over. She was relieved to see Simeon again and took comfort from the warmth of his smile and the lingering clasp of his hands before following Susannah to the window seat.

'Mother, shall I ring for refreshments?' he asked, seeing that Flora had done no more than nod at the rest of the party and was already whispering in Amelia Berrinden's ear.

'What? Yes, dearest one. Oh, I forgot to tell you. That bell pull broke this morning. You will have to go and find Burton yourself.' When he had left the room, she turned back to her friend and said loudly, 'Oh, the pangs of losing one's only child in this way!'

'As another mother who has been sorely disappointed in her offspring, I can appreciate your feelings.' Amelia replied, equally loudly.

Susannah turned scarlet and bent her head.

Flora sighed soulfully and flourished her handkerchief in the direction of her eyes.

'My dearest friend, you must allow me to express our gratitude for the effort you are making.' Lady Berrinden glared across the room at Cassie. 'I only hope you have not overstrained yourself. But then, you always did place your duty before your health.'

'I do my best and at least I have my dearest Jane to help me.'

Her companion concentrated on her embroidery, for she made it a point to remain as quietly invisible as she could in company, since anything else brought down recriminations from Flora about 'putting herself forward'.

Simeon returned, and they all made stilted conversation until the tea tray arrived.

While he was in the room, both the older ladies moderated their remarks, Cassie noted grimly, but when he was not present, their conversation was laced with acid, most of it aimed at her.

'Allow me to pour for you, my dearest Flora.'

'So kind! Yes, four spoonfuls of sugar, if you please, Amelia. I need to keep up my strength, given the sad circumstances.'

Simeon walked over to pass a cup to his fiancée, muttering, 'I'm sorry, Cassie. If I'd known how awkward my mother was going to be, I would never have suggested this party.'

Seeing his embarrassment, she tried to make light of it. 'She's no more awkward than my aunt! I've never spent such an uncomfortable two weeks in all my life. At least here I'll be able to escape for walks.'

Richard sauntered across the room just then to join his friend and there was no more chance for private conversation.

Cassie listened as her cousin monopolised his friend's attention for the next ten minutes with news of a mutual acquaintance who had recently sailed for India, then went on without a break to discuss horses, for he had just purchased a particularly fine hunter. She stifled a sigh. Was she never to snatch a word alone with Simeon?

After the rather meagre refreshments had been consumed, the guests were shown to their rooms. Cassie sank down on the bed and looked at her maid, who was setting out a dress for her to change into. 'Mary Ann, I don't know how I'm going to last for even two days with Mrs Giffard!'

'If the mistress is as miffy as the servants, we're both in the same boat. The trouble I had getting your hot water, you would not believe!'

'Where have they put you?'

'Oh, the room's all right, though it's a bit shabby. That housekeeper seems to know her business, I'll give her that, for the place is as clean as anyone could wish, but she's that starchy, it's a wonder she can bend her tongue to say hello.' She came across to give her mistress a hug. 'Don't let them get you down, lass!'

'I'll try not to. You – you won't let this change your mind about living at Stovely?'

'Stovely or the moon, it's all the same to me as long as you're there! I think your mother would have liked to see you as mistress here, don't you? So the sooner we get you wed and send that nasty old dragon to live in the Dower House, the better,' Mary Ann said.

'Is there a Dower House?'

'So they tell me.'

Cassie sighed in relief. Perhaps Simeon had simply assumed she knew about that.

In the afternoon, Simeon invited his fiancée to go for a walk, hoping for some private conversation with her, but Lady Berrinden insisted that Susannah accompany them, and Richard also attached himself to the group, monopolising Simeon's attention. When the two men disappeared round a bend in the path, talking of the horses they had ridden as boys, Cassie seized Susannah's arm. 'Let's go the other way!'

'Oh dear, ought we to?'

'I have *no* intention of walking behind Simeon and your brother like dogs on a leash and meekly waiting for the crumbs of their attention! Do you know where this path leads?'

'To the summer house. It was built for Simeon's grand-mother.'

'I have a burning desire to see it! I quite dote upon summer houses.'

That made Susannah smile. 'It's bound to be full of cobwebs.'

'I *adore* cobwebs!'

'And it's half ruined – or at least, it used to be.'

'Nothing could be more romantic!'

The path through the woods was peaceful, and opened every now and then on to beautiful vistas of the lake glinting in the sunshine. Cassie began to relax for the first time in days. 'Stovely is lovely, isn't it?' she said, sniffing at a pink rose she had not been able to resist picking.

'I'd rather have Bardsley. I like people better than trees.'

Cassie stared at her in amazement. 'You can't mean that!'

'But I do! I love to see the streets full of people. It's a pity the shops in Bardsley aren't better, but Will says the town is growing rapidly and they'll soon improve. And there's always Manchester. He's sure I'll enjoy shopping at the new Manchester Bazaar on Deansgate. Apparently Mr Watts has a splendid range of merchandise there, as good as anywhere in the North.' It was her turn to sigh. 'I do wish Will could have come down here with us today!'

'He'll be coming tomorrow. He still has business matters to deal with, you know, besotted as he is with you.'

Susannah turned rosy and a blissful expression settled briefly on her face.

Cassie could not help feeling envious.

They inspected the summer house very cursorily, for it smelled of mildew and rotting wood, and was the antithesis of romance, then they strolled about for half an hour before making their way back towards the house. Simeon and

Richard were waiting for them near the edge of the woods. Richard was obviously bored, for he was scowling and swishing away at the undergrowth with a stick, like a sulky schoolboy. Simeon was standing with arms folded, his face expressionless.

'How on earth did you manage to get lost, Susannah?' demanded Richard, before the two parties had even reached each other. 'Goodness knows, you've been here often enough before! *How* you will get on living in a strange town, I don't know!'

'Whatever gave you the idea that we were lost?' Cassie asked scornfully, seeing the ready tears brimming in Susannah's eyes. 'Or that we couldn't find our way around? You two were so engrossed in your conversation we decided to entertain ourselves with a visit to the summer house. I'm surprised you even noticed we weren't there.'

Hiding a smile, Simeon intervened before his friend could give vent to the indignation that was written on his face, for like his mother, Richard did not take kindly to being put in the wrong.

Simeon stepped forward. 'It was I who missed you, Cassie. I'd hoped to spend a few moments alone with you. Richard, perhaps you'd escort your sister back to the house? Cassie and I have some things to discuss in private.'

It was Susannah who demurred. 'But Simeon, Mama will be angry if I leave you two alone together, you know she will!'

Richard nodded. 'Susannah's right. M'mother's a stickler for the proprieties. Don't want to upset her any more than we have already, do we, old chap?'

Simeon was adamant. 'We shall only be a few moments. Please go ahead.'

'Oh, very well, if you insist! Here, take my arm, Suzie. You always used to trip up on these paths.'

'Yes, Richard.'

Simeon waited until they were out of hearing. 'I wanted

to say that I hope you won't allow my mother to upset you. She's been . . . um . . . rather difficult lately.'

'It's difficult *not* to be upset when—' – she saw him wince and modified what she had been going to say to – 'when she's so stiff with me.'

'I had hoped you would make allowances for her age and infirmity.'

Cassie was suddenly tired of everyone making allowances for two autocratic old women, who delighted in making other people feel uncomfortable, and said so. 'In fact,' she said thoughtfully, 'I don't know who is worse, *your* mother or *my* Aunt Amelia! Susannah was right to be afraid of coming back to London. My aunt seizes every opportunity to make her feel guilty – and me, too. But Susannah copes because she has Will to cheer her up! I have seen very little of you.'

Now he was becoming angry. 'Are you insinuating that I'm not supporting you as I ought, because if so—' He broke off as Richard's voice boomed back at them.

'Simeon! Simeon! Your mother's calling for you.'

'Damnation!' He glared in the direction of the house.

They stood there for a moment without answering. Simeon was angry, but so was Cassie. I've had as much as I can stand, she decided. Why should I sit there and let his mother insult me? Why does he let her do it? Why is he so strong in other things and so bad at standing up to her? But then she remembered that it was her own foolishness which had led them into the engagement and sighed, swallowing the hot words hovering on the tip of her tongue. 'I'm sorry, Simeon. I didn't mean to upset you. You've – you've behaved more than honourably towards me.'

His mother had not stopped harping on his nobility in offering for a mere Miss Trent ever since his return from Bardsley and he didn't feel it was noble to do what you wanted. 'It wasn't like that—' he began, longing to explain to

222

her how much he wanted to marry her, but Richard appeared at the end of the path just then.

'Didn't you hear me calling, old fellow? Your mother sent me to fetch you. Some visitors have arrived.'

'We're coming,' Simeon said curtly. 'You might have said you didn't know where we were. I did tell you that we wished to discuss some things in private.'

'There's no need to get your hackles up! There'll be plenty of time for discussing things in private once you're married. And anyway, Suzie needs rescuing. M'mother's been goin' on at her for leavin' you two lovebirds alone together. Told you she wouldn't like it!'

'Oh, come on, then!' snapped Cassie.

Simeon held out his arm. 'We shall continue our conversation later,' he murmured.

'Yes, Simeon!' She smiled at his amusement and felt his hand tighten on her arm. For a moment, as they walked, she felt a little closer to him. But only for a moment, because all too soon they arrived at the house, where they found that neighbours had called to felicitate the happy couple upon their engagement. Once again, Simeon was swept from her side.

The following day was dominated by preparations for the party. If Flora was not asking her dearest Simeon to give her the benefit of his advice about something, then the servants were, for they seemed unused to entertaining on any scale. Watching this, Cassie began to make plans to reorganise the household on more efficient lines as soon as Mrs Giffard had moved to the Dower House, which Susannah had told her was situated on the far side of the estate. It couldn't be too far away for Cassie!

A cold collation was served to the family in the middle of the day, so that the cook could concentrate on preparing the evening's offerings .

'A meal such as this is not what I like to set before guests,' sighed Flora as she picked at some food, 'but we have lived very quietly since my poor dear husband died, and for a party like this, I have had to bring people in from the village to help out. I don't like bringing in strangers, but dear Simeon can be a tiny bit parsimonious at times, and we really don't have the staff we need for a large house like this.' Her gaze settled on Cassie for a moment. 'Some people may enjoy living in understaffed households, but *I* was brought up to better things.'

When Simeon rejoined them, he noticed his fiancée's rigid expression and went across to her. 'Are you all right?' When she nodded, he asked, 'Can you bear it for ten more days, my dear? Once we're married, things will be better, I promise you.'

They were on their own in a corner, so she seized the opportunity to raise the subject that was worrying her. 'Simeon, what about your mother? I hadn't thought about it until we came here, but how soon will she be moving out? There's a Dower House on the estate, isn't there?'

'I haven't been able to arrange for her to move yet, but she has her own wing and need not bother us. I—'   At that moment his mother called, 'Dearest Simeon, could I steal you away for a few moments to deal with a tiny problem for me? Alas, that I am so weak! I ought to be assisting you at this time of trial, not demanding your help.'

'We'll discuss this later.'

Cassie watched him leave and waited for her two tormentors to start again.Once he was out of the room, the two older ladies began discussing the problems faced by young wives in adjusting to a new status and role. She had had more than enough of this. 'Come out for a walk round the rose gardens,' she said to Susannah, 'for if I stay, I'll not be able to hold my tongue.'

'Mama, I think Cassie and I will take the air,' said Susannah, in a voice fluttering with nervousness at her own temerity in making a decision.

'Then see that you don't go beyond the rose gardens! I believe Mr Trent is due to arrive soon and we shall need you to greet him. *I* never know what to say to a man like that! I realise I have always been too sensitive to the tone of a conversation, but I cannot help being upset by his blunt ways and lack of delicacy.'

The two young women fled.

Will arrived half an hour later, by which time Cassie's temper had cooled. Simeon rejoined them at the same time, and she smiled at him, feeling a little better about everything, after her peaceful saunter round the gardens.

After a few minutes of doing the pretty to the two old ladies, Will decided it was time he spoke to Susannah on his own. His poor little love was looking distinctly hangdog and needed cheering up. Since the old lady was reluctant to let them be alone together, he said breezily, 'How about showing me these famous grounds of yours, Giffard? I've heard enough about them from our Cassie. Susannah, you'll join us, won't you?'

'Oh, yes.' She moved to his side at once.

Simeon seized the moment. 'I'd be delighted to. Cassie, have you had enough fresh air?'

'On a day like this, I don't think you can have too much. Besides, the atmosphere in here is a trifle stuffy!'

'Simeon, dear one, could you just—'

'Later, Mother. You will not wish me to neglect our visitors.' He offered his arm to Cassie and led her out of the room at a rapid pace.

In the hallway, they met Richard. 'Simeon, old fellow, could you—?'

'No, I couldn't! I'm about to show Will the grounds, and I'm sure you would be bored by the tour, so I shan't even invite you to join us.' He pulled Cassie forward so quickly that a gurgle of laughter escaped her, and behind them, Will chuckled audibly.

'I'd forgotten how attractive your laugh was.' Simeon clasped Cassie's hand as it lay on his arm. 'And I owe you my deepest apologies. I hadn't realised that my Mother could be so – so—'

'Devilish!' she finished for him.

'Devilish is a good word.' He turned to the others. 'Susannah, why don't you take Will down to the lake? We'll meet again here in about an hour, so that we can return together.'

Will and a beaming Susannah strolled away, already deep in conversation.

'How happy they always are together!' Cassie exclaimed.

'Yes. She blossoms when she's with him. Um – we need to finish our discussion about my mother.'

Cassie sighed. 'I suppose so. Though it's a pity to spoil our walk. Simeon, I don't think I can live in the same house as her, not even if she's in a separate wing.'

'I know it will be – difficult, but unfortunately there hasn't been time to make other arrangements.'

'But there's the Dower House.'

'It's very dilapidated. The roof leaks and it's riddled with damp. And even if it weren't, she's always hated that side of the estate, because it's too near the village and has no views of the lake.'

And because there would be no one there to crab at, Cassie thought. Determined to find a solution, she suggested, 'Then could you not find her some comfortable apartments in Bath or Tunbridge Wells, or even rent a whole house for her there? The waters might do her good.'

'Apart from the fact that she'd refuse to go, it would cost a fortune to set her up in the style she'd demand. I – I don't have a great deal of ready money at present, not till after next quarter day, and possibly not even till next year. I've had to undertake a lot of renovations to the estate cottages. However, I thought that we could—'

'But Simeon, that's no problem at all!' she interrupted eagerly. 'I have plenty of money.'

'Thank you, but no.'

She felt his arm go rigid beneath hers. 'But why ever not?'

'Because I am *not* marrying you for your money!'

'Who said you were?'

Half the gossips in London, he thought, but he could not bring himself to share this distasteful information with her. 'Look, I don't need your money, Cassie. And if you'd stop interrupting me for just one moment, I'd be able to tell you—'

'Well, I think that's one of the most ridiculous—'

The next few minutes were spent in working off their accumulated frustrations in a sharp quarrel. Just as they were running out of steam, after tearing each other's families to shreds, and were getting ready to return to the debate about what was to be done with Flora Giffard, Lord Berrinden appeared, looking flustered.

'Why couldn't you two stay out of sight?' he demanded.

Simeon frowned. 'I beg your pardon?'

'Stay out of sight. I know you lovebirds like your little tête-à-têtes, but Amelia can see you from the window of our bedroom and she's *not* pleased that you're unchaperoned. Where have Suzie and that chap of hers gone? Amelia's upset about that, too.' He gazed round vaguely. 'Not that it isn't a dashed romantic place, if only roses didn't always make me sneeze.' He proved his point very violently and they moved away from the offending flowers.

'Did you want something, sir? Your niece and I are in the middle of a serious discussion.'

'Plenty of time for that once the knot's tied. You save your chats till then. It can be dashed difficult sometimes, fillin' in the silences, I can tell you.'

'We wish to discuss certain matters *now*, if you please!'

Lord Berrinden gave a scornful laugh. 'Well, you should

have stayed out of sight, then. Anyway, thing is, you've got to go back because your mother's had one of her turns. Fainted. Callin' out for you.' He gave Simeon a knowing smile. 'Nothin' to worry about, of course. We all know what Flora's like. Amelia says she's just over-excited and will soon perk up once you're with her. But we can't have her missin' the party, can we? It'd cause too much talk, what?'

Simeon groaned aloud. His mother's presence at the party was vital to protect Cassie's reputation. Beside him, he saw his fiancée close her eyes and her mouth go into a thin, straight line. 'I'm sorry,' he whispered. 'But I have to keep my mother calm – for your sake.'

'Yes. I suppose so.'

'You trot along, then,' said Lord Berrinden, prodding him. 'I'll bring Cassie back, but we'd better find Suzie first. Amelia don't like her wanderin' off on her own with that Trent fellow, though why she makes such a fuss when they'll be married in a week or two, I don't know. But there you are. Women! Once they get a maggot in their heads about somethin', there's nothin' you can do about it.'

Though Mary Ann fussed over her and tried to cheer her up, Cassie could not shake off a feeling of foreboding as she changed for dinner. This evening was going to be dreadful, she was sure. For Simeon's sake as much as her own, she hoped the stupid woman would not go too far.

But what worried her most of all was why he was letting his mother manipulate him, not to mention the fact that he didn't intend to touch the Trent money. If he cared about Cassie at all . . . and that was the problem. She cared about him, but she was growing more and more concerned that she had read too much into a mere physical attraction.

To hear her aunt talk, it only mattered in a marriage that both parties be from good families. To hear Mrs Giffard talk, Simeon was nobly sacrificing himself in giving Cassie the protection of his name. If Cassie could only feel Simeon cared about her, she could face anything and anyone, but at the moment she needed reassuring, and needed it badly. Indeed, she had decided during a bleak and wakeful night that she did not intend to marry him unless and until he did reassure her about that, whatever the social cost of not doing so.

'That's the prettiest dress you've ever owned,' Mary Ann said, putting a final touch to her coiffure.

'It is nice, isn't it?' The gown was made of soft aquamarine silk, decorated with white satin ribbon embroidery and languettes at hem and neckline. Mademoiselle Clunette had outdone herself in designing a flattering style and Mrs Keeling's stitchery was as exquisite as ever. Mrs Keeling was at present working on her wedding dress and Cassie was planning to offer her permanent employment as a sewing woman here at Stovely afterwards, which would be much better for the children than Garnett Lane. She was looking forward to having the power to do such things again.

She studied herself in a mirror, and twisted her head to and fro, admiring the new style Mary Ann had devised for her hair, which was caught up in a double knot on the crown of her head, with a fringe softening her forehead and short ringlets before each ear. White satin roses and a pearl-trimmed comb decorated this coiffure. Around her neck she wore her mother's pearls, and she fingered them before she left the bedroom, for they helped give her the courage to face Flora Giffard again.

With a nod of thanks to Mary Ann, Cassie opened the door and made her way reluctantly downstairs. She agreed with Mary Ann that she had never looked so well – but at the same time, she had not felt in such low spirits since her mother's death.

Fifteen

C assie and Susannah were the last to join the house guests downstairs, both having delayed leaving their rooms long enough to ensure they were not on their own with Flora Giffard and Lady Berrinden.

Their appearance caused Lord Berrinden to comment loudly, 'Well, you two will certainly take the shine out of the other females tonight. By Jove, you will! Come and give your old father a kiss, Suzie, my love!'

From the way he ignored his wife's glare, as well as the flush on his cheeks and nose, Cassie guessed that he had been drinking even before he breathed port-scented breath all over her as he claimed an uncle's prerogative of a kiss from her as well. He seemed to have decided to make a unilateral, if hopeless attempt to create a happy atmosphere about the engagements, and she accepted his fulsome compliments with gratitude for the effort he was making.

Susannah was, as usual, all in white, this time in satin with a net overskirt edged in several rows of lace. She wore her hair fluffed out, with a narrow satin bandeau across her smooth white forehead, and kept casting loving glances at Will. Cassie hid a smile as Lady Berrinden stiffened visibly, looking as if she were itching to slap her daughter's face.

Well, it might be unladylike to display one's emotions, but Cassie preferred to know what people were thinking. Will, who had actually dared to grin openly at Flora's more outrageous remarks, smiled across at his cousin

230

sympathetically, as if he knew how frustrated she was feeling, but he remained by his fiancée's side, protecting Susannah so well that she remained radiant with happiness.

As host, Simeon could not do the same for Cassie and indeed, he seemed very abstracted tonight. Suddenly her sense of foreboding returned. She sensed that this was going to be one of the most difficult evenings of her whole life.

The house guests had assembled in the blue drawing-room, a huge apartment whose faded furnishings were only too well illuminated by a blaze of candles. When carriage wheels were heard, Cassie took her place by Simeon's side in the hall, ready to help receive the other guests. Flora was seated next to them, rather than standing up, 'so that I shall not become overtired', and her presence effectively prevented any real communication. However, when Simeon gave Cassie a glance which said he understood how difficult this evening was for her, she could not help smiling at him and her sense of foreboding eased a little.

Flora glanced up from time to time, annoyed at the brilliance of Miss Trent's eyes, the perfection of her complexion and the tasteful and flattering nature of the garments she was wearing. It would have been better if the young woman had betrayed her vulgar nature, would have made Flora's task tonight easier, but no doubt Amelia had had a say in the dressing of her. Yes, that would be why she was looking so elegant and ladylike.

She glanced up at her son and frowned to see how often Simeon's eyes strayed towards his companion. If Flora did not do something about it, he, too, would soon forget his position in society and start showing his feelings for all the world and his wife to comment on. She detested the thought of her son marrying *that female*, absolutely detested it – but she had made her plans and they would soon see Miss Cassandra Trent irrevocably disgraced in the eyes of polite society – after which there would be no need at all for poor Simeon to marry her.

Cassie watched in amazement as Flora received her visitors with more majesty than the Queen of Sheba, and with a haughtiness that bordered at times on actual rudeness. It was equally astonishing that the guests put up with it, but they did, though one elderly gentleman breathed deeply and made rumbling noises in his throat at one of his hostess's remarks – until his wife dug him in the ribs.

The only persons to whom Flora unbent were the Earl and Countess of Elmsworth, but when these ageing specimens of the nobility were followed by their eldest son, Viscount Summersby, it was Simeon who became stiff and ungracious.

'Is something wrong?' Cassie whispered, marvelling that he had not even offered to shake hands with the Viscount, just given him a curt nod.

'I had no idea that *he* had been invited tonight!' he muttered.

'Why should he not be invited? He seemed pleasant enough to me.' At that moment, the Viscount turned and winked at her, giving a little wave of the hand.

Simeon glared across the room. 'Have you met him before?'

'No, never.'

'Then what does he think he's doing, waving at you like that! Summersby is *not* the sort of person I should wish my future wife to associate with, and he'll not be coming here again, I promise you!'

Cassie had not appreciated the familiarity of the Viscount's gesture, either, and had immediately revised her first opinion of him. 'Why do you say that?'

'Because he is an unprincipled libertine!'

'Goodness, how exciting! I don't think I've met one of those before.' But she too wondered why the Viscount had singled her out for a greeting like that when she had never met him before? It seemed very strange. The Brendanberes were announced just then, so she dismissed him from her mind and gave them her full attention, for they seemed very pleasant people and Lady Brendanbere was not much older than herself.

By the time the nearby drawing-room was full, Cassie had forgotten half the names. The guests were now chatting in animated groups – no doubt about her! – for people kept glancing her way. Simeon stood motionless by her side, bending his head occasionally to listen to his mother.

Flora heaved a weary sigh. 'Everyone *must* have arrived by now. I'm simply parched with thirst, Simeon.'

He helped her up and walked into the drawing-room with a lady on each arm. The servants were all busy serving the guests, so he had no alternative but to offer to fetch his mother a drink himself. 'I'll be back in a moment,' he murmured apologetically to Cassie. 'Wait for me here.'

She stood there in growing embarrassment, because Flora turned her back the minute Simeon left them and made not the slightest attempt to include her future daughter-in-law in her low-voiced conversation with the Countess of Elmsworth. From the shocked glance the latter threw at Cassie, it was only too obvious what they were discussing.

'I bet you've forgotten all our names by now,' said a voice in her ear, and Cassie turned to find the wicked Viscount standing beside her. The merest courtesy would have obliged her to answer him, but she was also glad to be rescued her from the humiliation of being the only person in the room standing on her own.

When Simeon returned with a drink for his mother, he glared at the Viscount, but was obliged instead to chat to his mother and then fetch a drink for the Countess.

A moment later, music struck up in the next room, from

which the carpet had been removed to allow dancing, and the guests began to make their way in that direction.

Since Cassie was not enjoying the Viscount's conversation and definitely didn't want to dance with him, she was relieved when Simeon returned and took in her difficult situation in one swift glance. Handing the glass of wine to the Countess, he made his excuses so swiftly that he had already turned his back by the time his mother opened her mouth to request something else.

With a curt, 'Please excuse us!' to the Viscount, Simeon led Cassie into the ballroom and swept her on to the floor, still looking angry. She had never seen him in quite this mood before and was intrigued. As he gazed down at her, the possessive look in his eyes made her heart lurch and his closeness was again making her tingle from head to toe.

'You look beautiful tonight,' he told her.

She looked up at him and could not speak for a moment, because her breath caught in her throat. He was beautiful, too, but you could not say that to a man.

Across the room, Flora Giffard, who was keeping an eye on things, moaned aloud as she saw the way her son and Miss Trent were looking at one another. 'Shameless!' She contemplated the efficacy of a dramatic faint for separating them, but before she could decide whether it was worth spoiling the whole evening in order to part them, the moment had passed and the dance had ended. Her view was then obscured by people leaving the dance floor.

With a hiss of annoyance, she turned to Jane Canley and gave her some very strict instructions.

'Are you sure this is wise?' Jane ventured.

'Of course I'm sure. Only *I* can save my son from this harpy now.'

With a sigh, Jane left her side.

Amelia Berrinden, who had more sense than to show her disapproval of Mr Trent in public, and who was beginning to grow a little annoyed with her friend for wearing her feelings on her sleeve, came across with the intention of diverting Flora's attention, and succeeded for a time by introducing the fascinating topic of the Queen's failing health. This inevitably led Flora on to remember the death of Princess Charlotte in childbed only the previous year. For once, Flora became quite animated, for nothing interested her as much as other people's mortality and tales of death beds. For a time she even forgot to keep an eye on her son.

Her heart buoyed up by the way Simeon was staying by her side, Cassie smiled and chatted to a seemingly unending series of people. However, a sense of irritation gradually built up again between the two of them, as person after person inquired as to when Mrs Giffard would be moving to the Dower House and Simeon avoided giving a definite answer. When he was driven by one lady into admitting that his mother had no immediate plans for moving from the big house, that lady ventured to hint delicately that an early move might be wise for all concerned, which made him grow rigid again.

When they were on their own, Cassie spoke her thoughts aloud. 'They're right, you know.'

'Who are?' Simeon was conscious mainly of a great weariness, after several days at his mother's beck and call, and was worried sick that she might have hysterics and bring on a fatal seizure. Cassie was so easy to be with that he had relaxed considerably in her company, but her sudden statement made him jerk to attention again and look at her inquiringly.

'Your worthy friends and neighbours are right,' she repeated. 'Your mother *ought* to move out of Stovely. We can have no hope of happiness, or even of peace, with her living here.'

'This is not the time to discuss it.'

'When is the time? As far as I can see, my aunt intends to prevent tête-à-têtes until the minute we get married, by which time it will be too late to *do* anything about your mother.'

Before he could respond to this, Will materialised at his side. 'Your mother's asking for you and she's getting quite upset. Apparently there's some domestic crisis. Anyway, you're not needed here, because it's more than time I danced with my cousin.' He took Cassie's hand and led her on to the floor.

They completed a circuit without speaking, then he said quietly, 'Giffard is caught in a cleft stick, you know.'

'What do you mean?'

'There's no doubt about his feelings for you –'

She could feel herself blushing.

'– for he can't keep his eyes off you. But I've been chatting to the head groom and he's rather talkative under the influence of a drink or two. It appears that Mrs Giffard nearly died last year after a fit of hysteria. Ever since then, Simeon has indulged her every wish.'

'However did you find all that out in such a short time?'

Will grinned. 'Oh, a common fellow like me can get into conversation with all sorts of low people.'

She had seen it before, his ability to gain people's confidence.

He looked over her shoulder and frowned. 'Who's that fellow who keeps staring at you? I don't like the look of him.'

She twisted round and realised it was the dreadful Viscount again. 'A neighbour's son. Rather disreputable, I gather.'

'Well, if he doesn't stop ogling you like that, he'll feel my fist on his mouth.'

'Ignore him. He'll be gone in another hour or two and we need never see him again, for I certainly shan't invite him when I'm in charge here – even if his parents are an Earl and Countess.'

When they rejoined Susannah, she needed to repair her hem, which had been caught by a clumsy partner during one of the dances, so Cassie accompanied her upstairs, glad to leave the noise and glare of so many candles behind for a time. While Susannah went into the bedroom designated as the ladies' retiring-room, where a maid was on hand to make such repairs, Cassie took the opportunity to go and sit quietly on a window seat at one end of the first floor, gazing down on the gardens, which were lit by flaring torches and across which shadows of the dancers inside the brightly lit ballroom twisted and moved.

'All alone?' a voice breathed in her ear and someone sat down and pressed himself against her.

She gasped in shock and tried to stand up, but the Viscount pulled her down again to sit beside him and would have made free of her body if she had not slapped his hand out of the way.

'Let me go at once!'

'Surely we've met before? In London, perhaps?' he asked in a voice slightly slurred by drink.

Cassie cast a quick glance along the corridor, relieved to see that no one else was around to see what might look like an incriminating situation. 'Take your hands off me!' she hissed, pushing him away with all her strength.

But he was stronger than she had expected and if Susannah had not come out of the retiring-room at that minute, Cassie might have been in serious trouble.

The Viscount lurched to his feet. 'Servant, Miss Berrinden. I've enjoyed our little chat, Miss Trent. We must continue it when we are less likely to be interrupted.'

'Are you all right?' Susannah whispered.

'I am now. Thank goodness you came back just then. He followed me up and would not go away. I'll make very sure that man doesn't get a chance to come near me again, believe me.'

Susannah's eyes large and fearful. 'I can't imagine why

Mrs Giffard invited him here this evening. She doesn't normally allow him into the house. He has a *dreadful* reputation – though I'm not quite sure what it is that he's done.'

'Well, we need not speak to him again,' Cassie said, taking her cousin's arm. 'Let's go back into the lion's den again and find Will for you. And please don't tell anyone what happened.'

If she had not been so immersed in her own troubles, Cassie would have noticed that the evening had been punctuated by Lord Berrinden's loud and prolonged guffaws. He had decided that Amelia was wrong to disapprove of Will Trent as a son-in-law. Why kick up stiff about little Suzie marrying a fortune, however it had been earned? It was damned useful to have a full kitty, and he'd drink to that any time.

Lady Berrinden observed her husband's rebellion with eyes chill with disgust, but could do nothing about it, because Henry, on the rare occasions when he got the bit between his teeth, only became more pugnacious under pressure. Besides, she was fully occupied with Flora, who had been hovering on the verge of hysterics for most of the evening and she did not wish her hostess to make a scene tonight. For once, Amelia's usual indulgence towards her old friend's posturings and megrims was wearing thin.

As the two cousins came down the staircase, Cassie heard her uncle laughing so loudly that she halted to stare at him. Even from this distance, she could not fail to see that he was 'well oiled' as her father would have said.

'Your father's been drinking too much. Go and fetch Simeon quickly,' she whispered, giving Susannah a push.

'Mama will be furious.'

'Go *on!*'

Cassie reached Lord Berrinden just as he grabbed another

glass of wine from a passing footman and took a loud gulp, slopping half of it down his shirt front.

'Uncle Henry, please let me help you to your room—' she began.

'Whaffor? Party's not over yet, is it? Plenty of wine left, ain't there? Want t'drink the health of you four lovebirds. Here's to you!'

Cassie took the glass from his slack grasp, just as it started to tilt. A quick glance round showed that people were staring, but they were all strangers to her and she could not ask them for help. 'I believe Simeon has some rather fine brandy in the library,' she murmured. 'Shall I pour you a glass?'

Lord Berrinden's eyes lit up. 'Good idea! Let's sneak away 'fore *she* sees me!' He graciously offered Cassie his arm, but nearly overbalanced as he waited for her to take it and if she had not grabbed him, he would have fallen over. However, he ignored this slight hitch and allowed his niece to guide him out of the hall.

In the library, he stared round, saying loudly, 'Where's that brandy, then? Got to keep m'strength up.'

Simeon hurried in. 'Heavens, I've never seen him so bad. Well done for getting him out of sight!'

'We can't find this brandy of yours,' his lordship complained, then giggled. '*She* won't be able to see me in here, will she? Can't spoil the fun this time, can she?'

Just then Will came in. 'Susannah said—' He broke off and grinned as he studied his future father-in-law. 'Didn't know he had the courage.'

'It only happens at his club, usually,' Simeon said. 'Look, we need to get him upstairs. Will you help me? We can go along the terrace and use the rear stairs.' He turned to Cassie. 'Will you be all right?'

She chuckled. 'I'll be fine.'

Between them, Simeon and Will managed to guide Lord

Berrinden's wavering steps around a table loaded with valuable china ornaments and out of the library.

'Does he often swig the juice like this?' asked Will. 'Fine father-in-law he's going to make me!' But he was smiling as he spoke.

'He very seldom gets the chance to indulge. And I would hate to be in his shoes tomorrow. Lady Berrinden will be furious.'

In his bedroom, his lordship subsided into an armchair, demanded 'a glash of your good shtuff' then fell asleep before they could reply. He looked like a crumpled elderly cherub.

'You go back downstairs,' Simeon said. 'I'll wait for his manservant, then rejoin you.'

He went to stand by the bedroom window, glad of a minute's peace. He had never experienced such a nightmare of a day in his whole life. What on earth had got into his mother? Even she had never behaved so badly before. And he wasn't going to allow her to do this to Cassie. He had reached the absolute limit of his tolerance tonight. Pity for his mother's genuine ill health was not going to make him spoil his own life – or Cassie's.

When Simeon left her alone by the open french windows of the library, Cassie decided to take a breath or two of fresh air before she returned to face the rest of this dreadful evening.

The weather was chilly but fine, and the breeze had completely dropped now. The moon had risen, turning the rolling lawns into dark grey velvet and making the lake look like polished silver. She took a deep breath and went to stand by the stone balustrade, savouring the quiet. But then her worries resurfaced again. If Simeon could not persuade his mother to move out and could not accept his wife's financial help, what chance did they have of happiness? She could not agree to a cool, formal marriage like the Berrindens had, but wanted a warm, loving relationship such as she had seen between her parents. Sometimes she felt it was possible with Simeon and at other times she felt in despair, especially when he refused to discuss things openly.

Oh, what a tangle this all was! Was she expecting too much of Simeon? Of their marriage? She didn't know what to think any more. Her emotions had see-sawed ever since their return to London and her virtual incarceration in Bransham Gardens. If only she could be certain of his feelings, she would not care about . . .

Suddenly she was grabbed from behind and a voice said, 'We meet again, fair damsel!'

Fury sizzled through Cassie as she recognised the voice. The last thing she needed or deserved was this fool pestering her. All her frustrations coalesced into action.

It was taking Lord Berrinden's manservant longer to answer the bell than Simeon had expected. From his post by the bedroom window, he saw Cassie come outside and stand in the moonlight like a pagan goddess, her head thrown back. He smiled as he saw enjoyment in every line of her body. Then he saw her sag against the balustrade and sadness shadow her face again. At one point, she shook her head, as if she was debating some point in her mind, and there was something so hopeless in that gesture that his heart went out to her.

Suddenly it all seemed very clear to him and he wanted to tell her how he felt. He loved Cassie. Loved her absolutely. And as his wife, *she* deserved and was going to get his first loyalty, not his mother, however much he pitied Flora. He not only owed that to Cassie, but every fibre of his being made him *want* to protect her, love her, cherish her. And he also wanted more from his marriage than he had seen in other couples of his acquaintance – he always had done, which was why he'd waited.

He would go down and speak to Cassie this very

minute and if anyone tried to keep them apart, anyone at all . . .

He saw a figure creep up behind Cassie and seize her. And there was no mistaking who that person was. With a growl of fury, Simeon turned, forgetting Lord Berrinden, who had sat up again and was making a feeble attempt to get out of the chair.

The door slammed back against the wall as Simeon rushed from the room. In the corridor, he pushed Lord Berrinden's startled manservant out of his way and clattered down the back stairs several at a time. When he reached the ground floor, fear for Cassie made him break into a run and he did not even slow down when he caught the edge of a tray and sent its contents flying. As the maid who had been carrying it shrieked in shock, he vanished round the corner.

Outside, Simeon ran along the back of the house, terrified of what he might find as he turned the corner.

What he did find was Cassie, arms akimbo, staring down at a figure sprawled on the terrace. There were pieces of broken flowerpot scattered everywhere and when the man raised his head and groaned, Simeon saw that he had smears of earth on his face and one or two cuts.

'Are you all right, my darling girl?' he demanded, taking her in his arms. 'He didn't harm you, did he?'

Summersby heaved himself into a sitting position with another groan, and cast a glance of acute dislike at Cassie. 'She *invited* me to meet her here, and if she hadn't heard you coming, she would be in my arms now.'

'See what an immoral female you have got entangled with!' came Flora's voice from the shadows to one side and she moved out of them like an avenging fury. 'Oh, my son, she is not worthy of you.'

Simeon's arm tightened around Cassie's shoulders. 'It is I who am not worthy of her,' he said, his voice sure. 'As for you, Summersby, you could never make me believe such a thing of Cassie.' He bent to press a kiss on her forehead. 'My darling, I'm so sorry I failed to look after you properly tonight. It'll never happen again, I assure you.'

She looked up at him, all her love showing in her face. 'What did you call me?' she whispered, as if she could not believe her own ears.

His breath caught in his throat at the sight of her loving expression and he turned her to face him. 'Cassie, darling, I— '

Flora's voice grew shriller and she darted forward to tug at her son's sleeve. 'You heard what Summersby said! She *invited* him to meet her here. She is a harpy. She— '

Another figure moved out of the shadows. Jane Canley, hands clasped tightly in front of her breast, said breathlessly, 'No. Miss Trent didn't invite him outside. *You* told him where she was, Flora. You never notice whether I'm there or not, but I heard it all, and even if I lose my position for this, I can't keep silent. You invited him here tonight on condition he try to seduce Miss Trent, or at the least, arrange to be caught in a compromising position with her.' Her gaze swept over the Viscount, who was swaying on his feet and still rubbing his head, and disgust burred her voice as she added, 'Though why *you* accepted the invitation, I cannot understand.'

The Viscount shrugged and laughed. 'Deuced boring in the country. Thought it'd be a bit of a lark, and if Mrs Giffard was right about Miss Trent,' he sketched a mocking bow in Cassie's direction, 'might have found something to while away the time while I'm rusticating.'

Simeon took a hasty step forward. 'You'd better leave before I—'

Cassie pulled him back. 'He doesn't matter, Simeon dearest.' Her tone was a caress, her eyes were bright with happiness.

'You ingrate!' Flora hissed at Jane. 'Get out of this house at once!'

At that, Simeon and Cassie broke apart and moved to stand either side of Miss Canley. 'Don't leave, Jane,' he said.

'I'm going to need some help,' Cassie added. 'Would you stay on and act as my amanuensis instead? There will be so much to do renovating this beautiful house and,' she turned back to Simeon with another glowing smile, 'I don't want to neglect my husband.'

Flora opened her mouth to let loose a scream that would have brought the guests rushing out to investigate, but Miss Canley moved swiftly to give her a light shake. 'Do you want to alienate your son's affections for ever!' she demanded. 'Do you? And what did the doctor say about giving in to hysterics?'

Flora gulped audibly and closed her mouth, but the look she gave Cassie was filled with undisguised hatred.

'I shall either renovate the Dower House or find you somewhere to live in Bath or Cheltenham,' Simeon said. 'You will be well looked after, Mother, but I'm not having you make my wife's life a misery – as you have made mine these past few years – whatever your state of health.'

Flora burst into tears, but as her former companion's grasp tightened on her arm, she sobbed quietly.

'I'm happy to accept your offer of employment, Miss Trent. Very happy indeed, 'Jane said in a brisker tone than usual. 'For now, please leave Mrs Giffard to me. I'll get her up to her bedroom and give her something to help her sleep.'

'Are you sure you'll be all right?' Simeon asked.

Jane smiled at him, then turned to include Cassie in that smile. 'Oh, I've had a lot of experience at dealing with her in the past few years.' She guided the still sobbing woman along the terrace towards the rear entrance.

When they were alone, Simeon took Cassie in his arms again. 'My beloved, can you ever forgive me?'

She put her arms round his neck. 'I might be able to if you call me that often enough.'

'My own darling.' He drew her close enough to kiss her in the way they had both been longing for.

When the kiss ended, he said softly, 'I do love you, you know, Cassie. I was too stupid to realise it at first, but now it's all very clear to me. I love you and want to spend my life with you. The money doesn't matter and, though I shall see that my mother is looked after, she has little love in her and will not really miss me, only,' he grimaced, 'the state and consequence of her position here.'

'She might – say things about me, though,' Cassie said, for this thought was worrying her still.

'No. I shall make everything I do contingent upon her saying nothing that will harm you. She has no money of her own, for my father gambled away her portion.' After a moment, he added, 'You do love me, don't you?'

Cassie sighed happily and leaned against him. 'I've loved you ever since that night on the moors,' she confessed. 'I was so afraid,' she hesitated, then finished, 'that you didn't know how to love.'

'You've taught me to love, because everything you do is filled with a love of people, not only your family, but even stray sewing women.' He smiled down at her, 'I now intend to spend the rest of my life proving how well I've learned the lesson.'

He bent his head again and as his lips hovered over her, he saw the tears tracing down her cheeks and froze. 'What's wrong? What have I said?'

She gave him a misty smile and pulled his head down again. 'You've done nothing wrong. I always cry when I'm as happy as this.' Daringly, she planted a kiss of her own on the firm flesh of his cheek, then moved her lips down to his and with a groan, he began to kiss her passionately.

When he pulled away, he said savagely, 'I don't care if my mother goes to live in the stables, but if you don't marry me soon, Cassie Trent, then I won't be answerable for the consequences.'

She raised one hand to caress his cheek, then lifted her lips for another kiss. 'Yes, Simeon.'

As he chuckled, joy flooded through her and more happy tears filled her eyes. She understood now exactly how her parents had felt about each other, and when Simeon's lips recaptured hers, she vowed that she would make her marriage as happy as theirs had been.

When he folded her arm in his and began walking towards the lake, with a muttered, 'I can't bear to go back quite yet,' she went with him gladly, feeling as if the night were full of moonlight and the perfume of roses. And him! Always, from now on, him.